ALSO BY
FRED VAN LENTE

Ten Dead Comedians

THE CON ARTIST

A NOVEL BY
FRED VAN LENTE

INTERIOR ILLUSTRATIONS BY
TOM FOWLER

QUIRK BOOKS
PHILADELPHIA

Library of Congress Cataloging in Publication Number: 2017951341

ISBN: 978-1-68369-034-4

Printed in the United States of America

Typeset in Sabon, Above the Sky, and Knockout

Designed by Doogie Horner
Cover illustration by 100% Soft
Interior illustrations by Tom Fowler
Production management by John J. McGurk

Quirk Books
215 Church Street
Philadelphia, PA 19106
quirkbooks.com

10 9 8 7 6 5 4 3 2 1

For Dad

NOTE

Due to ongoing litigation, many names of the companies, trademarked characters, and real people in the statement of Michael "Mike M" Mason have been changed upon the advice of the publisher's counsel. However, none of the artwork has been altered in any way; it has been reproduced exactly as it was found in the sketchbook confiscated by the San Diego Police Department.

WEDNESDAY

I heard about the first death from the girl who picked me up at the airport. She said her name was Violet and she was my biggest fan.

She looked Hispanic, no older than twenty. She had dark-blue eyeliner drawn in a kind of Egyptian curl at the edges of her sad, serious eyes. She was standing at the foot of the escalator holding a cheery hand-drawn sign with my name spelled out in magic-markered rainbows. I couldn't have missed it even if she hadn't started jumping up and down and waving it with one hand as soon as my face appeared on the arrivals level above. I was wearing sunglasses and had slung over my shoulder a beat-up bike messenger bag filled with art supplies, toiletries, and a single change of clothes. I carried a small, flat, black portfolio of original art from my comic books.

With my free hand I reached out to shake hers when I stepped off the escalator. "The con sent you?"

She had to shove the sign under her armpit to take my hand, which was when I realized that she had no left arm—or rather, her left arm stopped just above what would have been her elbow.

"I am so very very happy to meet you! My name is Violet—as you can see! Violent Violet."

I put two and two together finally and her outfit clicked. She was wearing a leather aviator helmet and from her belt jangled a riot of prosthetic arms—one ending in a claw, another in a popgun, another in a weed whacker—just like Violent Violet, one of the main characters from the indie comic book I made my bones on, *Gut Check*, a post-apocalyptic pro-wrestling action-drama-romance about the titular hero, an American who travels to Edo to learn sumo wrestling and goes on to become a superstar on the televised wrestling circuit before finding himself enlisted in an ancient war against demonic *luchadores* to prevent the Mayan end-of-days—

Yeah, the one the movie is based on, right.

Yeah, they had me on set to help out a little bit.

No, I—

Hey, listen, is it cool if we not talk about the movie? Or maybe save it until I get through my whole statement? Because it's kind of on the long side.

Thanks.

Anyway, like the girl picking me up at the airport, the comics version of Violent Violet—Gut Check's love interest—is a one-armed warrior who wrestles using her wide variety of prosthetic limbs or, from time to time, with none at all, just to prove she requires no technological enhancement to kick your dumb ableist ass.

"She is my favorite, and *you're* my favorite, I mean, seriously, you are my favorite artist of all time, I love *Gut Check*, I love the comic, I love the movie, I love your amazing run on *Mister Mystery*, I mean, I love everything you do."

I greet all praise with suspicion and believe every horrible thing ever said about me a hundredfold, so I just smiled vaguely and nodded, more in acknowledgment than agreement. "That's really nice of you to say, thanks. Thanks for volunteering for the con, that's really cool of you."

"Yeah, no problem. Anything you need, I'm gonna get you. I am, like, going to be right by your Artists' Alley table at the con, you need me to go get you food, you need me to bring water, you need me to sit at your booth while you go to the men's room, whatever you need, all of Comic-Con, I am going to be your sidekick, I am there for you, all the way, 24/7."

She said all of that without taking a single breath. I couldn't tell if she was on something or just naturally had the metabolism of a hummingbird. I didn't really mind one way or another. I'd seen worse. One time, I agreed to do what I was told was a quote-unquote small convention in Eugene, Oregon. I flew in, the owner of the local comic book store picked me up and took me to the quote-unquote show. Not to a convention center, not to a hotel ballroom, not even to his shop, but to the basement of his house, which was lined with framed copies of my comics and some of my original art he had bought online. There was no one else there except these two big, quiet white dudes. After we had been down there for a couple hours, hanging out, drinking beers and eating pizza, I realized, looking into the guy's eyes, that wait, there is no con. *This* is the con. He just wanted to meet me and have me hang out with him and his buddies.

Once you get through a weekend like that without anybody wearing your skin for a hat, the Violent Violets of the world seem fairly normal.

"I love it," I said. "Lead on."

Catching a ride from the airport with one of my own characters would ordinarily qualify as strange, except that fiction starts devouring reality pretty much as soon as you step off the plane at San Diego International Airport during the week of Comic-Con. The escalators leading down to baggage claim had been covered in vinyl and made to look like on- and off-ramps ferrying you into and out of the bowels of a massive gray spaceship: Up was labeled To ABDUCTION and down was labeled POST ABDUCTION. The baggage kiosks had been skinned to look like spinning UFOs. The whole thing was promoting some new extraterrestrial romance streaming on Netflix in two weeks.

I followed Violent Violet through the automatic glass doors of the terminal. The weather in San Diego was, per usual, insultingly perfect: cool, blue skies, a vague sweetness in the air. Across the palm-lined taxi stand was a squat concrete parking garage where we found her candy-colored Toyota Corolla.

"I have to warn you," she said, holding up her hand before getting inside, "the interior of my car is a reflection of my internal psyche."

I opened the passenger door to find what would have been my seat covered in In-N-Out Burger cartons, an empty Coke Zero bottle, and a half-eaten bag of Smartfood, among other dorm-room detritus.

"Oh, shit, shit, sorry, sorry." She reached across from the driver's side and swept the garbage onto the floor of the car. "I was going to do that before coming to meet you but I was so excited and my brain just started racing and—*brrrruuuggghhh!*" She mimed an EMP explosion mushrooming out of her cranium, or at least that's what I assumed it was.

"Believe me, I've been there." I got in the car, keeping my bags in my lap. My shoe soles settled atop the pile of garbage with an audible crunch.

Violent Violet maneuvered us out of the airport's pretzeled traffic. The car had an automatic transmission, unsurprisingly, and she only ever took her one hand off the steering to use her turn signal, at which point she leaned forward ever so slightly to brace the wheel with the tip of her stump. It looked like the most natural thing in the world.

"There is one thing I should probably tell you, though," she said once we got on the highway, and took a deep breath.

Before she could say more I interjected:

"Actually, real quick, if you're serious about being my helper, I've got a mission for you."

"I accept it. I pledge my honor and my life to its completion!"

"You are officially my hero. Thank you. There's this self-storage place, A1 U-Store, off I-5? I need you to go into my unit, it's number 616, and grab my banner, a FedEx box filled with prints, and a small suitcase and bring them to me at my table, okay?" I wrote the address on a Starbucks receipt I found in my pocket and put that plus the key on the dashboard where Violent Violet could see them. "Normally I'd do this myself, but I want to make it to my table before preview night ends."

"Oh . . . kay." She frowned, puzzled. "You keep that stuff here when you're not in town?"

"Yeah, I have storage units all over the country. Charlotte, Chicago, Seattle, Orlando. Wherever the big comic cons are."

"You don't keep them at home?"

"This is my home."

"Pardon?"

"I gave up my house three years ago. Now I live entirely at cons. They fly me out, put me up in hotels, and I go to my Artists' Alley table and draw sketches for people, and then another con flies me somewhere else. I just ask them to extend my stay past the weekend in either direction, instead of an appearance fee."

"So you were just coming from another con when you arrived here?"

"Yeah, a small one, in Cleveland. There was a ballroom dancing competition and a brewers' convention going on in the same hotel, which made for some interesting conversations at the breakfast buffet."

"You . . . live at comic book conventions." Violent Violet blinked. "Is that really, really awesome . . . or really, really sad?"

"Yes," I said with conviction.

Violent Violet didn't say anything, she just drove.

"I store my prints in the unit because they can get completely destroyed on flights, either in the overhead bins or from the barbarians in baggage handling. And I scatter changes of clothes everywhere because I find doing laundry in hotels super depressing.

"And another thing, Violet, if you'd be so kind. If you see me trying to talk to my ex-wife, or call her, or wave her over to me, I need you to take that arm on your belt with the spike on the end and ram it directly through my eyeball and into my brain. If you could do that for me, I'd really appreciate it."

"I, uh . . . " She swallowed. I met her five minutes ago and already discovered the limits of her devotion. I excel at that. "I don't really know what your ex-wife looks like, though? Besides, all my weapons are Styrofoam."

"Ah, well. My loss." I looked out the window. The Corolla was winging its way toward downtown, a modest row of skyscrapers rising up beyond a harbor dotted with sailboats and U.S. Navy warships. "I wasn't even going to come to this show when I heard through the grapevine she was going to be here too. For the first time in three years, we're going to be in close physical proximity to each other, like matter and antimatter. That's dangerous stuff. Like, *cosmically* dangerous."

"Why'd you change your mind?" Violent Violet's voice had softened to a peep.

"The committee that runs the Kirby Awards asked me to give a lifetime achievement award to Benjamin Kurtz—you know, Ben K, the creator of Mister Mystery? He's like my oldest friend and mentor in this business, so I couldn't say no."

"Oh." She practically swallowed the word.

"Oh?" I turned to her with a frown. "Oh, what oh?"

After a moment's hesitation she said:

"You haven't seen Twitter?"

– – – –

I am not a big social-media guy. My Facebook feed consists mostly of updates on people's cancer treatments, memorials to recently dead pets, and deeply misinformed political rants. But after Violent Violet said what she did, I pulled out my phone. On Twitter my feed was filled with many variations of:

"RIP, Ben K, you were truly The Great One"

"Raising a glass of brown to Teh (sic) Great One last night, Ben K, you were the best"

"A photo of me & Ben K from DragonCon last year, really devastated that this is the last time I'll ever see TGO"

Violet said something but I didn't hear her, so I looked at her with what must have been utter bafflement because she repeated without prompting:

"I'm really, really sorry."

I blinked. My mind reeled. As Violet's Corolla drew closer to the convention center, reality further loosened its grip on my surroundings. Comic-Con was such a draw for San Diego—I once overheard a retail clerk say it generated as much as a third of merchants' revenue for the year—that the city allowed itself to be more or less completely taken over by it. *Absolute Zero*, the nuclear winter HBO show based on the Steve Ellis comic, had constructed a massive ice castle that rose up and around the Wyndham hotel. *Westworld*, the latest season soon to be re-released on Blu-ray, had its own saloon. It was preview night at the con, and only VIP ticket holders could get inside, but still the sidewalks in front of the Hyatt and Marriott Marquis were crammed with people. A woman in a BURR SHOT FIRST T-shirt (*Star Wars* font) held the hand of a six-year-old in an R2-D2 cap. They passed a Golden Age Flash wearing his upside-down-bedpan Mercury helmet, the cuffs of his Spandex so saggy around his winged boots that it looked like he would run out of his costume if he started to jog. The sky was an of-course California blue and the sunlight beat down with brilliant indifference that Ben K was dead.

Ben K was dead.

He was the first comics artist whose name I actually knew, because he was the first comics artist whose name I actually bothered to learn, because that's how much I loved his drawings.

Comics were a minor thing to my dad; he had been a casual
reader as a kid. When I was growing up, he had this big red book
he got for some birthday when he was a kid that was still lying around our apartment in New Providence, New Jersey: Jules
Feiffer's *The Great Comic Book Heroes*. In addition to Feiffer's
original *New Yorker* essay about his teenage years in Manhattan
right after World War II, growing up among the comic book
"shops" (the early producers of the funnybook medium), there
were a bunch of reprints of superhero origin strips from the Gold-
en Age—Siegel and Shuster's Superman, Kane and (uncredited)
Finger's Batman, Simon and Kirby's Captain America, Eisner's
The Spirit, and of course Ben K's creation, Mister Mystery. Ben
dreamed up the character when he was a wee lad of seventeen,
and Mister Mystery became one of the few long-underwear men
to survive the fairly predictable postwar lack of interest in fan-
tasy fighting. It thrived a decade later in the revitalization of the
genre commonly called the Silver Age.

I didn't know any of that Comics History 101 crap when
I was four, I just knew Mister Mystery was kick-ass because he
was drawn kick-ass by the man known as the Great One. Of
course, when I was a kid, anything with capes and punching was
my jam. When I was old enough to ride a bike I would brave the
scary street with all the cars on it, the one by the Friendly's, to
go to the 7-Eleven and buy Blue Ribbon Digests off the spinner
rack, with the Mister Mystery reprints in them for the astronom-
ical sum of one American dollar. When I was old enough to drive
I would head to the nearest comic book store I knew of, Dewey's
Comic City in Madison, by Drew University, where I discovered
Ben K's non-superhero output, the racy stuff, like *Black Sky* and

American Wasteland.

By then I had been bitten by the drawing bug. I was filling my school notes with crazed sketches of pro wrestlers clothes-lining each other atop spaceships, and my parents, skeptical intellectual types, college professors, thought too highly of their open-mindedness to tell me to cut that out and fantasize about getting a real job instead. They moved to Park Slope once they accepted teaching jobs at Fordham, so I was able to go to the High School of Art and Design, and from there SVA, where one of our guest artists was, much to my shock and surprise, none other than the creator of Mister Mystery, the great Ben K himself. I had already moved on in terms of heroes, to the Jim Lees and Whilce Portacios of the world, the creators of the first Image Comics wave. But at my first sight of Ben K—tall, gaunt, with a reverse widow's peak, spouting rapid-fire profanity-laced tirades about our general uselessness and inability to understand shot selection, anatomy, and composition—I fell in love with him all over again, not just as some kind of abstract demigod anymore, not just an all-caps name in the credits box, but as a mentor, a professor. Someone I hungered to impress.

And then he gave me a job. Me and this other guy, Dirtbag, another SVA student. He was talented too. We called him Dirtbag because every day he sat down to draw in the studio and within an hour he would somehow manage to cover himself from head to toe in ink stains, graphite smears, and eraser shavings. He was like a baseball player always sliding headfirst into home, which you are absolutely not supposed to do because of the risk of injury to your head and, more importantly, your hands. But he just couldn't help himself. So we called him Dirtbag.

From that day on, for the last two years of college and for a few years after that, we worked for Ben K in his tiny rent-controlled studio on Fifty-seventh Street; it was lined with books, comics, movie magazines, art supplies, and every other thing he never threw away from his seven decades in the industry. Having kicked a nasty heroin habit in the late seventies, his drugs of choice were cigarettes and Maxwell House instant coffee, both of which he consumed incessantly as he pontificated on everything from politics to cinema to fine art to literature, all while drawing his comics stories for his employer, and the copyright holder for all of them, Atlas Comics. Me and Dirtbag inked backgrounds for him, erased pencil lines, and sometimes he made us draw whatever massive crowd scene the sadistic writer had cursed him with, during which he alternately praised our burgeoning skills and called us his favorite word, "cunts."

I loved him like the foul-mouthed whiskey-throated Tom Waits father I never had.

Sitting in Violent Violent's passenger seat, I tried to focus beyond what was outside my window. I turned back to my phone, looking for a more detailed explanation of Ben K's death. The consensus of the various fan sites was that he'd been discovered by a colleague, one of the Atlas editors, after mail had been piling up outside the door of the same one-room studio where I had worked with him as a kid. He'd been dead for maybe three days.

All of a sudden, my eyes felt a little too big for their sockets. I took a deep breath, and a hand touched my shoulder.

"Are you going to be all right?" Violent Violet asked. I was surprised at how shocked and worried she looked.

I decided to be strong. For *her*, don't you know. "Yeah. I

guess." I swallowed. "Although now I don't know what the hell I'm doing here, to be honest."

The con was putting me up at the Hilton San Diego Bayfront, which was a big flat monolith rising up on the southeastern side of the convention center. To get there, you have to drive up a ramp to what is essentially the second floor, and before I knew it, we had arrived. My thoughts were scattered and muted; I didn't know what to say, or what to do, or even how to do it if I did.

"Are you still going to Artists' Alley tonight?" Violet asked me.

I nodded.

"Okay. I'll head over to the storage place and grab your stuff now. I may not be able to make it back to the con until tomorrow, though."

The doorman, who was dressed as a blood-dripping zombie Hulk, came over and opened the door for me. "That's fine. Hey." I turned back to her just after I climbed out. "I thought you said you wanted to tell me something."

"Oh. Yeah." She looked guilty for a second, but then I realized that was maybe her default expression. Violent Violet suffered from Resting Shame Face. "I—I just wanted to say—it may not seem like it sometimes, but what you do matters. It matters to people like me. You know, people look at us and don't know what to say or do, but when you make your heroes look like . . . people like me . . . everyone around us takes a second look. So. Thank you."

I got a lump in my throat. "You're welcome. Your saying that means a lot to me. You're all right, Violent Violet."

"I know," she said cheerily and drove off.

As she did, I finally looked up, taking in the imposing facade of the Bayfront rising above me, and saw for the first time
that Atlas had completely covered it, from bottom floor to top,
with an ad for the just-announced Mister Mystery movie. Ben
K's shadowy trench-coated creation, for which he never got true
royalties, or even credit, scowled down on me and the festival
before him, his white eyes burning with the pitiless judgment of
an Old Testament God.

– – – –

The Bayfront Hilton's hypermodern, copper-colored lobby had
been transformed into a superhero team's space-station headquarters for Comic-Con. The front desk was even manned by
Superman himself, with a gelled curlicue of hair at the top of his
forehead and everything. His red-and-blue costume had big puffy
muscles sewn in, which didn't make him look like he had a super-
human physique so much as a rare Kryptonian eating disorder.

"Welcome to the Bayfront, sir," Supes said. "What brings
you to San Diego?"

"I heard there was some kind of a comic con going on? Little affair, real mom-and-pop operation?"

Kal-El laughed a loud, fake, customer-service laugh. "I believe I heard that too, sir. Can I see some ID and a credit card?"

I turned over my New Jersey driver's license but held on to
my credit cards. "I should be comped all the way through."

The Space Computer confirmed this as true. Not for funnybook royalty such as myself were the indignities of paying for
hotel rooms and Artists' Alley tables. Long ago, I made a drawing for the guy who's been running Comic-Con's guest services

since the late 1980s. I drew a spectacular Sailor Moon for his personal sketchbook full of lovingly rendered Sailor Moons. In gratitude he made me an Always Approved guest, meaning I could parachute out of an airplane in the middle of the convention center and still receive a badge, table, and hotel room. The barter economy was alive and well on the comic-con circuit.

"Behold, the prodigal artist returns. You never gave me a goat, so don't expect a fatted calf. Glad you're taking a break from devouring life with prostitutes."

I sensed the crackle of nervous energy surrounding Sebastian Mod before I heard his voice. He'd come right up to my shoulder and spoke right into my ear, looking around the crowded lobby as if expecting assassins to leap out at every corner. He had shaved his head completely bald and wore circular sunglasses on his beaklike nose—one red-tinted lens and one green one. He wore high tops, leather pants, a 1985 West German army jacket, and no shirt: as usual, he dressed like he was actively encouraging people to punch him in the face.

"Hey, Sebastian. You realize I only understand about every other sentence that comes out of your mouth?"

"As long as you understand me *here*, in the kidneys, where the eyes of the soul rest, that's all I care about," he said.

Every three or four years the big publishers elevate a new writer to megastar status by putting him on one of the five major franchises (historically, but not always, Batman, X-Men, Spider-Man, Avengers, and Mister Mystery). Sebastian Mod was our current moment's It Writer. As Abraham Lincoln once said (I'm paraphrasing), if you want to see what someone is really like, give them Geek Power. Within six months Mod's higher-profile status transformed him into a Frankenstein Monster of ego and entitlement, rampaging across the countryside terrorizing his editors with threats and demands.

Mod had spent the last few years reaping the benefits of his carefully crafted public image as an unapologetically pretentious techno-shaman bad boy. Hollywood executives, having long been to faux badassery what a nursing home is to a chain-email scam—easy marks—bought his schtick hook, line, and sinker; in addition to the four or five summer blockbusters that had been adapted from his own creator-owned work, Mod rented himself out to the studios as a consultant for their comic book franchises. He was a Crocodile Dundee for the Otaku Outback, guiding A-list stars to the essential graphic novels and cartoon episodes to consume in preparation for playing the Anti-Monitor, or Elsa Bloodstone, or whomever. There is a persistent urban legend within the comics community that as a result of meeting for several hours with Mod while preparing for *Batman v Superman: Dawn of Justice*, Jesse Eisenberg's manic turn as Lex Luthor was basically a thinly veiled Sebastian Mod impersonation.

I have no doubt in my mind whatsoever that the primary source of these rumors is Sebastian Mod.

"You may think it's a coincidence, us meeting here, now, in this lobby, but it is not, my friend. It is not."

"You haven't given me much chance to think about anything."

"My last ten or twelve orgasms? I made sure to picture your face while I came, to summon you here to me."

"That's funny, because what you're actually doing is repelling me." Sebastian Mod liked to tell people he worshipped some kind of pre-monotheistic serpentine sex god and was a practicing tantric magician. He once asked his thousands of fans to masturbate simultaneously on the same date at the same time and use their combined "mana" to keep one of his titles from being canceled. After what I like to call "The Wankening," the series lasted only four more issues before finally getting the ax, so trillions of spermatozoa gave their lives for a skinny $9.99 trade paperback; rarely have so many given so much for so little.

"I'm not staying in this hotel. I'm not even having dinner here. I'm just randomly passing through. You're here, though, aren't you? And so am I." He said it like that slammed shut any possible argument. "You know, I've taken over writing *Mister Mystery* and read the whole series dating back to the first Nixon administration, and I've got to say, the most striking run was yours. Despite what many people say, you're quite an effective storyteller."

"Stop. I'm blushing."

"I have a proposal that I'd like to imprint onto your DNA—something for us to work on together."

"Is that right? Well—yeah. I might be into that." Though Sebastian Mod's personality was the human equivalent of crawling through broken glass, you couldn't deny that he moved a lot of comics. Each of his first issues went through a minimum five printings, and that was even before one factored in Hollywood option money. As someone staring down looming alimony payments, I had to consider any project he suggested, no matter how exhausting I might personally find my potential cocreator. "What did you have in mind?"

"Not here," he hissed, looking out the corner of his eye at

the figures in black lurking in the Space Lobby. There were three of them, women, cosplaying as J, K, and young K. Sebastian Mod kept one eye on them while he talked to me, even though they weren't paying either of us the least bit of attention. "You going to Christine's birthday karaoke thing at the Gaslighter tonight?"

"No, Sebastian, I am not going to my ex-wife's birthday party."

"Really?" Mod reacted like Earth emotions were unknown to him.

"Really. Why, are you going?"

"Not now. I'd much rather talk with you about this project. It's burning its way through my gut like some alien parasite and I've got to pass it on or I'll die."

"You're really selling it."

He gripped my shoulders. "With our creative powers combined we shall shake the proverbial walls of heaven. What say you to dinner and drinks at the Marriott Marquis tonight, once preview night ends?"

"Sounds great. I'll meet you over there around nine."

"Chin-chin," he said for no reason, then walked sideways out of the Space Lobby while avoiding eye contact with the WiB like some kind of paranoid crab.

I got the sinking feeling I was making a terrible mistake; it wouldn't be long before I realized how right I was, but for the wrong reasons.

— — — —

I took the Space Elevator to my Space Room and removed a change of clothes and toiletries from the bike messenger bag, then turned around and carried it and my portfolio right back down to the Space Lobby and across the street to the convention center. A guy carrying a bullhorn from the Eastboro Baptist Church screamed at the fans and cosplayers streaming by:

"THE JEDI KNIGHTS CANNOT SAVE YOU, THE AUTOBOTS CANNOT SAVE YOU, GRIFFINDORS CANNOT SAVE YOU, THE JUSTICE LEAGUE, THE AVENGERS, THE X-MEN AND TEEN TITANS CANNOT SAVE YOU. BECAUSE ALL OF THOSE THINGS ARE UNREAL, THEY ARE THE WICKED THINGS OF THIS WORLD. OPEN YOUR EYES TO THE REALITY . . ."

These were the same charming souls who protest soldiers' funerals with hateful signs; this guy had a GOD HATES GEEKS placard sticking out of the back of his waistband. To my great amusement somebody in a delightfully retro cardboard robot outfit stood next to the religious ranter and held up a DESTROY ALL HUMANS sign. As I passed by, I gave the cosplayer a high-five.

Behind the preacher I nearly ran into some kind of steampunk ninja person wearing a jet-black intergalactic stealth suit with a helmet-goggles combo and heavily padded armored vest that completely disguised any gender, race, and waist size.

"Hey there! Hi!" Ninja Person pulled my gaze toward him/her/them with a wave. There was some kind of voice distortion box in the helmet, so it sounded like I was getting a telemarketing call from the killer in *Saw*. "Would you like to be part of history?"

"Not really," I said. "Usually you get to be part of history by dying."

"No, this is the good kind of history. The *amazing* kind of history. At a minute past midnight, when the first official,

non-preview day of Comic-Con begins, we *Dante's Fire* fans are going for the Guinness World Record for biggest group cosplay of any comics series, American, Japanese, or otherwise."

"I have no idea what that is—"

"No worries, you just need to put on a costume and join us! We have costumes that match all body types and gender identifications. I'd just need you to fill out this cosplay consent form . . . "

"No thanks. Good luck to you guys, really. But I'm afraid I'm running late as it is . . . "

The fire-and-brimstoner with the megaphone was wandering back toward me, and I had to shout a little to be heard over him. "THE WORST THREAT YOU FACE IS NOT INVASION FROM OUTER SPACE, BUT THE ROT OF INNER SPACE IN YOUR VERY SOUL!"

"But this is to prove *Dante's Fire* is the most popular manga to ever come from Japan to America," Ninja Person continued.

"THERE IS ONE ONLY ONE SUPERHERO WHO CAN SAVE YOU, AND HIS NAME IS OUR LORD JESUS CHRIST!"

"And that *Dante's Fire* otaku are the greatest, most dedicated otaku in history." *Otaku* was a Japanese word that had been adopted as a prideful self-identifying term by international anime fans. I'd met precious few Americans who understood that in Japan, *otaku* had as pejorative a connotation as *geek* used to have here, meant to describe basement-dwellers (as in *taku*, or "home") with poor social skills and even worse hygiene.

"THERE IS ONLY ONE COSPLAY TO DRESS IN THAT WILL SAVE YOU . . . "

"All you need to do is take a costume and report over there, the base of the steps to the Sails Pavilion, at midnight tonight to live on forever as a part of history—"

" . . . AND THAT IS THE BLOOD OF CHRIST, TO AC-
CEPT HIM AS YOUR LORD AND THE SOLE PATH TO
SALVATION."

Neither of these people were going to take no for answer, so
I basically just ran away. Ninja Person immediately turned to the
next hapless victim while the preacher blasted cosmic invective
at another random passerby.

I didn't want to belong to any eternity that would have me
as a member.

– – – –

The preview night hordes pushed their way through the four
sets of double doors into the main hall, advancing me with
them. The inside of the convention center simultaneously went
on forever and seemed far too small to contain everything; the
displays always seemed to get bigger and brighter and louder
every year. The *Jurassic Park* TV show booth was an eye-pop-
pingly detailed re-creation of a cloning lab, bordered by clear
tubes in which embryonic dinosaurs of various species—there's
a raptor, a T. rex, an ankylosaurus!—bobbed in colorful gel.
Masked *luchadores* hurled each other onto a raised mat with
teeth-rattling crashes; hooded dwarf wrestlers did the same with
slightly less noise—but only slightly. A LEGO airship covered
in stunted-limbed wizards and cyborgs quietly traced parabolas
in the air above the company's plastic wonderland of a booth.
The *Dragonriders of Pern* movie people were letting guests climb
into the saddles of a variety of roaring life-size wyrms and get
photographed. On a Jumbotron overhead a digitized man with

machine guns instead of arms ran through what appeared to be a college campus, perforating zombie co-eds with duck-if-you-hear-it booms. Superman and Captain America and Link (*not* Zelda, goddamn it) and the Teenage Mutant Ninja Turtles and *Game of Thrones* and Commander Shepard (male and female versions) loomed on banners in the cavernous room over their respective corporate parent's booths like fluttering flags on a medieval battlefield. The displays of T-shirt vendors with the Green Lantern logo and the Deadpool logo and the Venture Industries logo and "Bazinga!" climbed to the rafters. A woman in elf ears and a floral wreath hawked what appeared to be small knit busts of your favorite superheroes meant to go over the eraser end of a pencil. (Pencil doilies? Was that actually a thing?) The cube boxes of big-headed Funko dolls formed whole walls of vendors' booths like Minecraft bricks. A brochure-wielding NASA representative stood in a small canvas tent silkscreened with purple nebulae photographed by the Hubble Telescope and looked absolutely overwhelmed by the Lovecraftian vastness of it all.

If the con was an archeological site, this would be the uppermost strata, the bombastic bells-and-whistles mini-Disneylands that were the booths of the major Hollywood studios and video game publishers. Hollywood discovered Comic-Con not long after I broke into the industry: San Diego is a mere two hours south of Los Angeles and thus a great place to waste employers' expense accounts while acting all hip at the same time by pretending to enjoy these graphic-manga-comic-novel things. Movie people weren't used to having gatherings to which the *public* was invited: They were used to treating themselves more like distant royalty whom the huddled masses could just gawk at through the palace gates. But once they discovered Comic-Con as a marketing tool they quickly infected the event and took it over like show-biz vampires.

Even so, every once in a while at Comic-Con you might accidentally stumble onto, you know, actual comic books, even if the space allotted to the convention's original purpose had shrunk and shrunk until it was just a little corner of the hall. The dealers of original art and dealers in old comics would be the absolute lowest level of our hypothetical dig, where the origins of Geek civilization might be discovered. In the olden days, when the con was first founded, around the same time the great Jack Kirby moved to Southern California to ease his youngest daughter's asthma, this was the con: the comic book dealers replaced the childhood memories your mom threw away when you went off to college. Of course, you were an accountant now, with a job you hated, a wife you forgot why you liked, and kids you were too busy trying to keep alive to properly love. And now you finally had more than twelve cents in your pocket, now you could pay several hundred bucks for that book you read so much when you were ten that it fell apart in your hands. Back when I was twelve and I could cajole my dubious father into taking me to a "convention" in Manhattan, it was invariably inside the dingy ballroom of a struggling hotel on Tenth Avenue near the entrance to the Lincoln Tunnel. The vendors looked like carnies and smelled like ashtrays and talked like crotchety candy store clerks, perpetually vigilant against thieving children. They surrounded themselves with cardboard longboxes jammed to the gills with comic books in plastic Mylar sleeves, with or without the (hopefully acid-free) cardboard backing to keep them straight and flat.

The most coveted comics, like *The Incredible Hulk* #181 and *Giant-Sized X-Men* #1 and *Daredevil* #168 were mounted on a wire rack behind them—you had to ask for permission to look at them more closely.

Beyond the back-issue dealers was the self-deprecating alliteration of Artists' Alley, my domain, which still clung to the Comic-Con in the same way the back-issue dealers did, like a vestigial tail. The setup remained virtually unchanged since the 1970s: a grid of fold-out tables behind which sat comic book artists and the occasional writer, selling comics and prints, offering to do sketches for fans. The wannabes fresh out of SVA or SCAD, pushing their stylishly bound photocopied mini-comics, sat beside legends of the medium who had come to realize there was more money in drawing Vargas-style cheesecake pinups of Black Cat, Mary Jane, and various other female members of Spider-Man's supporting cast and selling them at cons than there was in actually drawing *The Amazing Spider-Man* comic itself.

One table had my name on it. I dumped my stuff on top; but before I could walk around to the other side Katie Poole rushed over to me. She had her trademark handkerchief tied around her cornhusk-frizzy blonde hair, perfecting a look that I would absolutely never tell her to her face I called "Hot '70s Mom." When she hugged me, the baby bump beneath her brown sweater rubbed against my side.

She instantly said, "Not fat, pregnant."

"Oh, good," I said, laughing. "Congratulations. I didn't want to assume, that's happened before and—it didn't go well."

"I hear you, I've been there."

"How far along?"

"Seven months."

"Wow. And you made it out this year?"

She looked at me like I was nuts. "What, and lose my table? Fuck that. Priorities, man, priorities."

San Diego Comic-Con was unique among conventions in that once you were granted an Artists' Alley table by the Powers That Be, you were grandfathered into the system. That table was yours forever, as long as you showed up every year to claim it. But miss just one Comic-Con, and you risked losing your table to the ravenous hordes on the waitlist who would gladly take it off your hands.

"So if I start going into labor prematurely," Katie said, "I need you to run and get me hot water from the men's room."

"Don't worry, I played catcher on my high school baseball team. You're in good hands."

The line of fans waiting in front of Katie's table was a half dozen deep when I arrived, and now that she'd arrived the crowd was growing. She was facing me and hadn't noticed. I nodded over her shoulder: "Your adoring public awaits."

She turned and saw. "Oh! Look at that." She waved at them. "Thanks for waiting, guys. Just let me get set up."

I had exactly one guy waiting for me. He removed a stack of my *Mister Mystery* issues from a vinyl case. I hadn't done a regular run on a book in my three years of self-imposed exile; the public forgets you quick. Katie, on the other hand, had replaced me on the *MM* ongoing and subsequently, as the kids say, blown up. It wasn't so long ago that I first met her on the con circuit, when she was the talented up-and-comer pushing mini-comics of her own creation in Artists' Alley. Back then she had asked me about tips for breaking in, and now she already vastly surpassed me in buzz. I tried to be proud of her success, the way a parent or a big brother would be, I really did.

But it was a struggle. Jealousy is the creative professional's constant companion. You hear your friend gets a gig and your first reaction isn't "Good for them," it's "Why didn't *I* get that gig?" Social media provides a steady stream of nourishment to the envy demon. Online it looks like everyone is getting better reviews, everyone's sales numbers are higher, everyone's follower count is bigger. No matter how many breaks you get, whenever you suffer a reversal of fortune you can still feel like the unluckiest sap in the world.

And then along comes someone like Katie, who in my mind was still a wide-eyed art school chick with bad highlights. In just a couple years since her first six-page Atlas Comics backup fill-in job she's metamorphosed into a seasoned superstar before my very eyes, zooming past me like I was standing still.

So, in my heart, I want to be happy for her. I desperately yearned to be a better person, a selfless person who could feel objective joy at her well-deserved success.

But it's hard. It's very, very hard.

Looking over the con floor, though, I found I still had so much affection for this world that had bludgeoned me so thoroughly over the years, with the persistence of a battered spouse. It's easy to be cynical about the con world, but walking through those doors every year reminded me of how much I goddamned loved comics. Under one roof was the entire process of the creative spark transitioning through different stages of being: from comics to movies to toys to baby tees. Caterpillars, pupae, and

butterflies adrift on a sea of interlocking references and knowledge points that you shared with a small army of strangers. I was
part of a continuity that began long before I arrived and would
continue long after I was gone, assuming society proceeded in
some similar form. That was why I wanted to get into this business in the first place.

This was geek culture.

– – – –

I don't mean to say I was without business, far from it; mine
just trickled in at a slower rate than Katie's. I kept a Commissions List on the corner of the table where fans would come up
to me and write down what they wanted me to draw, and I'd
charge them based on how big the drawing was, i.e., how long
it would take me: a pretty straightforward proposition. By the
end of preview night the list was three-quarters filled with characters: Deadpool, *Tomb of Dracula* Dracula, Captain America,
Mister Mystery, Batman, Baby Groot, Power Girl, somebody's
Dungeons & Dragons character (9th level Drow ranger/wizard),
another Deadpool, and so on. Before noon tomorrow it would
be completely full, and I'd have three days to crank them all out.
This, in essence, was how I made my living.

I could do a head shot ($50/ea.) in an hour, that was easy
dough. Half figures for $150; full figures twice that and the big-
gest moneymakers by far. For the fulls, if I worked hard and
didn't dick around and socialize too much I could do five of
those a day. Oftentimes, though, I had to work on them back in
my hotel room at night. In a show in the middle of the boonies
someplace where I didn't know any of the other pros, that wasn't

much of an issue. But here at San Diego, where everybody I knew was in attendance, it would be tempting to head out to parties and drink all night, so I had to get as much as possible done in Artists' Alley while the show was open.

I love drawing for so many reasons I could barely begin to tell you, not the least of which is that the ability to set images down on paper in the form of lines, for me, purges those same images from memory. The sight of the ranting Eastboro preacher next to the robot cosplayer was equal parts amusing and infuriating, so I sketched it out as a warm-up. I had my red Ziploc bag full of art supplies, which consisted of a Palomino Blackwing pencil, Microns, a refillable brush pen, various mechanical pencils, replacement leads, wedge erasers, and the phallic blob of gray putty that was my kneaded eraser.

Time kind of blurred in the eternally lit, windowless convention hall, and soon I was in the Zone, where others could not reach me and I could only leave when I chose. Set a line down here, set a line down there—wait, no, not there, here instead. They say sculptors dig a statue out of a block of marble by knocking away all the stone that isn't the finished piece; I was just covering all the white I needed to on the blank paper until the only thing left was the image floating in my head. And then my mind would be completely clear, because the image in my head was gone. Until the next one appeared a few seconds later.

For some reason, though, the thing I love most about drawing is that moment of completion, of transforming a stack of blank Bristol boards, one by one, into finished works of art. I was turning Nothing into Something. I wouldn't go so far as to call the feeling godlike, but there was something undeniably mystical and sacred about the process, even if all you had at the end of it was a headshot of Sonic the Hedgehog.

I'd knocked out that first Deadpool and the Dracula by the time preview night ended and so I could head over to the Marquis to meet Sebastian Mod guilt free. The comics pros were already three deep around the square cabana bar by the time I arrived. I looked for Sebastian there and then searched the dimly lit luxury grotto by the pool, but I couldn't find him.

However, I did find half a dozen friends from around the world I only get to see at Comic-Con. They hugged me and slapped me on the back, and together we commiserated about the loss of Ben. Even those who didn't know how close he and I were had been hit hard by the news, and we all wanted to talk through it.

And, more importantly, drink through it, with a rapidity that made our increasingly panicked server start with "Rough Night" in her eyes until, two hours later, became "Please Kill Me Now."

One of my guilty pleasures of attending a comics convention is visiting the hotel bar after hours and watching all the pros fill the place beyond capacity. The mounting horror on the bartenders' faces (or, even worse, bartender's) as they realize *these people won't stop drinking and I may not have enough stock to last the night, much less the weekend* is a truly awe-inspiring sight to behold, not unlike seeing the sun setting behind the Grand Canyon. The bartenders don't understand that—for a lot of us—the con circuit is the social circle we don't have at home, trapped at a drawing board round the clock, unless you have kids to drive to school or a wife who wants to go to the movies more than twice a year.

So, here I was, depressed and drunk, faced with impotence

in the face of death. I just want you to understand what my mental state was when I saw the person I hated more than anyone else in the world walk into the pool area.

Now my mother, bless her soul, is one of the most kind-hearted people I have ever met, and she always discourages me from saying I "hated" anybody. And for a long time I tried to pretend I didn't hate Daniel "Danny" Lieber. He was a lifer at Atlas Entertainment, which is what Atlas Comics renamed itself once they started making movies. He started out as an editor when I was an artist on the regular *Mister Mystery* comic book series, and I tried to make my mother proud and not hate him when he would take some of my pages away and give them to another artist whenever there was the slightest hint of me missing a deadline. I tried not to hate him when he tried to have my A rate slashed by $20 a page. I tried not to hate him when he was condescendingly informing me that I was never big as I could be because I didn't ape the work of Artist X, Y, or Z.

But I would have to say I gave up all pretense of trying not to hate him when I returned to this very pool bar from the men's room three years ago and discovered him making out with my wife.

Yeah, I'd have to pinpoint that as the exact moment I was pushed over the edge.

I saw that on the last night of the con, and I walked out of my, let's be honest, already disintegrating marriage. I happened to have another con in Toronto I was going to right after San Diego that year. So I threw my stuff in a storage unit and flew off to Canada. And I booked another con after that, and another con after that. And so on and so forth. I never returned to our home in New York. Or any other home at all, for that matter. I just embarked on an infinite tour.

One of my drinking buddies, the bearish English artist Ian Smallwood, leaned over like a ruddy-faced devil on my shoulder and muttered in my ear:

"Aw, what is this . . . Can you believe this wanker, showing his face around here?

I looked and saw Danny, dressed like a generic entertainment-industry douchebag, which is to say he was a fifty-year-old trying to dress like he was fifteen: hoodie, gray T-shirt, overpriced jeans, limited-edition high-tops.

He was carrying a portfolio not unlike my own, covered in colorful stickers. "Pathetic," Ian said. "Tooling around with that portfolio. Probably got samples from some poor Estonian art student he can pay in blue jeans to take our gigs away."

I saw Danny through the palmetto bushes, seeming kind of lost by the edge of the pool, checking his watch and then looking around as if he didn't have anywhere to go. My drinking buddies, maybe half of whom knew that the Editor-Makes-Out-With-Freelancer's-Wife Incident was what precipitated the end of my marriage, followed my gaze. This half erupted in a combination of gasps and giggles.

When I got out of my chair and started walking toward Lieber with terrible purpose, I could sort of hear the scrape of chairs behind me as somebody tried to stop me, but then Ian Smallwood stopped them:

"No, wait. I want to see this, it could be brilliant."

A small footbridge connected the bar area to the pool area over a bubbling rock-lined tropical fountain. Lieber was staring at his phone as he crossed and didn't even see me until I walked into him, shoulder first.

Hey, it's not like I'm proud of this. I'm really not. Truth is I had a jet-black serpent of bile inside me that was rattling and squirming and trying to get out. I was pissed off at just about everything and I had drowned with booze any part of me that might have stopped me from surrendering to my worst impulses.

My mother was a literature professor. What does Ishmael say at the beginning of *Moby-Dick*? He goes to sea because the damp, drizzly November in his soul makes him want to knock strangers' hats off in the street.

I really wanted to knock this motherfucker's hat off is what I'm saying.

After we collided, Danny Lieber looked up, into my eyes, and he did not like what he saw there. I couldn't blame him. He took a few steps away from me.

"Isn't Christine's birthday thing tonight, Danny? Shouldn't you be there?"

"We're not together anymore," Lieber said, eyes downcast. "She moved to L.A. last year."

"What?" My pickled brain roiled, unable to process this information. "Really?"

I had walked over here with a vague plan to kick his ass, but now I was just standing in place with my mouth open. Did he really say that Christine was single?

"Yeah, so." He shrugged. "There's one thing we have in common. She dumped both of us. I guess I did you a favor. Anyway. I got a meeting, so . . . Good to see you? Maybe? I guess?"

He tried to get past me, across the bridge, but I stepped in front of him.

"What third-world penciller are you exploiting today, Danny?"

I made a drunken lunge for the handle of his portfolio, but Lieber leaped back. "Dude, find some coffee," he growled. "Stop fucking the corpse of your career. It's not a good look."

In my peripheral vision I could see my drinking buddies stirring, exchanging worried looks, as in, gee, maybe throwing the lit match into that lake of kerosene wasn't as much fun as we thought it was going to be.

Danny sized me up and the fear left his face, along with the anger, replaced by contempt: the default setting of the bully. He knew I knew I wasn't going to do shit to him because I thought I was above that; I thought I was better than him. That was what gave the Danny Liebers of the world a leg over you and me: they were whatever they needed to be, good, bad, or indifferent.

"I don't even know what you're doing here. This show is for comic book artists—you haven't drawn an actual comic book in years."

"I was supposed to give Ben K a lifetime achievement award."

"Little late now," Danny sneered as he tried to walk away.

That did it, as far as I was concerned.

I punched him.

Which is to say, I tried to punch him. It was more of an attempted punching. I'm not a violent person, I swear. I don't know what the other witnesses told you, but I've never even been in an actual fight before.

Up until this point of which we're speaking, I mean. I'm not counting the one I get into later on.

I was drunk, the lighting was dim, we were on the apex of a curved bridge, and Danny saw my fist coming from Tijuana. He easily dodged out of the way. He kind of slapped at me and missed, and I instinctually understood the easiest way for me to lay a glove on him would be if I was literally on top of him, so I bear-hugged him in that pathetic bar-parking-lot-fight sort of way.

I was dragged off by Ian and some of the other guys, joined by a very large bald black man in a green Oxford with the word SECURITY on the back. A phalanx of dudes separated Danny from me, and the security guard hustled me away from the bar, pool, and hotel, toward a gate in the low fence beyond the palmetto-concealed in-ground Jacuzzi. From the outside, you needed a Marriott room keycard to get in. From inside, a large security guard could just open the door with one free hand and eject a drunk cartoonist with the other.

I stumbled down a half dozen steps but was spared the indignity of sprawling onto my face. When I turned back the guard was slamming the gate closed.

"Sleep it off," he said. "And don't let me see you coming around here."

"I won't," I said to the back of his head, "until I can think of a better comeback than that."

A forest of white masts crowded the marina on the other side of the harborwalk railing. It was pretty late, the day before the con actually started, so only a couple cosplayers and tourists witnessed the shame of my ejection from the Marquis.

Idling in the small paved patio between the rear of the hotel and the harbor was that longtime San Diego institution: a pedi-cab. The driver was a woman dressed like a famed video game explorer, with a ponytail braid and khaki shorts. She sat on her bike seat thumbing through her phone. The passenger cab, or whatever you called it, had been transformed into some kind of lost Mesoamerican throne, all skulls and obsidian daggers, like a set piece in the stage show of an Aztec death-metal band. Throughout the city I had seen similar jitneys turned into famous furniture from pop culture, like the Iron Throne, or the New Gods' Mobius Chair, or a Batbike.

"Where to?" the driver asked as I climbed into the Mayan Popemobile. She had an accent I couldn't have placed even if I was sober. Russian, maybe?

I took a deep breath, the air briny. Metal halyards clanged against masts in the distance. A Viking longboat floated along the bay, flying the History Channel flag, presumably venturing out for raids on other basic cable channels.

"I . . . " I suddenly had the burning urge to get away from here, away from the commercialized womb of the con. "Take me to your favorite place."

The driver turned back and looked at me blankly. "My favorite place?"

"Yeah. Anywhere but here if you would, madam."

"I can't bike to my favorite place."

"Your favorite place you can bike to would be perfectly fine."

She considered this request for a second. "That I can do."

Then she stood on the pedals and started pumping away.

− − − −

The bay slapped the gray rocks heaped at the edge of the Seaport Village shopping district as the rickshaw rocked past the marina's quaint faux–New England gables and tiny lighthouses. The edges of my Aztec throne were highlighted with green and orange track lights that lit up as the driver pedaled, along with a green glow from the undercarriage that made us look like the ghost of Tron cycles. We glided in our incandescent way through the erupting riot of coral trees planted on either side of the path, beige lightning trapped trying to crackle skyward.

We passed a large abstract pink marble monument against which a forlorn bronze Bill Mauldin serviceman leaned, helmet drooping from his hand. Then the driver turned left onto a parking lot embarcadero that jutted into the sea. The bike path continued along a row of mottled eucalyptus. On one side loomed a massive aircraft carrier. Red, white, and blue Christmas lights twinkled diagonally from the control tower at this hour. A row of retired gunship helicopters slumbered on its deck.

"Here we are," the driver called back as the pedicab squeaked to a halt.

We'd stopped before a huge, four-color monument that took me a couple seconds to recognize because previously I had only ever seen the subject matter in black and white. Looming over me was a giant U.S. Navy sailor—blue uniform, white kerchief and hat—with one arm crooked around a nurse in a white skirt and hose and shoes, leaning her back and kissing her. These were the central figures of the famous V-J Day photo from Times Square taken in August 1945, now rendered in three dimensions and three stories high.

Craning my head up at it, I laughed. "This is your favorite place?"

"That I can bike to. Yeah."

"How come, if you don't mind me asking?"

The driver shrugged. "So many statues, all around the world, are raised to death and war. This one is raised to love. To a kiss. If that's not magical, I don't know what is."

I got out of the wheeled obsidian throne to walk all the way around the statue. It was underlit below and I resisted the childish urge to look up the giant nurse's white skirt. I returned to the side where the pedicab waited, glowing, the driver smoking a cigarette. It was a striking scene, so I sat down on a marble bench near the statue and started sketching.

"So where is your favorite place?"

"What do you mean?"

"You know, the one you said you couldn't bike to."

"Oh. It's a forest. Białowieża, this big national park in Poland. When we were teenagers we'd drive up there and go camping for the weekends in the summer. Get drunk. Hike. It was awesome. Some of the oldest trees on planet Earth are in that forest. And you can feel it. It's not like going back in time. It's like time . . . stopped."

"How'd you wind up here?"

"In America? I went to school here."

"You went to school in San Diego?"

"No. I graduated from Penn State. I wound up in San Diego . . . " She blew the thin strands of hair that had fallen across one eye onto her head. "I don't want to talk about it. It's stupid."

"Aw, c'mon."

"No, it's embarrassing. It's because of a boy."

"Not a man?"

"Oh, no. A boy. We started dating in school and I followed

him here after. But he left a long time ago. And I'm still here."

"I know what that's like."

She grunted a deep central European laugh: centuries of perennially justified cynicism expressed in a short, single breath. "No you don't. You're a man."

I had no interest in arguing with that, so I kept my mouth shut. I turned to look back at the water bobbing between sea wall and battleship and laughed.

"You better not be laughing at me," she said.

"No, not at all," I said. "I just realized I'm sitting here by the sea, thinking about your forest. If I was in the forest, I'd probably be thinking about the sea." I shook my head. "Sometimes I feel like I've been trained to look at everything except what's really there."

She nodded. "You know I'm charging you for this whole time, right?"

"Yeah, that's fine." I held up my sketchbook. "Finished."

She took it from me and smiled at the drawing, of which I was proud. "It's lovely," she said. She flipped through the pages and then handed it back to me.

"It's yours, you can have it gratis."

She took a long drag on her cigarette, then shook her head as she exhaled.

"Thanks, but you can keep it. I don't want you to have to rip a page out of your beautiful book. Besides . . . I'm not one of these people who needs to look at herself all the time."

"Fair enough," I said, and climbed back into the pedicab for the ride back to the Bayfront.

"You're pretty good. What kind of art do you usually do?"

"Comic books, mostly."

"Really?" She turned back to me, nose wrinkled in puzzlement. "They still make those?"

THURSDAY

Christine and I were arguing over the check in a restaurant. I had ordered the great white shark and it never came, but she said you got the kraken and that's basically the same thing, and I said no those are two sea monsters that don't taste anything alike, and over the lava river in the kitchen staffed by gum-cracking roller derby girls a phone kept ringing and ringing and no one was picking it up.

Finally, I woke up. It was still dark, and I didn't know where the phone was. So I flopped around a bit in the too-big bed until I found a light switch. Whatever rocket scientist designed this room had put the phone over on the glass-lined writing desk near the window. Its ring was a high fluttering trill, rising and fading before striking again, like a delayed-reaction heartbeat. It just sounded excited that someone wasn't using their cell phone for once.

I managed to untangle myself from the sheets and staggered over to the receiver. "Hello?"

"This is the front desk." Flat, nasal woman's monotone.

I looked and looked until I found the clock: 4:35 a.m. "Uh-huh?"

"Some detectives from the San Diego Police Department would like to speak with you."

I became aware of the throb of my hangover and the dryness of my mouth. It was the same story, every con: I overdid it with the drinking the very first night and then felt like shit the rest of the weekend. I really needed a glass of water, and also—

"Wait. Did you say *police*?"

"Yes."

"They're here now?"

At that moment there was a knock on my door.

I blinked. I had stripped down to my boxer shorts after I got home and belly-flopped onto the bed. I remembered being at the Marquis poolside bar, and the fight, and then going to the kiss statue after the fight, but I had no memories whatsoever of returning to the hotel and going to sleep.

I didn't know if the desk clerk said goodbye or not; I didn't. I hung up and shouted "Just a second" at the door.

I somehow managed to find last night's jeans crumpled on the bathroom floor but couldn't find my shirt before whoever was at the door knocked again and said, "Police." His voice was at a normal volume but the word boomed loud and clear.

"I hear you," I called. "Just getting dressed."

I gutted the drawer beneath the flatscreen TV until I found a plain olive-green T-shirt and pulled it over my head.

Through the peephole I could see two men in suits who, beneath the gaudy fluorescent light of the hallway and my currently compromised cognitive capacity, reminded me of the detectives in Todd McFarlane's *Spawn* comic books, Sam and Twitch: one short, broad, and angry-browed; his partner tall, slim, spectacled, with the pale shock of a widow's peak rising like an eternal flame off the top of his head.

I opened the door and Sam said hello and mumbled each of their names, which were neither Sam nor Twitch, but I didn't quite catch them.

"Mind if we come in?" Twitch said.

"Ah . . . " I suddenly became self-conscious about the clothes I had strewn all over the floor hunting for my shirt. "It's kind of a mess in there. I'd rather . . . "

Neither of them reacted visibly. "That's fine, we can talk in the lobby," Sam said.

"Can I ask what this is about?"

"Sure you can," Twitch said.

I waited for them to tell me but they just stared at me in silence. At last, Sam chuckled and slapped me on the shoulder. "Cop humor."

"Oh." I blinked. "Oh."

"Sorry. There's just been an incident that happened earlier tonight. We were hoping you could help us out."

"Provide some insight, like," Twitch said. "Shouldn't take too long."

I looked down at my bare feet. "Should I . . . ?"

"Nah," Twitch said. "I mean, you don't have to if you don't want to. That's how quick this should be. Shoes and socks optional."

"Also, it's easier to catch you if you try to make a break for it," Sam said.

I must have blanched because Sam barked a laugh and slapped me on the shoulder again:

"Cop humor, brother. Cop humor."

– – – –

My room was on the eleventh floor and it was an endless Space Elevator ride to the Space Lobby, me wedged in between the two cops.

"So you here for Comic-Con?" Sam asked.

"Yeah," I said, smiling for no reason other than I was nervous.

"Who are you dressing as?" Twitch said.

"Sorry?"

"What's your costume?" Sam said. "Like, Captain America, or Winter Soldier, or the Joker, or what?"

"I think I seen more Winter Soldiers than Captain Americas wandering around town this year," Twitch said.

"I think you may be right. A lot of lady Winter Soldiers too."

"A lot of hot lady Winter Soldiers."

"You got that right. Makes me question my sexuality. It truly does."

"Well, when you find out the answer, keep it to yourself."

I felt the need to say, "I'm not a cosplayer, I'm one of the guests—I'm an artist."

Sam said, "Is that right? That's cool. Oil or watercolors?"

"Comic books."

Twitch frowned, puzzled. "They still make those?"

– – – –

Spider-Man had passed out in the far corner of the Space Lobby, his head thrown back against a couch. He had really let himself go since Gwen Stacey died. The upper half of his Spandex had peeled away from his waistline and rolled all the way up to his man boobs, exposing a great white beer belly that gleamed like a giant pearl. A security guard texted by the front doors and paid him no mind at all.

The detectives walked toward a couch close to those doors and I followed them, my bare feet making *slap-suck-slap-suck* sounds on the marble floor tiles. There was no one else here this early in the morning except for us, the guard, a weary Mexican American front desk clerk with a Wonder Woman tiara resting on her hair, and Spidey.

Twitch produced a neat little black Moleskine notebook from his inside jacket pocket and undid the elastic strap. As if I had already commented on it, he grinned apologetically and said, "My kid got it for me for Christmas. I know, it looks too fancy to be a cop's pad, right?"

"I call it his Book of Special Thoughts," Sam said and winked at me.

"Ball-buster," Twitch said. "Like I'm writing poems in it and shit."

"Dear Book of Special Thoughts," Sam said with a lisp, "this is my Ode to the Crackhead Who Shot His Baby Mama."

"But my little girl got it for me for Christmas, so, you know." Twitch gestured to an empty armchair opposite the couch he sat on. Sam draped his ham hocks over the arm on the other end.

Twitch asked me for the spelling of my name, which he dutifully wrote down in the Book of Special Thoughts. "Okay, and for profession, we got comic book . . . artist? Is that right?"

"Penciller, technically, I guess, but comic book artist is fine."

"Sounds good. And where in God's green Earth did you come from to visit us here in San Diego for our famous Comic-Con today?"

"Cleveland," I said.

"Cleveland. And is Cleveland where you make your permanent residence?"

"No . . ."

"Okay, and where is your permanent residence, sir?"

"I . . . " I smacked my dry lips. I never did get that glass of water. "I don't really . . . have one at the moment."

Sam and Twitch looked at each other. It was the first time they had any visible reaction to anything I said so far.

"No permanent residence?" Sam said.

"No," I said. The next words came out slowly, deliberately, well-worn from constant repetition. "I gave up my house three years ago. Now I live entirely at cons. They fly me out, put me up in hotels, and I go to my Artists' Alley table and draw sketches for people, and then another con flies me somewhere else. I just ask them to extend my stay past the weekend in either direction, instead of paying me an appearance fee. So, technically, if you're asking me my permanent residence . . . " I looked around the lobby, spotted Spider-Man snoozing in the corner, and jerked a thumb at him. "You're looking at it."

Twitch's eyes had narrowed quizzically at the beginning of my explanation and remained so. "But there are no comic cons during, like, Christmas weekend. Or New Year's. Where do you go when there is no con?"

"I . . . I have my car."

"Your car," Sam said.

"You live out of your car," Twitch said.

"Only when I absolutely have to. Around the holidays, like you said. When my parents are truly driving me crazy and I can't deal staying with them."

"Where is your car now?" Twitch said. "Is it in Cleveland?"

"No, Newark Airport," I said. "Long-term parking."

"So your permanent residence is in Newark?"

"It's where my mail gets sent."

"To your car?"

"To a UPS Store."

"Huh," Twitch said. "You're like a gypsy."

"Or a hobo," Sam said.

"Okay, okay, I feel like we're focusing too much on the residency thing," Twitch said, raising his hand to forestall an objection no one was making. "We'll get your cell phone number and that's how we'll get in touch with you if we need to. So can you tell us your whereabouts from, let's say, eight p.m. yesterday evening to . . . well, when the desk clerk phoned you in your hotel room."

"Be as detailed as you can be," Sam said.

I blinked. "Why?"

"Generally speaking, sir, we prefer to ask the questions. Gets everyone home quicker that way."

"Those of us with homes," Twitch said.

"You know a Daniel Lieber?" Sam said, glancing down at his notes. "Also known as Danny Lieber?"

"Yes."

"How do you know him?"

"Professionally," I said. "He was my editor for many years."

"An editor—for comic books?"

"Right."

"Was this before or after he was fucking your wife?" Sam said without expression.

I looked at him slowly. I made sure to match his expressionlessness.

"Before," I said.

Reading from the Book of Special Thoughts, Twitch said, "Sir, witnesses say they saw you drinking at the poolside bar at the Marriott Marquis down the street here from about nine p.m. to about eleven-thirty this evening, is that correct?"

"Sounds about right."

"And where did you go after you left the Marriott?"

"After you were *thrown* out, we heard," Sam said.

I shook my head in disbelief. "Is that piece of shit pressing charges against me? After everything else he's done to ruin my life? You've got to be kidding me. I didn't lay a finger on him!"

"Not for lack of trying," Sam said.

"Mr. Lieber was found dead by a bunch of folks in costume trying to take a picture on the steps of the convention center at just a few minutes past midnight," Twitch said.

"Shot," Sam said. "Twice. In a very unfriendly fashion."

I looked at the cops.

The cops looked at me.

"Are you serious?"

"No," Sam said, "this is all part of our stand-up comedy routine. Which we practice late at night in random hotel rooms to audiences of one."

The world narrowed then, becoming very cold and small

and focused on the men sitting directly in front of me.

"Where did you go after the Marriott?" Twitch asked again, more gently this time.

I didn't know what else to do other than answer. "I . . . I got in a pedicab outside the hotel and asked the driver to take me . . . somewhere. We rode around for maybe an hour. We hung out at that big statue, out by the battleship, what is it called? *The Kiss.*"

"It's called *Embracing Peace,*" Sam said.

"We're very proud of our landmarks here in San Diego," Twitch said.

"Big military presence here in town."

My brain was only now beginning to resynchronize with reality. "I support . . . uh. I support the troops," I said, almost like a sleepwalker.

"I'm sure that means a lot to them. Then what did you do?"

"Then I asked her to take me back here, and I went to bed. Must've been just after midnight."

Twitch's ballpoint pen hovered over a fresh page in the Book of Special Thoughts. "The driver was a woman?"

"Yeah."

"You get her name?"

"No. She said . . . she said she was from Poland?"

"A lot of people are," Sam said.

"Polish people, mostly," Twitch said.

Sam said, "Did you catch the name of the company on the side of the cart?"

"No."

"You pay with a credit card?"

"Cash, I think."

"You think. You get a receipt?" Twitch asked.

"I don't think so."

Sam and Twitch looked at each other.

"Well," Twitch said, putting his pen down without having written anything.

"I didn't kill him," I said suddenly, with more force than I meant to. "Do I have to say it out loud?"

"Doesn't hurt," Twitch said.

"Doesn't help much either," Sam said.

– – – –

"I . . . " I looked at the ground, then looked at the detectives.

"Yeah?" Twitch said.

"I think I should get a lawyer before talking more to you guys," I said.

"Why? Have you done something wrong?" Sam said.

The instantaneous way it came out of his mouth, like an actor responding to a cue, led me to believe he had offered that response to the same question the same way many, many times before.

"No," I said, but then that was pretty much all I had. Flop sweat had broken out on my brow, which made me nervous, which caused flop sweat to break out on top of the original flop sweat, and so on, in the usual manner of flop sweat.

"Look." Twitch held up his hand again—I was such a pathetic suspect that the detectives felt like they needed to help me along a little bit. "You can absolutely have a lawyer present if that's what you want, but as a legal requirement that only comes into play if we place you under arrest. But, you see, we haven't arrested you for anything."

"So," Sam said, "no lawyer."

"So then I don't have to talk to you guys?" I said.

"You're asking me?" Twitch said. "You're asking me, I would say, I would really like it, and in general it's in your best interest, and if you're interested in finding out who killed your friend, your editor, and see that person brought up on charges, then you most definitely should speak with us. But no, you have no legal obligation to speak to us, no."

"Of course, we have no legal obligation to not arrest you," Sam said, and smiled as soon as he saw understanding sink into my face.

"You'd need a charge," I said even as the threat center in my brain finally shook off the cobwebs and punched the Emergency Alarm button, alerting my mouth to the idea that perhaps being so argumentative with the police was not the wisest of strategies.

"That we would," Twitch said.

"Say, what do you have there in your Book of Special Thoughts, partner?" Sam said.

Twitch looked down at the Moleskine. "Oh, hey look, 'no permanent residence.' It says it right here. See?"

"Uh-oh." Sam didn't take his gaze off me. "The charge would be vagrancy, then."

I scowled. "I have a hotel room."

Twitch said patiently, "A vagrant, in the strictest sense, is a person with no *fixed* residence or income."

"'Idle' is what the law books say," Sam said.

"Who travels from place to place, living off the charity of others."

"That's kind of like, literally what you just told us you do."

"And vagrancy is illegal within the metropolitan limits of the city of San Diego."

"Then you'd have to arrest half the people at this convention," I said.

"We don't have to do anything," Twitch snapped.

"Just like you," Sam said.

"But we'd like you to talk to us."

"That's a very *strong* like."

"So what do you say we start all over again, at square one, in the cooperation department? And you tell us your movements between eight p.m. yesterday until now, like I asked in the first place. Or we could go down to our offices, which I would really rather not do, because, frankly, the cushions there are lumpy as shit."

I didn't need to think about it long.

"Sure. Just let me get some coffee."

Sam and Twitch didn't say anything as I stood up and walked over to the array of thermoses on a marble countertop to one side of the front desk. Wonder Clerk didn't look up from her computer. Nor did the security guard from his phone. The cops watched me the way a house cat on a windowsill watches a robin hopping across the front lawn.

But they looked up when I pressed on the plunger of the Space Thermos and out hissed a thin stream of brownish water, as if milked from the barren udders of the world's oldest cow. My efforts barely yielded enough alleged coffee to cover my thumbnail.

Yet somehow this puddle of caffeine represented the last remnants of my autonomy and dignity and I clung to it like a cherished heirloom. I very deliberately walked over to Wonder Clerk. She looked up long before I got there because my bare feet went *slap-suck-slap-suck* on the marble.

"Your coffee needs refilling," I said.

"At six," Wonder Clerk said.

"Good," I said, but didn't know why.

And then I walked back to the couch and sat across from the detectives.

– – – –

The Space Janitor showed up to replace the Space Lobby's Space Coffee just as the night sky filled with light and I wrapped up with the cops. I went back to my hotel room, which was still dark except for the narrow sliver of dawn where the curtains didn't quite overlap.

I kicked my jeans off and got under the covers and laid my head on the pillow and didn't sleep. I was frightened and anxious and depressed and angry all at the same time. Once I was relatively confident they weren't going to arrest me on the spot, I was able calm down a bit and outlined my movements as best I could. I know they say never talk to the cops without a lawyer present, but I did it for the same reason everyone else does: it was the quickest way to get rid of them. Any more tactical misfires and I would have spent the better part of the first day of Comic-Con in the police station, and the first day of Comic-Con was when I filled up my commission list and made most of my money. There was no way I was going to miss that.

I did not hold anything back. I told them about going to wait for Sebastian Mod in lieu of going to Christine's karaoke party. I told them about spotting Danny Lieber and our non-fight and me getting thrown out of the Marquis. After that I had no one to back up my story except the faux archeologist pedicab driver and the half-coherent homeless people we passed along the waterfront on our way to *Embracing Peace*.

Sam and Twitch looked like they believed me. But I bet they were old hands at looking like they believed people.

They left without taking me with them, so I had that going for me at least. They took my cell phone number and gave me their business cards and told me to contact them if I thought of or learned anything else that might be relevant to the case. (They didn't say "case," they said "incident," but I had seen too many TV shows to not think of it as a "case.")

They asked the time and flight number for my plane out of town, which was to Austin on Monday, where I was supposed to attend the Lone Star Comic Con starting on Friday. Every answer I gave, including that one, was probably preceded by a hesitation, as I subconsciously considered lying, but in the end I was completely earnest with them.

I jokingly asked, as they left, if I was going to make my flight, and they did not laugh back. I got the distinct impression I was still under suspicion, if not under arrest. Yet.

The con floor didn't open for another four hours. Because I had nothing else better to do, and I wanted to purge my mind of the image, I gave up on sleeping and got out of bed and opened the curtains to let in the dead-channel early-morning Southern California sky.

I sat at the writing desk with my sketchbook and pencil and roughed out the scene of the crime as best as I understood it from the cops' description. They answered only a third or so of my questions about the murder—mostly, I imagined, because they were in the information-gathering business, not the information-sharing business. If I was the killer, they wouldn't want me to know how much they knew.

But I knew enough to know this:

The *Dante's Fire* cosplayers gathered to take their photo at a few minutes before midnight, with an iPad-wielding Official Observer from the *Guinness Book of World Records* standing close at hand. This allowed for the cops' timetable to be unusually exact for what transpired.

The primary character they were dressed as was Ulee-o, a kind of steampunk stealth pilot in a full-body helmet and goggles, with lots of patches and weapons and things all over his costume. The guy with the clipboard who had accosted me outside the convention center was dressed the same way. This was the most beloved character in the series, cosplayed as often by women as men. There would be other major *Dante's Fire* characters in the record-breaking picture, a smattering of Dantes and Fergies, but mostly one would see Ulee-os of all the genders, fat Ulee-os, black Ulee-os, Asian Ulee-os, immigrant Ulee-os, Ulee-os in wheelchairs, Ulee-os with service dogs, mommy Ulee-os carrying baby Ulee-os in Babybjörns strapped to their chests.

Near midnight the horde of Ulee-os gathered in the middle of the San Diego Convention Center, where a long row of steps leads to the Sails Pavilion. The kilt-wearing judge made the final count and the photographer's tripod was set up and he began to take pictures.

But then the top row of Ulee-os stopped looking at the camera; they looked up instead, at the Sails Pavilion, the white circus-tent upper terrace running across the top of the convention center. A figure emerged, staggering, uncertain, assumed to be drunk at first. But after the figure pitched forward and half the Ulee-os cried out in surprise and shock, he skidded face-first down the stairs and finally slid to a halt in the erupting, screaming mass. The snail trail of crimson he left behind was clearly visible.

At this point he was surrounded by a pandemonium of Ulee-os, some trying to help until discovering he was beyond help. The Guinness judge held down his kilt demurely as he ran across the trolley tracks to a pair of uniformed SDPD, their attention drawn to the eruption of cries and wondering whether it was something or just a bunch of adolescents freaking out for no comprehensible reason, which happens during Comic-Con every ten minutes.

It was Danny Lieber. He had been shot in the chest and once in the back for good measure. The blood trail suggested he had been attacked somewhere between the rear of the convention center and the Marquis and somehow managed to make it up the stairs at the rear of the building and across the Sails Pavilion to the steps on the other side before running out of life.

I finished my rendering of the scene and set my pencil aside. I often found I could purge emotions by setting their cause down on paper, but a dull ache in my heart remained. I had little love for Danny Lieber. But still. I couldn't help but feel a little bit guilty about his death. Though I didn't actually kill him, was it possible my hatred for him caused the karmic climate that allowed him to be killed?

I was even guiltier for being angry that Danny Lieber had, in going out and getting himself murdered on the first day of Comic-Con, managed to screw over an artist, me, while doing so, like he had screwed over artists every day of his miserable life. How appropriate. He was like a bee, lancing a fatal sting with his last breath.

But I was innocent. The cops wouldn't find any evidence that I *did* do it, so I was in the clear, right?

Right?

– – – –

Fittingly for Comic-Con, the first thing I saw when I walked out of the airlock of my Space Hotel was a line. It stretched all the way from the convention center across the street to the front doors of the hotel and curved around to the edge of the harbor and followed the water along the marina as far as I could see, behind the enormous big-topped concrete building. Most line-goers had prepared for the merciless Southern California sun, holding umbrellas and sitting in nylon folding chairs or hiding beneath tents or blue lean-tos on stilts. Encamped like refugees waiting for safe passage, they mingled with the actual homeless who passed out on the lawns between the snaking queues, clothes faded from the sun, skin baked to the color of orange brick.

A steampunk alchemist whose breasts peered over the uppermost edge of her lung-constricting corset walked up to a blood-soaked Ash standing in line. He was looking at his chainsaw arm as if trying to figure out how to scratch his nose with it.

"What are you in line for?" she asked him.

"Hasbro booth. Comic-Con exclusive figure."

"What is it this year?"

Ash looked at her as if she'd lost her mind. "Who cares?"

I waited patiently, one amongst the horde, for the SDPD traffic cop to let us ooze relentlessly across the street to the convention center. Six or seven massive high-arched white tents had been erected on the narrow lawn out front. I wasn't sure if this was the same line in front of the Bayfront or another one, with an army of fans of all ages and races waiting droop-shouldered for their anointed hour. Others sat crosslegged on the sidewalk and played Uno or Magic: The Gathering. I passed a pony-tailed woman in thick glasses arguing with a yellow-T-shirted Eastboro Baptist megaphoner. They grinned contemptuous smiles at each other as one waited for the other to stop talking so they could start, neither one listening to a word the other said.

Violent Violet was waiting for me at my table when I arrived. She bent her right arm and was pushing her hand into the end of her left stump. I wasn't sure if this was an isometric strength exercise or simply her way of "crossing" her arms, but I was pretty sure it'd be rude to ask. She had added a purple con-volunteer oxford and a four-day badge to her postapocalypse warrior woman's ensemble.

"Good morning!" she cried. "I brought your things from your storage unit; sorry I couldn't make it back last night. I had, uh, stuff. How was your night?"

"Uh . . . " I blinked. "Ask a different question."

The first thing I did was unzip the carrier and take out my banner. It was rolled up inside its stand, with its collapsible stake inside. I pulled it up and held it aloft. Like most artists' banners, mine featured the two characters I was most associated with: Mister Mystery and good ol' Gut Check, duking it out with killer robots and ninjas, with my name emblazoned over the top.

I removed a black felt dropcloth from my knapsack and draped it over the tabletop. I laid out my prints on the table, also mostly of Mister Mystery and Gut Check, but there was a Boba Fett I particularly liked as well as a Supergirl.

"Do you need anything? Water? Food? Do you want me to sit at your table so you can use the men's room?"

The throb of my hangover lanced through the dull ache of my general depression, demanding tribute. "Actually, if you could find me some Tylenol, you would become my personal superhero."

"*On it*," Violent Violet said with an intensity usually reserved for '80s action-movie heroes. In her zeal to execute her mission, she nearly knocked over the *Donnie Darko* bunny shambling down the aisle.

"What's her deal?" Katie asked from the next table. "The con didn't assign me a valet. Why are you so special?"

I just shrugged, wincing because it made my head ache. "Miss Poole, I live my life by what I call the *Ghostbusters* principle: if someone asks if you are a god, always say yes."

- - - -

There are various types you always see at every con, no matter where in the country, or the world, the show is being held. The vast majority of fans are the nicest people you could ever meet; they just want to come up to your table, shake your hand, get some comics signed, buy some new ones, take a picture with you, tell you how much your work means to them, ask you about why you made this or that choice in a story, ask you what you're working on next, and so on. A lot of pros grumble about going to conventions but I figure if you have a problem with sitting behind a table for a weekend letting people tell you how great you are, the problem isn't with cons, it's with you.

As I said, those are the vast majority of fans.

Then there are the exceptions.

Like the Voyeurs, the people who just like to watch people draw, as if they could somehow capture with their eyes whatever alchemy it is that allows the artist to put what is in her head onto a formerly blank piece of paper via her arm. A lot of them will film you with their phones while you're doing it, which is more than a little creepy. My favorite Voyeurs are the parents of bored children who make their kids stop and stare, as though I was churning butter in a bonnet at Colonial Williamsburg:

Look, kids, here's someone actually *making* something. With his *hands*.

Also common are the Lurkers, the ones who flip through every page of your portfolio of original art on the table. They'll pick up and stare at each print for so long you'd think they were imagining what it would look like hanging on every wall in their house. Lurkers spend upwards of an hour at each table in Artists' Alley and never say anything to anyone and absolutely never, ever buy anything.

For a long time the cohort I despised the most were the Models, the cosplayers who seemed to be laboring under the delusion that they were actually the con's main attraction. They leave their poster tubes or swag bags on top of my table, on top of my portfolio, on top of my prints, without asking, and stand and pose for a succession of photos from other randos' smartphones, completely blocking my table and preventing my own fans from getting near me. For the first few years after the whole cosplaying thing really took off I had fantasies about sweeping them away from my booth with a giant hockey stick. But after a while I learned to accept them as part of the landscape. Honestly, a lot of people *do* come to cons to cosplay or gawk at cosplayers, and if I can't convert those people into customers, I guess that's on me. I do wonder when cosplayers will figure out that they don't have to pay ridiculous entry fees and stand in line for forty-five minutes for a twelve-dollar hot dog; they could just mill about taking photos of each other in the parking lot to basically the same effect. Of course, as soon as enough of them decided to do that, the comic con industry would collapse and I would have to find some other way to make a living, but I almost think it would be worth it.

The Fetishists always want a super-specific sex-themed commission of some character they made first contact with when their hormones started bouncing around in puberty; their initial attraction to that fictional love had never quite faded. These requests range from the relatively harmless ("Cheryl Blossom lifting her skirt up so you can see her panties") to mildly disturbing ("Catwoman, on all fours, lapping up a dish of milk with her tongue but, like, she's spilling some of the milk on her boobs") to I'm calling the cops ("Can you do Freddy Krueger standing on a hotel balcony railing jerking off into the swimming pool?"). I almost always turn down the Fetishists, even though they are willing to pay way, way, *way* above the going market rate to have their kinks indulged. The problem is that rarely is the money quite enough to have whatever crazy image they want out of their head put into *my* head while I'm working on the damn drawing.

When the Disco Mummy guy walked up to my Artists' Alley table, I thought at first he was another classic con type: the Narrator. These guys can never not tell you exactly what thoughts are going through their heads at any given moment. They will also immediately begin talking to you as if they've known you all their lives; they might continue a conversation they'd started with you two cons ago, as if you'd been in cryogenic suspension since the last time they laid eyes on you.

The kid was in his early twenties, African American, with lenses so thick it looked like his pupils were painted right onto the glasses. He had no chin or shoulders to speak of; his head and neck just kind of oozed right into his torso like a partly melted candle. He was wearing what appeared to be a replica of Ryan Gosling's silk scorpion jacket from *Drive* over a striped Izod shirt. A gold VIP badge dangled from a lanyard around his neck.

"I don't know why there isn't a Plastic Man movie," this dude said as soon as he walked up to my table, without any introduction or salutation whatsoever: classic Narrator move.

I didn't look up from the commission I was drawing into a fan's sketchbook, which was full of various artists depicting Batman perched on a gargoyle. Not the most original theme for a fan sketchbook in history, I guess, but I like drawing Batman so I didn't really care. "I know, right?" I said. "Plastic Man is a great character. The Kyle Baker run is one of my all-time favorites."

A conversation with a Narrator is entirely one-way; they

could be having the exact same talk with the wall. The lack of eye contact and rushed monotone led me to believe that this particular Narrator fell somewhere on the Spectrum. Or Spectra, for that matter. "I mean, I don't understand why, I mean, superheroes have to be so serious all the time, you know? Like, I mean, they all have guns and tragic origins or whatever."

"You're preaching to the choir, Reverend," I said, still without looking up. Half the time a Narrator will just wander away if you avoid eye contract, still talking as if you're still there, giving you a good idea of how crucial you were to the conversation in the first place.

This one was just getting started, though. "I mean, Plastic Man's powers are really cool, and, like, back in the day, in the eighties, maybe the effects would be pretty bad, I mean pretty cheesy, but CGI has gotten really good now and with computers you could do stretchy powers really good, not like that lame *Fantastic Four* movie, I mean, but better."

"Computers! Is there *anything* they can't do?" I started to render the cathedral looming behind Batman in completely unnecessary levels of detail just so I wouldn't have to make eye contact with this guy, who was starting to get on my nerves a little, to be honest.

"And I mean Plastic Man has a lot of great villains too, like Disco Mummy. It'd be great to see Disco Mummy in live action."

I looked up instantly. "I'm sorry, I thought you just said Disco Mummy?"

"Yeah, Disco Mummy, she's a great character."

I set aside my Bristol board. "Please continue. In fact, I insist."

On cue, the Narrator swung his backpack off the knobby

protuberances that were not entirely shoulders and dropped it at his feet. From it he produced a dog-eared manila file folder and from that file folder he removed a half dozen screenshots ink-jet printed off the internet from the 1979 Filmation *Plastic Man* cartoon. In one, Plas was talking to a curvaceous woman with black hair and a purple half jacket. Beneath these she was covered from head to toe in mummy wrappings. In another, she appeared to be disco dancing to a jukebox in an underground cavern. They all looked utterly bananas.

"I'll need a full body drawing of her," he said, "dancing, or whatever, but with her butt facing us and turning back, you know. Dancing."

And this was how I discovered that this Narrator was actually a Fetishist.

I picked up the printout of Disco Mummy disco dancing: the animators had indeed designed her with a perfect apple-shaped butt beneath her bandages. I could see the appeal to a hormonally discombobulated tween. "Sorry, man, I'm only doing black and white sketches this con, my list is too long."

"I'll give you five hundred dollars," the Narrator/Fetishist said without missing a beat.

I blinked. As Fetishist requests went, this one was fairly milquetoast. I didn't even feel all that ethically challenged by it; after all, I'd be drawing Disco Mummy fully clothed. The wrappings completely covering her body were how you knew she was a mummy in the first place.

"Okay, you've got a deal," I said. "But I have a pretty long list, so I may not be done with it until Sunday."

I shook the guy's hand to seal the deal and tried not to make a face. The Fetishist's palm was cold, sticky, and wet all at once, as though not twenty minutes ago he had been licking it.

––––

Katie Poole was drawing; I was drawing; there was an eddy in the crowd around our tables, a gap where no one was around.

Two women dressed as the same *Steven Universe* character spotted each other across our aisle and ran to meet, screaming like long-lost sisters.

A man sat to one side of my table rebagging all of his signed comics, the tear of the Scotch tape on Mylar not quite drowned out by the *Doctor Who* and *Game of Thrones* themes played on an endless loop.

A train of Handmaids filed by in their crimson habits, dour faces framed by winged white bonnets, silent harbingers of oppression.

"Did you see the article on Bleeding Cool?" Katie said, not looking up from her DCAU Batgirl done in a very un–Bruce Timm realistic style. "About Danny Lieber?"

My pencil froze halfway through completion of Black Widow's hourglass belt-buckle design (the John Romita Sr. redesign from *Amazing Spider-Man* #86, that is, not the ScarJo MCU version, per my patron's request). Out of the corner of my eye I could see Katie wasn't looking at me, so I didn't have to worry whether or not my expression was giving anything away.

"Yeah?" I said with what I hoped was no discernible emotion.

"Be honest," she said, and it was only then she set her Bristol board aside and grinned directly at me. "Did you click your heels for joy? Or just squeal silently like a little fangirl?"

The roots of my hair tingled with heat. I wanted to keep working out the drawing, but I had to set it aside too. "C'mon, Katie. A guy's dead."

"Shut. Up. You don't fool me for a second, boy scout. I mean, look, am I happy he's dead, like, actively? No. But then people die all over the world, little kids in some hut somewhere from a disease you get from, like, drinking out of the same pond where the water buffalo poop. People die daily in wars and terrorist attacks and having flying robots drop bombs on your wedding party from the sky because somebody said the groomsman was ISIS. Those are abstract people I feel sad for in the abstract. But Danny Lieber? Come on. You don't get to spend so much of your life being such an unfathomable prick and get the same amount of sympathy as little kids who die in a bus crash in Mongolia or wherever. You don't get that! It's not fair. Otherwise what's the point of doing the right thing in your life at all?"

I frowned. "What did Danny do to you? I'm afraid to ask."

"Oh, my God, I've never told you this story? Really? Well. Anyway:

"Three years ago, when I was just starting out, I was tabling at WonderCon in Anaheim and he comes over to me and goes through my portfolio and is all like, you've got really good sequentials. I'm all freaking out because I know who he is, he's a big deal at Atlas, he gives me a card, and he takes my number so he can bring me over to meet some line editors at their booth later in the weekend, Sunday, maybe, when it's less crazy."

I made a face. "Uh-oh."

"So, like, later that night I'm at dinner, I can barely eat I'm so excited. Then I get a call. It's, like, eight at night and it's Danny and he goes—you're not even gonna believe what he says—"

Just then a colorful giant lumbered through our aisle. He wore yellow armor and a bright red winged helmet, clown make-up and a red nose, a long gold beard and gold cape, red boots, and a war hammer with an oversized foam Big Mac for a head. Happy Meal boxes garlanded his belt like Rob Liefeld pouches.

"*McThor!*" Katie screamed when she saw him and clapped her hands together. "Wait wait wait!" She pulled out her phone and handed it to me.

She ran into the aisle and threw her arm around McThor's shoulders and I took the picture.

"Your costume is *amazing,*" Katie said.

"It really is," I said.

"Thanks, guys," he said and glanced at the prints on Katie's table. "Your art's really good too."

"Thanks, man!" she said. "Have a good con!"

She walked around to her table, took her phone back from me, and returned to her Batgirl drawing. Because of the size of her pregnant belly she couldn't pull herself all the way up to the edge of table, so she had one of those lap desks with the beanbag underneath that tilted the Bristol toward her, and even then she had to hold her wrist at an odd angle to lay down the lines where she wanted. "Some really good cosplay this year, don't you think?"

"Katie," I said after a minute.

"Uhmmh?"

"You were telling me a story?"

"Oh! Sorry." She set her pad aside and turned toward me again. "Where was I?"

"Danny called you at dinner."

"Yeah, so he calls me at dinner and he's like, yeah, I wanted to take a closer look at your sequentials before we take it to the other editors, here's my hotel room number, come up around ten."

"Jesus Christ."

"Right? And I'm totally, like, thunderstruck, I don't even remember what I said. I was like, sorry, I can't, I'm tired, I've got commissions to finish, whatever. I think I even tried to make a joke about having a husband. And he's like—'Your loss'—and just hangs up on me."

"'*Your loss.*' Yikes. This guy."

"Wait, it gets worse."

"He really wanted to get into your sequentials."

"Seriously. My husband was like, I've never heard someone use 'come up and show me *your* etchings' as a pick-up line before. Anyway, the next day, I'm talking with a bunch of other people in Artists' Alley, mostly women, like Ming and Colleen, and he sees me across the room, and maybe he thinks we're girl-talking about him or something? Because I just happen to catch his eye and before I can look away he waves and booms out—so all of Artists' Alley can hear him, mind you—'*Good luck with your career!*'"

"God. What a piece of work."

"And I was devastated. I mean, just devastated. I cried in the ladies' room for a half hour, and I never cry like that. I thought my career was over. After I got back home I didn't get out of bed for a week. And it wasn't, you know, until I did that *X-Files* stuff at IDW and a completely different Atlas editor hired me that I got anywhere. They asked for me, and Danny couldn't just arbitrarily block me, you know, so here we are, but it took *two freaking years* after I refused to go up to his hotel room."

"I'm sorry."

"A bunch of people in Artists' Alley have stories like that. They're not all about Danny Lieber, but a lot of them are. That mugger doesn't know how many comics people he made happy by accident last night."

She winked at me before returning to her Batgirl. "But you better hope *you* have an alibi. After that whole thing with Christine."

Fuck me.

– – – –

I got off the Space Elevator a little before six in the evening and turned the corner to head to my room and saw Twitch standing in front of it, barking instructions to someone inside. My heart sank.

Twitch saw me coming halfway down the hall and nodded. "Good afternoon. How is your day going?"

"Getting better and better all the time," I said. Inside my room, uniformed SDPD officers were going through my drawers and my suitcase and my toiletry bag. Sam was nowhere to be seen.

"Glad to hear it." Twitch put a search warrant from the superior court of the State of California into my free hand. I looked at it. It looked to be signed by a judge; at the very least, it had been signed by somebody.

"Have you even bothered to check my alibi?"

"You mean the phantom lady pedicabbie? Yeah, you gave

us a lot to go on with that one, thanks, we'll get right on it."

I lifted the portfolio in my hand. "You mind if I drop my stuff off?" The only things I'd bothered to bring back from the con floor were my messenger bag full of art supplies and my portfolio filled with original art and commission sketches.

"You mind if we search anything you leave in your room?" said Twitch.

"Knock yourself out," I said. I could afford to be cocky because I knew there was nothing to find.

The uniforms stood still and watched as I dropped the portfolio and messenger bag on my unmade bed. In the mirror I touched up my hair with water and then nearly left without my sketchbook, but thought better of it. I went back to the bed and fished it out of the bag, along with a couple of pencils and pens.

"Thank you for your cooperation, sir," Twitch said as I walked out the door.

"If I complained, wouldn't you tell me you were just doing your job?" I called back.

"I never *just* do my job, sir," Twitch said to the back of my head. "I *love* my job."

– – – –

A Google search for "San Diego pedicab" garnered shockingly thin results—both were listed as "advertising agency," and only one was within walking distance. I could've called first, but going there was an excuse to stretch my legs.

Directly across the street from the convention center were trolley tracks where traffic cops blew whistles and kept the masses of cosplayers and large concentrations of black T-shirts and glasses from ducking under the clanging barbershop-striped crossing barriers as they lowered so the San Diego MTS trolley could roll past. Some shame-challenged studio marketer had decided it would be a smart idea to reskin the cars as a high-tech concentration camp transport for the *Man in the High Castle: Ten Years Later* TV movie.

The mob and I lumbered across the tracks and through the archway proclaiming the entry to the Gaslamp Quarter. The first few blocks of bars and restaurants were crammed with revelers of the Nerd Mardi Gras: a brass band in Syfy Channel shirts blasted a Sousa-style version of "The Imperial March" at krumping Stormtroopers. A small SDPD command pod rose up on a scissor lift over the scrum like a Walmart panopticon.

Beyond Island Avenue the con crowd thinned out considerably. As I trudged up the hill along the brick-lined sidewalk of Fifth Avenue, I was stuck behind an old Mexican woman in a track suit and carrying a cane, who was trying to walk a pitbull not much older than a puppy. The dog kept turning and biting at the leash and her owner kept clucking at her.

"*No, no, Mama*," the old lady said. "*No más.*"

Yellow Pedicab was on G Street between a vape shop and a Brazilian steakhouse. The storefront window was plastered with testaments to the benefits of advertising on a pedicab and a DRIVERS WANTED sign hung on the door.

I stepped inside and took off my sunglasses so I could see. The place was dark, with bikes and pedicabs hanging along three walls like carcasses at a butcher shop. The place reeked of grease and rubber. A white guy, whose skin was leathered in a very specific way that only Sun Belt white guys have, was cursing to himself in the middle of the room as he pulled the tire off a rim to get to the flat tube shriveled up underneath.

"Pardon me?" I said once, then again, louder, until the man looked up as he pulled the deflated tube out of the tire like a bra through a sleeve. He had circular wireframe glasses and shoulder-length hair that began somewhere near the middle rear of his skull; if you could yank his hairline forward, I was pretty sure it would adjust into a Beatles bowl cut.

"You a driver?" the bike guy said.

"No, but now that you mention it—"

"All our cabs are rented out now, man. You wanna drive, you're gonna have to take it up with the drivers themselves. Good news is most guys got kids, they take trips, they want to take the night off, they'd be happy for you to take over for a day, make a few extra bucks."

"No, I don't want to drive, I'm actually looking for a specific driver."

"Why?" Bike Guy flashed a grin. "You a cop?"

"No, I just—"

"You don't look like a cop."

"Well, there's a really good reason for that."

Bike Guy's eyes narrowed. "Process server?"

"No."

"Repo man?"

"No, it's nothing like that. I'm a passenger—*was* a passenger. I really need to speak with a driver I rode with last night. She's a woman, with blonde hair—"

"Oh, so that's how it is." Bike Guy nodded slowly. "You're a stalker."

"No, I swear to God, I'm not. It's just important I get in touch with her. She can really help me with something really, really important."

"What is it?"

I shook my head. "Look, it wouldn't mean anything to you, man. But it means everything to me. And—it is absolutely nothing weird or creepy, I promise."

Bike Guy shook his head too. "No can do, brah. For one thing I know all our drivers, and there ain't any chicks workin' for us right now." He held up a hand. "It's not because we discriminate, it's because no chicks have applied recently."

"Okay, but what if she isn't one of your regulars, what if one of your regulars rented their bike to her. Could I maybe talk to whoever had your bikes last night—"

"No can do, brah," Bike Guy said again. He picked up a clipboard off the counter and held it to his chest; it must have been the list of drivers.

"Aw, c'mon—"

"Sorry, man, that's, like, driver/dispatcher confidentiality and shit."

I opened my mouth to say there was no such thing, but immediately knew it was futile. I turned to leave, then turned back again. "Wait. If you know all your drivers, why did you ask if I was a driver when I first walked in?"

"That was a test, man. To make sure you weren't a cop or a perv." Bike Guy pointed the clipboard at me and peered over his glasses. "'Cause I don't talk to neither."

- - - -

Neither cop nor perv, I stood on the sidewalk outside Yellow
Pedicab and let pedestrians jostle me while I stared pointlessly at
traffic. Seemed like my investigation had been stymied before it
even really began.

A pedicab approached from down G Street, its driver out
of his seat, calves outlined like eggplants as he manfully pumped
the pedals, five hundred pounds of human distributed between
a pair of con-goers seated in the Starfleet Captain's chair with
wheels behind him, their faces completely obscured by the mam-
moth *Attack on Titan*–branded swag bags in their laps.

As the cab rolled past, a symbol on the back made me do
a double-take: it was line art of a muscular superhero, with a
saipan hat completely covering his head, pulling a rickshaw
holding an old dowager whose own head was covered by his
fluttering cape.

That sparked something in the deepest recesses of my
brain—I whipped out my sketchbook and flipped through the
pages until I found my drawing of the pedicab driver. Completely subconsciously, perhaps my eye was drawn to its vague rac-
ism, I had made a point of capturing that same symbol from a
sticker on the side of the Mesoamerican throne.

By the time I looked up, the Starfleet pedicab was already
gone, but that was okay: I had an idea. I typed "library" into the
Maps app and was delighted to find the main branch was literally around the corner from where I stood. San Diego was a pretty
small town when you got right down to it.

The main library was impressively cavernous, all metal and
glass, cleverly concealing any visible evidence of books. Two
homeless guys played chess near the wall-to-ceiling windows.

"We close in ten minutes," one of the front desk librarians said before I could even get through the door.

"No problem. Where are your phone books?"

She pointed, and I found. Turning the tissue-thin paper of the San Diego Yellow Pages made me feel like I was churning butter at Colonial Williamsburg. There looked to be six or seven businesses listed under PEDICABS, including a picture ad for Super Rickshaw.

I could have just ripped out the page, but that would have triggered my well-honed guilt complex. Up the main escalator I found a photocopier and fished some coins out of my pocket and copied the whole page.

"Kicking it old school," I muttered as the huge ancient machine rumbled through its task with a sliding light and ungodly racket. "Kicking this Hardy Boys shit *old school*, yo."

– – – –

I deemed my efforts sufficiently impressive to be rewarded with beer. I found a lovably awful dive bar back on G Street that had just the one tap, defiantly dedicated to Bud Light. I paid for a cold pint and sat alone in a corner booth, my butt crinkling on its descent.

I reached into my jeans and removed the search warrant I had shoved in my back pocket while riding down in the Space Elevator:

"The People of the State of California to any peace officer in the county of San Diego," it read, "Proof by affidavit having been made before me by Detectives (Sam and Twitch, whatever their real names were), San Diego Police Department demonstrates that there is substantial probable cause pursuant to Penal Code section 1524 for the issuance of the search warrant, as set forth in the affidavit attached hereto and made a part hereof as is fully set forth herein, you are, therefore, commanded to make search at any time of day, good cause being shown herefore, of room 1134 at the Hilton San Diego Downtown/Bayfront, 900 Bayfront Court . . . "

I set the paper aside. "Probable" and "cause" were the two words that leaped out at me. Probable cause that I shot Danny Lieber to death. Two words I had heard in countless TV shows and movies, but had never applied to me, personally, in real life, and now they chilled me to the bone.

I had to find a way to make *my* cause more *im*probable.

I called the number for Super Rickshaw, but got a recording about office hours, which were 9 to 5. It was currently 7:30. No opportunity to leave a message was offered before the robot hung up on me.

Did I really have to gumshoe this girl down myself? After all, I wasn't exactly poor. I had mid-five figures in checking this very instant. My current rootless lifestyle meant my overhead was laughably low. As a man of means, I could do what men of means did, which was hire other men to do the shit I didn't want to do for me.

I googled "San Diego private investigator" and was impressed to find so many that they merited a Top Ten list on Yelp. I could probably find someone before heading over to the con tomorrow morning, assuming one call to the Super Rickshaw offices didn't clear up this whole mystery.

The fact that I had developed a plan of action that wasn't

completely moronic put my mind at ease. I decided on the spot
that this deserved to be further rewarded with additional beer.

– – – –

I stayed at the bar until sunset, not sure what to do next. Normally I would amble over to the Marriott pool area and discover
which old friends were hanging out, but in light of recent de-
velopments I wanted to stay as far away from there as possible.
Ultimately I decided to try my luck at the Grand Hyatt bar next
to the Marquis, which had been the main pro hangout for the
decade prior to the Marriott's ascendance.

As I went back down the hill to the convention center area,
I tried Becca Kurtz's number. I got more than a busy signal, but
it was a leave-a-message from her, so I did:

"Hey, Becca, it's Mike again. I, uh, wow. I'm glad I got
through to you. I can only imagine what you're going through
right now."

I stumbled over my last few words because I had stopped on
a corner and turned back and was certain I was being followed.

"I'm really sorry about Ben. I was gonna ask if you wanted
to talk about it, but . . . I think the truth is . . . *I* need to talk
about it?"

And not by the sort of people you wanted to be following
you: they were big, scary white dudes with shaved heads and
anarchic beards and tattoos on their necks, none of which were
likely to say "Mom." If they had been wearing furs instead of
leather they would have looked like they had just come home
from a long, hard day of sacking monasteries.

"I know you must have a lot on your mind right now, but if

you could possibly . . . uh . . . call me . . . "

When I turned the corner I glanced back and saw the men striding purposefully toward me, increasing in pace. I could see vivid Gothic script of the same word inscribed across both of their Adam's apples:

M E H

Our eyes met at the same time and the MEH twins instantly lunged for me. I dove sideways into the street without looking at traffic, causing a Lexus to screech to a halt and the driver to scream high-pitched invectives at me. The bikers, not quite as suicidally mindless as me, looked both ways before crossing the street and got caught behind a double-decker bus blaring Tears for Fears. "COSPLAY KARAOKE" was emblazoned on one side. On the upper deck a guy in very realistic Doctor Doom armor clanked his way through the band's "Everybody Wants to Rule the World."

"Fancy meeting you here," said a voice in front of me. I nearly ran at the sight of its source, thinking that these two had brought one of their blonde Aryan gun molls with them. But it took me less than a second to recognize Katie Poole.

"You going to the H4H party too?" she said with a smile and jerked a thumb at the open doors of the hotel directly to our left, all potted palms, red carpets, and bronze nymphs.

"Uh, yes, yes I am," I said, grabbing her by the arm and pulling her into the lobby.

"I think it's on the roof—oh, here we go," Katie said, and walked toward an elevator dedicated via signs to the Sky Lounge. In front of its doors stood a large bouncer in a tuxedo and a chipper middle-aged woman holding a clipboard and wearing a

T-shirt emblazoned with "HEROES 4 HEROES," a charity that helped down-on-their-luck comics creators with medical and other life-changing expenses. It was a substitute for the insurance none of us had, or were ever offered, as we toiled away for decades in the comic strip mines.

"Are we on the list?" I said, glancing behind me.

"The email said as long as we had a collection bin on our tables, we'd be on the list," Katie said. Heroes 4 Heroes handed out Tupperware bins with their logo on it, and creators in Artists' Alleys were supposed to ask their fans to contribute money as tips for signatures or sketches. I intermittently remembered to do this during the day; most fans, God bless them, did so without prompting.

Katie gave our names to the H4H volunteer, who checked them off her clipboard. "Yup, you're all good—have fun, and thanks for your help," she said. The bouncer very slowly walked over to the Sky Lounge elevator and very slowly pressed the call button, which, I hoped and prayed, heralded its very slow descent to the lobby.

"How's your show going?" Katie asked, totally oblivious to my mounting panic. "It's really slow for me, man. I feel like people are paying less for commissions. Maybe it's the economy? I just feel like there's so much competition for the dollar in San Diego. But maybe it's just me. I worry I peaked on Mister Mystery. That would suck if my whole career was downhill from here."

I kept looking back toward the lobby entrance to see if my hirsute pursuers appeared. I didn't spot them before the elevator doors opened with a ding. I grabbed Katie by the arm and dragged her inside.

"Boy, someone really wants to get his drink on," she laughed. "Don't get too excited, tough guy, I'm pretty sure it's a cash bar."

As the elevator doors closed I saw the MEH brothers break into a sprint right at me—but the bouncer stepped forward and blocked them.

I breathed a sigh. What the hell was that all about? Did it have anything to do with the whole Danny Lieber business, or had Goodreads reviewers started deploying death squads?

The elevator doors opened to the Sky Lounge, which provided a predictably spectacular panorama of the city skyline. A turquoise Olympic-size reflective pool shimmered in the center of the roof, around which creators and editors and publishers clustered, drinks in hand. Cleverly projected on the side of a glass office tower across the street were huge photos of the many creators that H4H had helped over the years. None of them were household names, not that comics generated many of those beyond someone like Stan Lee. The graying heads and brown-spotted faces were attached to barely remembered names from the credit boxes on the splash pages of my youth, writers and pencillers and inkers and colorists and letterers who toiled away when comics were still mostly staples of spinner racks in drugstores and foot-level shelves in cigar shops. They had been successful in their days as weavers of childhood adventure, but were not among the lucky few who broke into wider acceptance in novels or movies. Some had given it the old college try, lighting out to Hollywood, but got only a couple Saturday morning animation gigs here or there. They discovered the hard way that breaking into another medium like television was as difficult as breaking into comics in the first place; and by the time they had no choice but to return to comics, comics didn't want them anymore. The generational turnover was quick in the comics pages, when styles no longer what the readers wanted were overtaken by younger, newer models, closer to the ages of those readers, as I had done to Ben K and Katie Poole had done to me. For these guys, once old age set in, with its myriad tiny ailments and its several major ones, their savings had been spent and their current earning power was all but nil. It was left to charities like H4H to step in and pay for their treatments, from dialysis to chemotherapy. These golden-aged artists literally depended on the kindness of strangers; but thankfully the artists were no strangers to the fans who donated to their cause—no, these were grateful readers, grown up and able to give back to those who had provided them with so much grist for adventure and laughter when they were younger.

I was surprised, in that it made me stop and stare, that one of the photos of the elderly comics creators on the side of the nearby building was of Benjamin "Ben K" Kurtz.

As I stood there stunned looking at Ben's photo, another artist—I'm not going to say his name, but anyone in the industry would know it immediately—passed by and patted me on the back.

"'Atta boy," he said, and kept walking to the other side of the roof before I could ask what exactly I had atta'd.

A widow's-peaked caterer handed me a Jameson on the rocks.

"Thanks?" I said.

"Thank your friend at the bar," the waiter said, pointing in the direction of the northern end of the pool, where a bar was flanked by two potted palmettos. Ian Smallwood was leaning there, a twinkle in his eye. He raised his glass in my direction and mouthed what I thought was:

Well played.

I started to walk over to ask him what the hell was going on but Allan Boelle, the director of Heroes 4 Heroes, stepped in front of me with an oustretched hand. Before landing his current gig at H4H, Allan had bounced around the comics industry in a variety of roles—retailer, editor, marketer, animation writer—as had many before him. Comics was the stranger with candy of careers: once you agreed to get into the white van, you never got out again. Allan had told me once his mother wanted him to be a doctor, and you could see why: he had big, sad eyes, horn-rimmed glasses, a graying Afro, and a calm singsong of a voice. He was exactly the sort of person you wanted to tell you that you had cancer. Odds are he'd sound like he felt really bad about it.

"Sorry for your loss," he said to me in a well-practiced funeral director purr.

"Thanks." We shared a manly one-armed hug.

Allan shook his head. "These things come in threes. I'm waiting for the next shoe to drop."

"What do you mean?"

"First Ben K, then Danny last night. Deaths, they're like waiting for a bus. Nothing comes forever, then *wham*—a bunch show up at once."

Anger welled up inside me at the thought that the tragic passing of Ben K, who was one of the most generous, gifted men I had ever known, would now be forever intertwined with the random killing of my archnemesis Danny Lieber, who was, um, not.

I had to figure out some way to change the subject before I said something I'd regret. I nodded at the projections on the opposite building. "I had no idea Ben was one of the people you were helping."

"Yeah, well . . . " Allan cast a conspiratorial eye around the terrace then leaned in close. "We weren't until very recently. I don't need to tell you Atlas is one of our bigger corporate sponsors. I'm ashamed to say out loud what percentage of our annual operating budget comes directly from them."

"You mean so you can help out the freelancers who don't get a pension or retirement benefits from them? Yeah, they're great humanitarians."

Allan rolled his shoulders. "It is what it is. And you know, Ben K was suing them to get the rights to Mister Mystery back."

"I had heard that, yeah. Well, now I guess Becca will have to decide whether or not to continue with the suit."

Allan frowned. "You don't know?"

"I doubt it. I've been trying to get her on the phone, but it's been impossible to get through."

"You didn't hear it from me, but they settled."

"No! Really? Out of court? Ben K didn't get the rights back, did he?"

"Hell, no. Ira Pearl would give up his left nut first. But supposedly—I mean, what Ben K told me was that Atlas would actively help him recover his stolen artwork."

"Stolen artwork?"

"Yeah, he must have told you about it sometime. All those

original *Mister Mystery* pages, I mean the seminal stories—the Atlas executives, they would just give them away. To licensors, you know like toy company guys, foreign rights holders, producers who maybe might make a movie. Anybody who dropped by the offices in New York. A lot of them started popping up on the art market in the past year or two, and Ben caught wind of it. Atlas said they'd do their best to help him get that art back if he dropped the suit. I mean, it's not like paying his lawyers hadn't completely ruined him in the first place. Getting his art back and selling it would have gone a long way to building a nest egg."

"I just . . . " I blinked. "I had no idea he was in so much financial trouble. I just wish . . . " I couldn't quite bring myself to say "I wish he had come to me" out loud.

Allan patted me on the shoulder. "Keep your chin up, man. He is in a better place. I do know that. Buy a raffle ticket! Buy ten!"

"Okay, okay, sure," I said, but I was already lost in thought as Allan peeled away to join another conversation. Why did Ben K have to reach out to me? Why couldn't I be the one calling, checking in? This was a direct result of my vagabond ways. I had cut myself off from not only the pain of my past but all the good I could do in the present as well. I almost wanted to cry.

I turned toward the raffle sales table, but then another big-time writer—and, again, I'd rather not say who—patted me on the shoulder and whispered, "Good going, killer."

Killer? Damn. Danny Lieber was clearly well-loved in the artistic community. I was actually starting to feel sorry for him. He was just a hatchet man for Atlas, really. It's not like he woke up every morning plotting new ways to backstab his coworkers.

More disconcerting was the idea that everyone naturally assumed I was the one who did him in, as payback for the
Christine Incident. Were the cops assuming this too? I no longer
felt so sanguine about the decisions I had made today. My head
throbbed in irritation.

Then I spotted Sebastian Mod hanging out on the other side
of the pool, and the throbbing only increased. He wore a purple
suit, purple shirt, purple shoes. His perfectly round bald head
gleamed like a snowball. He was talking to a group of artists that
had twenty-eight Kirby Awards between the five of them.

I strode over and tapped Sebastian on the shoulder. "Where
were you last night? I waited for you at the Marriott for hours
but you never showed."

He shook off my complaint as a parent would a child's.
"You know how the con hours ebb and flow. I got caught up in
the whitewater rapids of confluence and wound up at Christine's
karaoke birthday thing. I was a little surprised not to find you
there, to be honest."

I summoned all the strength I could to keep my voice down.
"I don't know why you would be surprised at that. Because *you*
told me to meet you at the Marquis."

"My friend." He clapped both hands on my shoulders.
"Learn to live in the moment, huh? You have to let the universe
provide, you'll be a lot happier. Stress is a side effect of resisting
destiny. You're here now, I'm here now, so let's talk now. Step
into my office."

He led me to an empty corner of the terrace that looked
down on the yawning expanse of Petco Park below. The Padres
never played in their downtown stadium during Comic-Con at

the pleading of every traffic cop in San Diego County, and this weekend the ballpark had been taken over by an obstacle course sponsored by *Cell Block Z,* the popular cable show about attractive rapists and murderers trading witty banter while fending off a zombie apocalypse inside a surprisingly well-lit maximum security prison. Constructed below on what was usually a baseball diamond was a sprawling jungle gym that sort of looked like a prison, where gnats were chased around by groaning, clawing gnats dressed like zombies.

"So my friend, I hear you're still walking the Earth like *Kung Fu.* You have to come in from the cold sometime, though. As a wise man once said, home is where you have to be taken in."

"I think that quote's the other way around."

Sebastian looked genuinely wounded. "What do you mean? That was from my Earth 2 *Black Canary* OGN. You know it's become a feminist bible."

"Really? Do they give out a Kirby Award for mansplaining?"

"Just hear me out," he said, not so much ignoring the insult whistling over his head as the fact that someone other than him had said something. "I think I have just the project for you to make your triumphant return to monthly comics."

"I can't wait to hear it," I said, and despite my best efforts, that was actually true.

"So Atlas flew me up to Comics Pro, that's the retailers thing in Portland? Every single shop owner was talking about how we need to get more big name teams on big name books. That sound you hear is Comics Twitter collectively jizzing when it is announced that you and Sebastian Mod are teaming up for a twelve-issue maxi-run on . . .

"Wait for it . . .

" . . . *Mister Mystery*."

I blinked. "*Mister Mystery?*"

Sebastian wagged his pale blonde eyebrows. "I know. Genius, right?"

"Sebastian . . . I already pencilled *Mister Mystery* for three years."

"I know, that's why it's genius. Make your triumphant return, like Frank Miller when he came back to do 'Born Again' in *Daredevil*. Bring back those lapsed readers. I've already pitched this idea to Atlas and they creamed their jeans. Heidi Macdonald at The Beat has already promised me an exclusive interview. Don't quote me but I bet you could name your rate."

"Isn't that Katie Poole's regular gig?"

"Not for long." Sebastian thew up his hands. "You didn't hear it from me. And for God's sake, don't leak it to Rich Johnston at Bleeding Cool. I'm going to do that on Tuesday."

"She's leaving?"

"Not voluntarily." I must have visibly paled because Sebastian added quickly, "She's just not working out, it's really a shame. She's not ready for prime time. Circ has dropped by twelve, thirteen percent since she came on board."

I rolled my eyes. "Yeah, but . . . " The gravity of the month-to-month circulation of serialized comic books was as constant and inexorable as the gravity between planets and stars. Even on the most successful series, you'd hope to bottom out at a two to four percent monthly negative drop rate. What Sebastian was describing was unusual, but well at the high end of normal parameters, and couldn't necessarily be attributed to one specific factor.

Which was why when I said, " . . . correlation versus causation, man," Sebastian knew exactly what I meant.

"No, no, I have a feel for these things," he said. He pointed at the elderly faces projected on the building next to us. "You know how we don't wind up like those poor penniless schlubs up there, begging for fans to pay for our hip replacements? You stay one step ahead of everybody else. The editors, the retailers, the fans, everybody. That is the one thing that has kept my head above water in this business: I can sense vibrations. Like a small animal that starts running from the earthquake hours before it hits."

"Is that like a Spider-Sense type of deal or do you have the Shining?"

Sebastian jerked his head at Katie, who held a Sprite in her hand and was chatting with some people by the bar. "I mean, clearly she's sweating it. Don't take my word for it, look at how much weight she's gained."

"Dude, she's pregnant."

"It's rude to just assume that."

"She is, she's like seven months along."

"You can't tell that just by looking at her."

"I'm . . . " I closed my eyes, mustering patience. "Sebastian, she told me to my face. Because *I* am psychologically capable of having a conversation that's not about myself."

"Don't change the subject," Sebastian snapped. He got a far-off look. "Okay, okay. This could work in our favor. They're going to need a fill-in artist for at least two issues; it's not like she's going to go into labor and then start roughing out thumbnails the next day. So we bring you on to fill in, make a big deal of it. Atlas maybe can even get us on one of those morning talk shows the network owns, put some asses in seats. And then, you know, you just don't leave. This could be a killer strategy. Danny could never get rid of her himself, you know, politically, because she made up that bullshit sexual harassment story a couple years back. Optics of that would have been terrible. But this . . . Everyone's happy."

"Everyone except Katie."

"I know, it's awful, it's unfair. She's great, I'm a huge fan of hers, but the market, you know? In the world I want to live in, Martin Luther King and John Lennon would have died in their beds. I would have taken the bullets for them both. But that's not the world we live in." He spread his hands. "The market isn't responding to her."

The great god Market, to whom all the petty, selfish acts of Man are offerings.

"Even setting Katie aside for a second, I don't think I'm ready to get back into the monthly grind. I did that for seven years, it wore me down to a nub and basically ruined my marriage."

"I bet you're going nuts, sitting on the sidelines. C'mon, what do you say? Are you in or out?"

"Out."

"Stop screwing around. You joining this Round Table of Knights of Totally Fucking Awesome or not?"

"Not."

"Final offer, take it or leave it."

"I'm leaving it."

Sebastian looked unblinking at me for a second.

Then he held up a hand. "What if—"

"Sebastian, I'm not drawing your book, okay?"

He pointed a finger at me. "Don't think I'm giving up this easy." And then he walked away.

I was about to leave too, but when I turned around I found myself looking at Christine Black for the first time in three years.

"Hey, you," I said, eloquently.

— — — —

"Hey, you." She looked incredible, which she always did, which I couldn't help but take personally now. Her bangs were cut à la Clara Bow while her hair went long in the back. She was in a black and gray cocktail dress and high heels, with minimal make-up. She was half German and half Japanese, which prompted me to call her "The Axis" in the first few weeks of our relationship until she made it clear how unfunny she thought that joke was.

She was smiling at me now, though, which was relatively unique in our recent history.

"The cops chat with you too?" she asked.

"Yeah. You—they talked to you?"

"Yeah," she said. "Someone at the Marquis must have told them about the, uh, incident. Three years ago. These two detectives asked me where I was at the time of the murder. Just like in the movies."

"You have a pretty good alibi."

"Yeah, surrounded by twenty people in a karaoke bar will do that. Mostly they wanted to talk about you, though."

"No kidding."

"Yeah, whether you beat me, whether you were always homeless, that sort of thing."

"And of course you told them yes."

Her eyes twinkled. "It was tempting. Maybe. Just a little. But no. I told them you weren't really the crime of passion type." She took a sip of her vodka tonic. "Or the legal acts of passion type, for that matter."

"Gee, thanks."

"I'm *here* for you."

"You . . . I mean, did you get the impression that they think I did it? Everyone else here does."

The ice in Christine's glass tinkled when she shrugged. "Honestly, I don't know. They asked me a whole bunch of general questions too. If you put a gun to my head I'd say they have no clue who did it and they're just throwing a bunch of stuff at the wall to see what sticks."

"They searched my hotel room too. Jesus. I just don't know what to do . . . "

Christine looked down at her feet. "I don't want to add to your worries, but I don't want you to hear it secondhand. This business is so small, the gossip travels faster than at an old folks' home." She took a deep breath and looked at me. "Sebastian and I are . . . together."

I knew the meaning of all those words, but they didn't mean anything to me strung together. "Sebastian? You mean— Sebastian Mod Sebastian?"

"Yeah. You know we were pals from the old Warren Ellis message boards, and I'd moved to L.A., and, you know. You know."

"Do I?"

She looked into her glass. "I didn't know if he had already told you when you were out last night, but, before it slips out of nowhere, you know how he is . . . "

"He and I didn't meet last night. He went to your karaoke thing instead."

Christine frowned, puzzled. "Okay. Well when he showed up late to my party he said he had been at the Marriott. With you."

"Trust," I said cheerily. "It's a two-way street."

She laughed mirthlessly. "Well, fuck you too, then. Okay, I just came over to tell you that and say I'm glad you're not in prison, and I hope you remain that way. Oh, and there are divorce papers waiting for you in your mail drop in New Jersey whenever you want to stop playing wandering ronin and go back to get them. My lawyer wanted to serve you as you stepped off a plane or something, but I thought that was a bit aggressive." She blinked through wet eyes. "My bad. I shouldn't have come over here. We really should only talk through the lawyers."

Like all our fights, this one seemed to spring up from nowhere. As always the rumblings had been on the horizon, ignored as nasty jokes were traded until one actually landed, followed by a flash flood of invective. "No, I'm sorry. It's cool. It's—"

"No. No, it's really not." She trotted off toward the ladies' room, head bowed.

I could feel my heart dissolving into a mixture of black bile and ash, melting away into a bottomless cavity that had opened up in my chest.

I had to leave this party right now—even if it meant jumping off the roof to do it.

_ _ _ _

Anger made me deaf, dumb, and blind for the whole elevator ride back down. It wasn't until I was halfway to the door that I snapped back to reality, which in this instance was the two huge dudes who had chased me into the lobby, and about whom I had completely forgotten, barreling toward me like runaway trains with "MEH" tattoos.

"Wait right there!" one roared in a tone that inclined me to do the opposite. I was already almost to the front door anyway, so I sprinted outside and tore down the sidewalk.

At the end of the block loomed the colossal bulk of Petco Park. A pair of teenage workers in prison guard uniforms patrolled the gates with plastic truncheons. "Last call," one of them yelled. "Last call for the *Cell Block Z: Dead Men Running*!"

I turned to look behind me and saw the big dudes tearing down the street in my direction. I leaped onto a parked car and slid across so I'd have the straightest beeline into the ballpark. I was able to jump onto and swing my legs across the fold-out table where more security guards were checking bags. It was late and the employees were tired and looking everywhere but at me, so I was able to push through the turnstiles and into the park before anyone could stop me.

Just beyond the gate the last stragglers of the evening, con-goers squealing in anticipatory fear, boarded a bus blocking the field. Steel grating covered the windows. As we filed on board, speakers growled: *"Your crimes have been deemed severe enough that you have been sentenced to the highest-security facility in the federal prison system, San Lazarus Penitentiary, for the rest of your natural lives."* We entered on the driver's side and were supposed to walk down the aisle until we reached the open rear door at the opposite end. Plexiglas barriers prevented anyone from sitting in the empty seats.

I tried to look through the window screens, but it was impossible to see if the bikers had followed me. I was going to pause for a second longer but a teenage boy bumped into me and the whole bus shook violently, causing everyone inside, including me, to jump and scream.

"You will obey guards' orders at all times. You will not touch guards or your fellow inmates. You will dispose of all food and beverages before entering the facility. Flash photography and videography of any kind is strictly prohibited.

"Cell Block Z: Dead Men Running is brought to you free of charge by Skittles. MMMM SKITTLES: TASTE THE RAINBOW."

I hopped off the bus with the others and followed a wide faux-concrete tunnel dimly lit with flickering red lights until it opened into a large, bright room marked INTAKE. Metal shelves at the far end were piled high with folded towels and orange prisoner uniforms. A bald turnkey stood next to it, slapping his fake nightstick into his free palm.

"Welcome, inmates, to your new home, the Laz!" he boomed out in the too-loud nasal monotone of the amateur actor. "I am Officer Downe, and I will be conducting your cavity searches today! Stand facing the walls shoulder to shoulder. Spread your legs and plant your feet on the floor and your hands on the wall where the painted guides indicate."

Officer Downe was making a great show of snapping on clear plastic gloves to the nervous giggles of con-goers when a fist started banging on the frosted glass of the door to the guards' station. Everyone against the wall turned, and before their very eyes were bloody crimson handprints stamped on the glass with each rhythmic slam.

"Inmates, do not take your gee-dee hands off that gee-dee wall!" Downe roared as he ran toward the door.

He fumbled through a big ring of keys on his belt, but before he could fit one in the lock, the window exploded outward. A growling zombie in an orange uniform lunged through the hole and caught Downe under the chin with the chains of its wrist manacles, pulling him through the jagged glass opening. His palefaced attacker took a huge bite out of his neck that jetted blood across the room, and then Downe vanished inside. He screamed, I screamed, we all screamed. Two-thirds of the "new inmates" leaped away from the wall and cowered and giggled in a clump in the center of the room.

The lights went out, inspiring more screaming, before red emergency lights came on. Alarm klaxons sounded.

At that moment the bikers walked into the intake room. They spotted me immediately and I spotted them.

"*This is not a drill,*" boomed a voice from the ceiling. "*I repeat, this is not a drill.*"

The bikers made their way toward me, but when they tried to push past the screaming clump of teenagers, the human barrier just screamed more. Thinking the "MEH" twins were part of the show, they fanned out, startling the men.

"*A heretofore undiscovered virus has been unleashed on the prison populace, causing extreme violence and cannibalism. Corrections officers have lost control of the situation. All visitors are asked to leave the grounds immediately before you are infected.*"

I backed up toward the metal shelves and made a run for

the door with the window: it opened to a blank wall.

"*Emergency Apocalypse Protocols have been activated. The CDC has calculated you have exactly three minutes to evacuate the facility before the germ vector multiplies beyond any possible containment. Escape in this time, or be trapped forever.*"

I started slapping the wall, trying to find whatever triggered the opening, but found nothing.

The bikers had made it past the screaming fans.

They were almost on top of me.

There was no way out.

"*Your time . . . begins . . . NOW.*"

At that moment the entire wall to my left opened outward like a pair of giant doors, revealing a sprawling cell block with various spinning red and strobe lights flashing. A small number of guards and inmates fought off a growling horde of walking corpses with blood-smeared faces. With a collective shriek, everyone in the room except the bikers ran hell-mell out of the intake room like the starter pistol had been fired at the Summer Olympics. I joined them.

It was at this point it dawned on me that I had quite literally trapped myself inside a maze: there was no obvious way out of the room. As they dodged the fairly convincing lunges of the zombie actors, con-goers were running into cell doors and pounding on walls, looking for secret doors.

This gave the thugs a clear path. I looked around desperately and saw a Rita Hayworth poster hanging in an open, currently unoccupied cell.

Shawshank! I ran into the room. The poster was silkscreened on a single piece of wood that slid sideways when I tried to move

it, revealing in the wall a large hole "dug" by a prisoner. I dashed inside. Many other escapees saw and followed me, once again impeding the bikers' pursuit.

A makeshift tunnel wound away from the cell block, low enough that I had to stoop slightly to get through. Ultimately it sloped upward and ended in a hatch, which, when I pushed, opened into the wide exercise yard, enclosed entirely in barbed wire. More zombies loped around the basketball court, moaning. The tunnel exited onto a weight-lifting area where a zombie guard was swinging a barbell as a club.

"*TWO MINUTES,*" the loudspeaker blared.

The exit from this area was a chain-link corridor garlanded with razor wire, through which zombies struggled to reach out and claw the escapees as they ran through.

At the end of it all I burst through a door into several interlocking corridors with solid metal doors—"The Hole"—through which were solitary confinement cells with nothing more than metal cots and toilets. Con-goers were dashing in and out of doors waving their arms like they were in a Benny Hill skit.

I threw open one door and a zombie prisoner with half-eaten feet lunged at me, roaring from the floor.

I slammed the door shut and opened the next one: Empty.

And the next one: Empty.

The bikers ran into Solitary and spotted me.

The next one: empty.

They ran at me.

The next one: there was a hole dug in the floor. I dove for it and slid into a plastic chute that curved around and around until it dropped out in a bin filled with orange jumpsuits. I tumbled out of the cart and found myself in a laundry room, surrounded by rattling machines and flickering fluorescents.

The bin was on wheels; I had the presence of mind to pull it out from under the chute so the bikers would crash down to the floor. I didn't stick around to see whether that was the result, but as I ran out of the room a zombie popped out of another laundry cart and yelled, "Dude, not cool!" at me, but that was partially drowned out by:

"*ONE MINUTE.*"

I ran blindly through hallways twisting and turning, through a cafeteria set and a death row set, until I wound up in the viewing gallery for the gas chamber, where a zombie priest had been strapped into a gurney, a lethal-injection needle inserted into his arm. With a flex of his biceps he broke the leather straps around his arms and lunged screaming at me.

A hand grabbed my shoulder and I pulled away, spinning around, fist cocked.

It wasn't a biker—it was one of the zombies.

"Hey, you guys aren't supposed to touch people," I said.

"Dude! It's me," the brain muncher said through a grin. "Dirtbag."

"Dirtbag?" It was my oldest friend in comics.

"Come with me if you want to live," he said, and pulled off his mask. His wide grin grew even wider. "You know, I always wanted to say that."

"*YOU'RE ALMOST OUT OF TIME,*" the loudspeakers boomed.

– – – –

Like me, Dirtbag had been one of Ben K's assistants, back in the day, but while I ultimately wandered off and did my own indie self-published comics, he went in the opposite direction. He took a staff production job at Atlas Comics as the bullpen artist, the guy sitting in the heart of the cubicle maze in company headquarters who redrew or touched up or corrected or patched any piece of art before it went to the printer and there was no time to get the originating artist to do it. Ultimately, that position fell victim to Photoshop and the relentless cost-cutting drive of Ira Pearl; it was eventually eliminated along with a lot of other midlevel production and sales positions.

I had forgotten when we last crossed paths on the con circuit that he told me he and his wife and daughter had moved to San Diego, where he had taken a position with some tech company, 3D printing I guess? Just as with Ben K, I lost touch with Dirtbag over the last few years when I got sucked into the La Brea Tar Pits of my own personal apocalypse. I was happy to see him—as much to redeem myself in the lost-friendship department as to be delivered from the hands of the bikers.

Dirtbag led me out a side door through the gas chamber, he and the zombie priest nodding at each other as we went:

"Thought you weren't working tonight?"

"I was trying to pick up some extra hours, but now I think I'm going to take my friend out for a beer."

"Sounds good. See you tomorrow, D-Bag."

The side door led out to the concessions area ringing the stands, and through there we exited near his minivan, which was parked on a side street. At my suggestion, we drove down to South Mission Beach. On the way, we grabbed a six pack of Tecate and some microwave burritos from a rest-stop gas station.

In the beach parking lot he opened the side door of his Dadmobile and we sat and ate truly atrocious overheated tubes of graying refried beans. We talked and drank beer and watched the surf stutter against the sand over and over like it was desperately trying but not quite able to remember something of the utmost importance.

"Man, am I glad to see you."

"Yeah, I just, uh . . . Look, man, I don't mean to get all in your face after not having seen you for a couple years and all, but . . . "

"What?"

"Are you, like, on something?" He looked around and whispered: "And if you are, I'm not judging. I just was wondering if you had any left for me. It's been a hard day's night in the zombie apocalypse, you know what I'm saying?"

How must I look under the parking lot streetlamps, wide-eyed, pale, and sweaty? I laughed and shook my head. "No. Just an overabundance of adrenaline if anything. I've had . . . I mean, I've had some crazy cons before. Like, remember that con in Houston where the *Sons of Anarchy* cast stopped signing autographs because the organizers weren't paying them and the cops had to flood the convention center because of all the fights breaking out?"

"Do I? How could I forget? Geez, that was back when I was still looking for inking work. Is that the last time I saw you?"

"Well, this whole con has been the insanity of Houston but cranked to, like, eleven."

I told Dirtbag the whole thing, or most of it anyway, starting more or less from my arrival at the Marriott pool bar up until right now, including what I learned at the party. I even drew a quick sketch of the bikers to show Dirty what I meant.

"MEH?" he said, squinting at the image. "I have no idea what that's supposed to be. Are they from a really militant fan site?"

"Who knows. Maybe I look like somebody who owes them money."

"I can't tell you that, but I bet I can run down that lady pedicab driver for you. "

"What? You mean it? I'm still trying to make some money here, so I'm kind of chained to my table for most of the con."

"You got it. I'm mostly working nights at the Dead Men Running anyway. That 3D printer company went belly up, and Suzie and I split . . . "

"Aw, shit. I'm sorry, man. I know what that's like."

"Yeah, you do. So I can be your eyes and ears on the street while you're doing the cogitating. You were thinking about paying a private investigator—screw that, man. I know the area. I've lived here for a couple years now, and I could use the extra scratch. Let Dirty do your dirty work for you."

"No pun intended."

Dirtbag frowned. "What do you mean?"

"Nothing. Sure, man. That's actually a great idea. Find out whatever the usual daily rate is for this kind of stuff and I'll pay you that."

I pulled the folded-up photocopy of the pedicab page from the San Diego Yellow Pages from my sketchbook and it disappeared into Dirtbag's pockets.

"You got it. I'll be like the, what do you call them, the little homeless urchin shits that run around for Sherlock Holmes."

"The Baker Street Irregulars."

"Yeah, I'm like your One-Man Irregular."

"I doubt they reeked as strongly of weed."

Dirtbag scowled. "How do you know? You weren't there in Jack the Ripper times."

We both laughed, then lapsed into smiling silence.

"Did *you* know Ben K was in so much financial trouble?" I finally asked after a while.

Dirtbag shook his head. "I haven't spoken to him or Becca in years, to be honest with you."

There was a tiny sliver of beer at the bottom of my last Tecate can and I sucked it down. "Once, maybe, the first couple months we started working for him, I showed him these Atlas samples I'd been working on, some generic Mister Mystery fight scene. I was so scared to show them to him, I was worried what he would think. And so finally, near the end of a workday, I broke the pages out of my portfolio.

"And he just flips through them real quick—just like that." I waved my hand four times. "And he goes"—I made my voice gruffer, deeper, more staccato:

"'You know what this is like, kid? It's like a hamburger. It's a damn good hamburger, and a damn good hamburger is a damn good thing. But I've been around for a long time. I've eaten a lot of hamburgers. And you know what the difference between a good hamburger and an okay hamburger is? This much.'

"And he held up his fingers like this." I brought my thumb and forefinger together before my eye until they were almost touching.

"So I go, because I was twenty years old and didn't know shit about shit, 'Well, that just shows you've never had a really bad hamburger.'

"He's like, 'Bullshit! Of course I have. But I also know there's a lot more to life than just hamburger. Every menu in the world has a goddamn hamburger on it. You know why? It's for people who can't decide anything else they might want beyond what they already know. It's for people who are afraid to get outside their comfort zone. It's a guaranteed seller because it's perfect for dull minds with no imagination.'

"And I'll never forget what he said next; he said:

"'That's what your art is right now, kid. It's a coward's meal.'"

Dirtbag barked out a laugh. "Shit, man! Ben K in a nutshell."

I smiled down at my empty can. "Yeah. But I tell you, it made me bust my ass. It was the slap in the face I needed. I don't think I would have gotten anywhere without that crit."

"When I showed Ben K my portfolio," Dirtbag said, "he told me about this class he took with Burne Hogarth when he was just a kid. And he said Hogarth said, basically, don't be afraid to steal. Find an artist you love and just copy him until you erase all distinction between you and him. When you learn to destroy that thinking part of your brain, the one getting in the way of your eyes . . . that's when you'll finally start to see."

I nodded. "The man was a goddamn Jedi Master."

Dirtbag raised his Tecate high. "To Ben Obi-Wan K Kenobi." He poured out the rest of his beer, splattering onto the tarmac. "You deserved better."

Even though my can was basically empty, I did the same. "I

don't know if any of us get what we deserve."

"Tell me about it. Look at that Sebastian Mod. He is such a phony piece of shit and he just keeps failing upward."

"Tell *me* about it," I said, sucking bean sludge off my fingers. "Although, you know, come to think of it . . . "

"What?"

"He *was* the only person who didn't mention Danny's murder to me at that party."

"Huh." Dirtbag belched. "You don't think . . . you don't think Mod's in on it?"

"Hard to say." I looked out over the ocean. "I'm beginning to think everybody's in on it. Everybody but me, anyway."

FRIDAY

I was late for a comic book convention; I was late for the train that would take me to the bus that would take me to the ship that would take me to the convention, which was on the beautiful island nation of Corto Maltese.

But I had accidentally told the mystery lady pedicabbie to take me instead to the ancient keep at Winterfell. The men-at-arms standing beneath the fluttering Stark banners would not let me leave without paying the toll; unfortunately, the card reader attached to the pikeman's cell phone wasn't recognizing the chip on my Visa.

"You don't understand," I pleaded with the apathetic north-man. "The toll should be when I enter, not when I leave."

"You're the one who let us inside your head in the first place," Jon Snow said, fixing his sad brown cow eyes on mine. "If you're the foreigner in it now, you only have yourself to blame."

"Jesus, will you answer that?" I heard a voice say off in the distance, and within a few seconds my eyes were open. Dirtbag strode over from my hotel room couch, where he had been lying beneath a meager sheet. My cell phone lay on the bedside table, trilling the *Mission: Impossible* theme.

Dirtbag checked the lock screen before handing it over.

"Whoa," he said.

I instantly saw what he was reacting to: the incoming call was from Ben K.

"Hello?" I groaned into the phone, rubbing my bloodshot eyes. I am *not* drinking tonight, I swore.

"Oh my God, I'm so sorry, did I wake you?" A woman's voice. "What time is it there?"

I squinted at the clock. "Seven-thirty."

"Oh, right, it's three hours *behind* on the West Coast, I'm such a dummy. Here I was calling early because I thought *you* were ahead—"

"It's okay Becca, really, it's all right. How are you feeling? I am so, so sorry about Ben."

"Thank you, honey, you are a sweetheart. I saw that you called on my phone, but, you know, things have just been . . . you know."

"I know."

"It was all so sudden, really," she said. "I mean, in the sense it wasn't sudden at all, not surprising. I mean, he treated his body the way he treated me. Neglectful." I laughed weakly. "Is that awful? You must think I'm awful. Well, I'm not, I just have to laugh instead of cry."

"You go right ahead."

The toilet flushed and Dirtbag emerged from the bathroom in his tighty-whities. He was carrying a full paper cup of water, which he poured into the tiny, cheap coffeemaker resting on the mini-bar fridge. I had to cover my ear to hear Becca when the little machine started sputtering brown liquid into the cup.

"Are you calling from Ben's studio?" I said.

"How do you know that? Oh, yeah. Caller ID. Everyone knows everything about everyone now, or so they think. The more information people get, the dumber they seem to me, but what do I know?"

"Is that Becca?" Dirtbag whispered from across the room. I waved him off.

Dirtbag mouthed, *Tell her I say hi.*

"Aw, geez. I mean, if you could see this place . . . Such a mess. I mean . . . I don't even know where to begin." Her voice tightened. "The man hasn't thrown a single thing away in fifty years. There's just art and paintings and old comics and science-fiction pulp magazines and books everywhere. I don't even want to go in the closet where he slept."

"Where he . . . slept?"

"Oh, yeah." She paused. "We'd split up, didn't you know that?"

"No, I didn't."

"I just couldn't take being treated the same way he treats his liver, you know? He was just so angry. At Atlas. The way they were treating him, not giving him his artwork back, not letting him share in the rights to Mister Mystery." Deep breath. "The thing is . . . "

"What is it?"

"You . . . haven't been here recently, have you?"

"Did you tell her I say hi?" Dirtbag whispered, and I had to shoot him a "WTF?" look.

"No," I said, "I haven't been over in—geez, I think the last time I visited the Atlas offices. That's, like, four years ago."

"Because I've got to tell you, it looks like someone's been

all through this place. I mean, Ben has always been a hoarder. There's just stacks of stuff in these cubbyhole shelves on every wall and stacked in the corner and by the bed and next to the toilet. There's got to be sketchbooks here dating back to when he first started at Atlas, and blank paper, and office supplies, and everything else, but . . . I don't know, it's usually an organized mess. Now it looks a hurricane tore through here. Some stacks are tipped over, drawers are open—there's something funny going on here. I can always tell. I got a nose for funny."

As I mulled over her words I happened to glance over at Dirtbag, who spread his hands in an accusatory "WTF?" look of his own.

"Uh, hey, Becca, guess who's here too—Randall. He crashed the night in my room."

"Who?"

"Randall. Dirtbag."

"Oh, Dirtbag! Put him on, put him on."

I handed the phone to Dirtbag, who said, "How's it hanging, girl?" I zoned out for the rest of the conversation as I absorbed the new information. Did it have any bearing on my own predicament? I was still inclined to believe Ben and Danny's deaths were a coincidence, but that stance was becoming harder and harder to maintain with each new revelation.

Soon enough, Dirtbag was handing the phone back, and I could hear Becca crying.

"The hell, man?" I hissed over at him, but he was crying too. He waved me off.

"It's me again," I said into the phone.

"Sorry, it's all so fresh," Becca sniffled. "That man," she

said, her voice quavering with a combination of fury and grief. "He had so many good qualities, you thought he could figure out a way of getting rid of all the bad ones. Part of me, even after I got fed up with him, hoped that he would still try. But now . . . " She took a deep breath. "He's all outta chances to change."

"Yeah," I said, inadequately.

"So, listen, do you still live in Jersey?"

"Sort of."

"Once you're back from San Diego, do me a favor. Please, come by and help me sort through all this stuff. Some of it maybe needs to go to the Society of Illustrators, maybe I'll sell some of it, I just don't know. And the lawsuit! With Atlas! I guess that's my responsibility now too, huh?"

I didn't know whether or not to say anything about Ben K's settlement, but since I knew that information secondhand anyway, keeping my trap shut seemed wise. "Yes. I will definitely come by as soon as I can."

"Great. And could you bring Christine too? She has such a good eye for the original art. She handles your pages online, right? Is she there too?"

I swallowed. "No. She didn't come with me this year."

"Aw, that's too bad. But the conventions can be a trial for the wives. I know more and more ladies are getting into the comic books now, but when I was a kid I was all Barbies and ponies. I mean, when I was sitting there with Benjamin at his table . . . I was always amazed at the love the fans would just shower on him. How Mister Mystery meant so much to them. It'd fill my heart with so much joy, that he meant so much to them and their childhoods, like this living legend, and I would always say something like, 'Can you get the Great One to remember to leave the toilet seat down from time to time?' I meant it in good fun, but maybe . . . maybe I was jealous." She was crying openly now. "I'm gonna have to go now. Thank you for calling. I'll speak to you when you're back to the city, okay?"

"Okay, Becca, talk soon. Bye."

I set down the phone. Dirtbag emerged from the bathroom again with a wad of tissues in both hands. He had mostly recovered but was still sniffling a bit. "Death sucks, man," he said.

I nodded. "Indeed it does."

Dirtbag heaved a sigh. "I need to eat through my grief."

"The living need breakfast. Let's go."

– – – –

We went down to the Space Restaurant and got a Space Booth. After we returned from the Space Buffet with plates heaped with Space Breakfast, Dirtbag noticed me staring off strangely into the distance.

"What?" he said.

"That's weird," I said.

"What?" Dirtbag turned and immediately saw the bearded and bespectacled buddha sitting in the booth behind us, wearing a Mets cap and suspenders. He interrupted his meal to sign a napkin brought to him by two quavering thirteen-year-olds.

"Holy shit," Dirtbag whispered. "That's George R. R. Martin."

"Yeah, and I think I had a *Game of Thrones* dream this morning." I shook my head. "It's just a weird coincidence."

"Not at Comic-Con it ain't. What was the dream like? Were

you with Cersei? Or Daenerys? In combination with Sansa, per-haps?"

I chomped contemplatively on toast. "Jon Snow, I'm pretty sure."

"Well, that's very progressive of you."

"You are shocked that my subconscious likes to get freaky?"

"No, I just thought . . . well, I just thought you were dream-ing about Christine is all."

"Why do you say that?"

"Because you kept saying the same thing over and over in your sleep: '*No más, Mama, no más.*'"

– – – –

"Shit," I said too loudly, looking up from my Deadpool full-body sketch in Artists' Alley. I had dispatched Dirtbag on his day's sleuthing so I could go to the con and get some work done.

"What's wrong?" Katie Poole asked without looking up from her work. She was using a red marker to dab blood onto Red Sonja's blade.

"I'm pretty sure I forgot to file another extension on my income taxes. *Shit.*"

Katie laughed. "Christine used to do yours, I bet."

"She met with the accountant, yeah. After we split it took me a year to figure out the guy's name. And how to get in touch with him."

"Yeah, Javier does all that financial crap for me. Although he does our taxes himself. He says he actually enjoys it. He's such a weirdo."

"He's a good weirdo to have. Wish I still had one."

Common in the comics community is the phenomenon of the Hyper-Competent Spouse. Few were the creators I knew who supported their families: that role fell to the wife or husband who worked as an X-ray technician, landscape architect, estate tax lawyer, et cetera. Mostly women and the handful of men who had adult, human, capital-J jobs with health benefits and retirement strategies that allowed their life partners to weather the swells and squalls of intermittent freelance employment and unpredictable income in pursuit of the arguably frivolous dream of drawing stories in their waking hours.

Christine had been my Hyper-Competent Spouse. She had made stabs at becoming a colorist and got some gigs as a flatter, but she found it too tedious and worked instead as a sales rep for a furniture wholesaler until my career took off. This was really the best-case scenario a Hyper-Competent Spouse could hope for, that hubby or wifey's career was one of the lucky one percent that landed a big payday so that comics could put the kids, hypothetical and otherwise, through college.

Once my earnings ballooned, Christine quit her job to essentially become my manager, coordinating con appearances, dealing in my original art, and basically managing all the financial and business side of Life for which I have long shown zero competency. Since we split up, I gained no additional competency in any of her many major skills. Like an escaped zoo animal, I was wandering around backyards and parking lots, free from captivity but also free to be run over by a tractor trailer at any moment.

"He's back home with your boy?" I said while drawing. "Javier, I mean?"

"Yeah. He wasn't thrilled about me coming out here seven months in, but I was like, I'm the most popular girl in school right now. Gotta make hay while the sun shines, you know?"

"I hear that. Javier's off from school now, right, or does he teach summer semester too?"

"Well . . . " She put her Zebra marker aside. "He's going through a tough time. The university made all these cuts to the music department."

"He has tenure though, right?"

"No, that's the thing. He was just adjunct faculty. But then he got knocked down to assistant. They slashed him back to two classes and if he's just a part-timer . . . we get kicked off the school health insurance."

"Oh my God."

"Yeah, not ideal in my condition." She tried to pick up a pen but had to arch her back, wincing. "He can give private lessons for, like, violin and piano, but there's only so much of that to go around. Thank God for this *Mister Mystery* gig."

Swallow. "Yeah?"

"I would be completely screwed without it. It was stressful enough when the guy who sexually harassed me was my editor, but now maybe I'm safe. I better be. For both Javy and I to lose our jobs now . . . You know what, forget I brought it up. I don't like to think about it."

"Totally. It's forgotten."

I tried to turn back to my drawing, mind seething with renewed hatred for Sebastian Mod, but I nearly leaped out of my chair because Violent Violet was standing right in front of me burning twin holes in my skull with her come-at-me-bro gaze.

"You need anything? Water? Food? More drugs, like yesterday? I brought a whole bottle of Tylenol with me today. Also, Tums. Also, some weed. Do you need me to sit at your table while you go to the men's room? Do you need anything at all?"

"Actually," I said, "I could use my faith restored in the essential goodness of humanity."

"*On* it," Violent Violet said with her endemic intensity, and then she disappeared into the teeming costumed hordes.

———

I returned to the zone, drawing Green Lantern (John Stewart—no, not that one, the fictional one), so I didn't know how much time had passed before I saw Violent Violet again, but there she was, standing over my table, and she handed her phone to me.

She had the black band of an Apple Watch wrapped around the end of her six-inch-long left arm and she tapped at it with her right hand. Instantly, the screen on the phone in my hands burst to life and I was looking down from a security camera's vantage point onto a fairly nondescript office space. An Asian man in a bulletproof vest was sitting amiably on the edge of a desk chatting with another man standing in the doorway with a hand pointed accusingly in his direction.

"What am I looking at?" I said as the two figures mouthed silent words to each other.

"This is a police station in Bangkok," Violent Violet said. "That man on the right there has walked in with a knife. He wants to die. He's hoping the police will shoot him. But that policeman on the left? He doesn't shoot him. He just starts talking to him."

While I watched, the guy with the knife took a few steps

toward the cop. At first it looked like he was going to stab him, but instead he held out the knife and the cop took it off him. Then the cop walked forward, knife still in his hands, and gave his would-be attacker a great big hug. And tossed the knife away.

The video stopped.

"You see?" Violent Violet said. "There is good in people. And sometimes . . . sometimes people do dumb things. And get forgiven for them."

She said that last part with a very meaningful look on her face. I guess I should have realized that she was trying to tell me something else, something very important.

But unfortunately I was in the zone and unable to focus on anything other than the drawing in front of me. So I just said, "Thank you, Violet, that was awesome," and went right back to my Green Lantern.

Because I am not very, you know.

Smart.

— — — —

Dirtbag didn't have a Comic-Con badge so I had to meet him outside the convention center for a late lunch. He drove me out to this folksy eatery over on El Cajon that was legendary among San Diegans for its amazing chicken pies.

"So anyway, I tracked down my old buddy Dinesh, he's running the *Absolute Zero* immersive thing for Syfy. He used to be the talent coordinator at Atlas, so he's still pals with people over there; they're members of this massive text chain where they trade gossip with each other. And wouldn't you know—Atlas wasn't planning on dumping Katie from *Mister Mystery*."

"Let me guess: they were gonna dump Mod."

"Hells to the yes. Danny Lieber had been advocating for it for months. *Months.* It was kind of an open secret around the office. Mod's numbers were really weak, he just wasn't moving the needle. Not just *Mister Mystery*; his titles across the board were soft and getting softer."

"Any idea who they wanted to replace him?"

"They begged Joss Whedon, but he passed. Like, he passed a million times."

"Damn. Go big or go home."

"But now Danny's out of the picture and who inherits his books is still up in the air. Word is, though, Mod's got Danny's assistant editor wrapped around his little finger. So if she gets bumped up because Danny got bumped off . . . "

"Right. He's safe. For now." I frowned. "But would a guy really kill another guy just to not get fired off a freaking comic book series? That sounds nuts."

Dirtbag shrugged. "Who gets into this crazy business in the first place? I'll tell you who: crazy people."

"I guess." I thought about it some more. "Though . . . who-ever is writing the *Mister Mystery* comic when the movie comes out is going to make a nice chunk of change. See a healthy boost in the royalties on his backlist from all that other media exposure. I know that from *Gut Check*. It's not inconsequential at all."

"But there's not really going to be a Mister Mystery movie. The rights are still tied up in Ben's lawsuit."

I blinked. "No. They're not." I looked into Dirtbag's face. "Ben reached a settlement with Atlas. And Danny must have known that."

Dirtbag's jaw dropped. "Holy shit, dude," he said. "Holy shit."

"I guess we'd better run down Sebastian's alibi a little harder. And, say, speaking of alibis, did you get a chance to check out those pedicab places?"

"Nah, brah, haven't had time yet. But isn't you finding the guy who really did this the best alibi you could possibly have?"

– – – –

The Gaslighter karaoke bar didn't open until five in the afternoon. Dirtbag and I pushed our way inside at 5:15. Half the lights were off and the big room smelled of dried beer stains and mop water. A leathery old white guy was already hunched over something brown with ice at the bar in the front of the joint. In the back a dozen tables and their attendant chairs surrounded a big stage with a bigger screen behind it and an enclosed DJ booth off to one side. Doors ran along the left-hand side of the room, opposite the bar, and through the portholes set into them I could see smaller karaoke booths: vinyl couches lining the walls inside, facing a central screen.

A good-looking Korean bro in a black T-shirt and a flat-brimmed Golden State Warriors cap bumped through a door marked EMPLOYEES ONLY, carrying a box full of bottles that clinked when he dropped it onto the bar. He opened the box and started transferring various random bottles of Asian beer, Hites and Sapporos and Singhas, into the waist-high cooler behind him.

He glanced over at me and Dirtbag, the patiently waiting newcomers, and said, "You want a booth or just a drink? Main stage don't open till nine."

"No," Dirtbag said, whipping out his wallet and flashing his Sam's Club membership card at the bartender. "We want to ask you a few questions about a birthday party that was here the other night."

"Wednesday night," I said.

"Wednesday night, to be precise," Dirtbag said.

The bartender rested his fists on the bar. "You guys are cops," he said, not like it was a question: "*You* guys are cops."

"Do we look like cops?" I grinned.

"*He* doesn't," the bartender said, pointing at Dirtbag.

"Aw, c'mon," Dirtbag muttered, wounded.

"No, we're not cops," I said. "We're just trying to help out a friend of mine. You know the birthday party I'm talking about? I think they took over this place."

"Yeah." The bartender crossed his arms. "Half-Asian chick? She was hot."

"That's the one," Dirtbag said.

The bartender had turned toward the iPad that controlled the cash register and tapped through a multitude of screens until a printer below spat out five or six sheets of paper. I pointed at the bank of tiny monitors over top-shelf liquor behind the bar. Each showed the interior of one of the private karaoke booths. "I was wondering what you had recorded from that night."

The Korean guy looked down at the paper and cracked a smile. "You think she's cheating on you, dog?"

"Well . . . something like that."

He shook his head. "Sorry, man. I'd love to help you, but I don't know if they want me handing this stuff out."

"What if you got something in return?" Dirtbag said.

"Like what?"

Dirtbag pointed at me, incredulous. "Don't you know who he is? A *New York Times* best-selling comics artist?"

"Before the *Times* discontinued that list," I said.

"Creator of *Gut Check*?"

The bartender slapped his hands together. "Oh, no shit, really? That was you? I loved that movie."

Dirtbag looked around the room like a bad imitation of a drug dealer and leaned over the bar. "My friend here is in town for Comic-Con, obviously, and would draw any character of your choice, right here, right now, in exchange for helping us out. What do you say?"

"What, you're my pimp now?" I said.

"Yes, because you constantly undervalue yourself," Dirtbag said, then turned back to the bartender: "So who do you like? Wolverine? Jean-Luc Picard? Thundercats? Power Rangers? Superman? Spider-Man? Batman? C'mon, everyone likes Batman."

The man thought about it only for a second. "Me," he said.

"You're your own favorite fictional character?"

"Yeah, do one of me, here at the bar, so I can put it up, you know, on the mirror or something."

"I admire your self-esteem." I knocked out the sketch in less than ten minutes, sitting at the bar, adding as much of the decor as possible so people would know at a glance it was supposed to be the interior of the very establishment they were standing in.

When I shared the sketch, the bartender took a picture of it with his phone. "Thanks man, I appreciate it. This is going right on Facebook."

"Good, glad you like it. And now can you, uh . . . ?"

"Yeah, sure, dog, a deal's a deal." The bartender put the printouts he'd been holding into my hands. "Boomski!"

Mike flipped through the pages. They were a bunch of time-stamped songs with people's names attached. "Chandelier . . . Blister in the Sun . . . Sorry, I don't get it. What is this?"

"Records, like you said—the set list for the party," the Korean guy said. "I don't know, maybe you can figure out which dude's balling your girl from the names people put in to sing with?"

"No . . . " I shook my head, pointing at the screens above his head. "I wanted to take a look at your security cam footage."

The bartender turned around. "Aw, man, sorry, no can do. Those cameras are just so we know nobody's giving out coke or BJs in the private rooms. We don't bother holding on to the recordings; we flush 'em every night. I don't even have a camera on the main stage. I can see it with my eyeballs. And then, when shit goes down"—he brandished a baseball bat from beneath the bar—"I break out Lucille."

"*Walking Dead* reference," Dirtbag muttered at no one in particular.

"Who knew investigating crimes would be so hard?" Dirtbag said as we walked back down the hill, past the gabled Victorian manses of the Gaslamp to the convention center.

"Like, literally everybody, ever, since Cain hit Abel in the head with a rock and told God 'I didn't do it,'" I said.

"*God: The First Detective*," Dirtbag said. "That's your next comics series. Wait, no: *The Old Testament Mysteries*."

"You know," I said, ignoring him and flipping through the karaoke set list, "this isn't completely useless. Sebastian's first song pops up a few minutes past midnight. That fits within the timeframe of the murder."

"What song did he sing?"

"Bowie. 'Space Oddity.'"

Dirtbag scoffed. "Figures." He was thumbing through pictures on his phone. "He doesn't show up until late in the photos, either."

"Where'd you get photos of the party? Why didn't you tell me you were there?"

"No, dummy, I wasn't there, I just know how to use Instagram. She made a hashtag. See?" He handed his phone to me, and I flipped through the feed. In the images, the dreary mainstage of the Gaslighter was transformed into a purple- and fuchsia-lit cauldron of energy, like the heart of a sun: there was Christine onstage, singing "Goody Two Shoes" (I could tell by the lyrics lit up on the screen in front of her: You-Don't-Drink-You-Don't-Smoke-What-Do-You-Do). Other photos showed various pals singing onstage, Christine rejoicing behind a Great Wall of wrapped presents and gift bags, her and her friends lifting shot glasses, and the same basic repeating shot of drunkenly grinning revelry. Then, almost forty pictures later, was Sebastian and "Space Oddity" (Tell-My-Wife-I-Love-Her-Very-Much-She-Knows).

"You don't follow Christine on Instagram?" Dirtbag said. "Her feed is pretty awesome. She eats such photogenic food."

"No, Dirtbag, I do not follow my ex-wife on Instagram, for

the same reason I don't cut myself."

We had passed under the arch to leave the Gaslamp and were waiting to cross the train tracks amongst a motley crew: a woman in Princess Leia hair walking a small dog in a Yoda costume; a white guy in a Black Panther outfit carrying his helmet; hooded members of the Assassins Brotherhood; and a tall, skinny man dressed as Wonder Woman who somehow managed to precariously navigate the space between the tracks while teetering atop his high-heeled red boots, without breaking both of his ankles.

"This is good, but all it does is show Sebastian *could* have committed the murder," I said. "I can't show any of this to the cops. Not with some kind of, you know, corroborating evidence."

The sidewalk in front of the convention center was mobbed with traffic stopping and starting as people gathered around groups of accidentally themed cosplayers to take shots: an Elektra squaring off against a Daredevil, or an H. R. Giger Xenomorph and a Predator frozen at each other's throats.

At one point we were stuck right in front of a yellow T-shirted, bullhorn-wielding young member of the Eastboro Baptist Church:

"DO YOU HAVE THE BADGE YOU NEED TO ENTER HEAVEN-CON? IT IS NOT A FOUR-DAY PASS, NO NOT A THREE-DAY PASS, NOT EVEN A SINGLE-DAY PASS. NO, THIS BADGE IS FOR ETERNITY!"

I had to cover my ears until the crowd started moving forward again. "How those guys avoid getting punched in the face every day is completely beyond me."

Dirtbag nodded in the street preacher's direction. "They're

worried about that too. Must be why they all wear body cams."

The Baptist kid couldn't have been much older than eighteen, with bowl-cut brown hair and so much acne on both cheeks that they had turned the color of pinot noir. He had a satchel slung over his shoulder; attached to the strap just above his solar plexus was a small, cockroach-shaped object with a single unblinking eye. In the sketch I had done of the church group at the beginning of the con, I captured that object without recognizing what it was.

I grabbed Dirtbag. "Hang back and keep an eye on me," I said. "Don't step in unless it looks like I'm in serious trouble."

"What are you going to do?"

"Dance on the fine line between incredibly stupid and incredibly brilliant."

I pushed my way through the crowd until I reached the preacher kid.

He yelled from the bullhorn five or six steps up the stairs leading to the Sails Pavilion. He saw me approach and stop at the base of the steps, and he warily kept one eye on me as he continued his rant.

"ONLY ONE HERO HAS THE POWER TO GIVE YOU THE HEAVEN BADGE! HIS ORIGIN STORY WAS DYING ON THE CROSS FOR YOUR SINS! HIS SECRET IDENTITY WAS A SIMPLE CARPENTER BUT IN REALITY HE WAS THE SON OF GOD!"

Once it became clear I wasn't going to jump him, the teenage preacher slowly lowered the bullhorn and looked at me, not saying anything.

"Hi," I said, looking around, still smiling. "I'm sure you get this a lot, but I'm a real fan. I really like what you guys are doing here. Sorry, I'm kind of fanboying out here, but I was wondering . . . where do I join up?"

— — — —

The Eastboro Baptist Church pitched their tent, literally, across a quartet of undoubtedly exorbitantly priced parking spaces in a lot across the trolley tracks from the Hyatt. It looked like a cross between a football tailgate party and a bivouac for Christian soldiers. A congenial grandpa type flipped burgers and dogs on a charcoal grill. A red-faced young woman who couldn't be much older than eighteen sat in a big canvas lawn chair under the tent, with a wet towel wrapped around her neck; she panted and sweated and fanned herself with a small battery-powered pinwheel.

"Listen up everybody, I made a friend outside Hall H," the acne-spotted preacher announced as he led me into the tent.

"Yeah, I was just wondering if you guys had a mailing list or something I could sign up for," I said.

"What's your name, young man?" asked a grandmotherly woman wearing a tennis visor and holding a clipboard with a mailing list on it.

"Sorry?"

"Your name?" she asked again.

"Oh, sure. My name is Danny Rand. That's R-A-N-D," I spelled out slowly.

"And are you ready to accept Jesus as your Lord and Savior?"

"Oh, yeah, yeah," I said, nodding my head vigorously. "I mean, I've been a real big fan of the Bible for a long time. It's a great series. I know some people complain it's got long stretches of windy exposition and an unlikable main character, a classic peak TV antihero type, with all his strict boundaries and anger management issues.

"I knew the scuttlebutt for a long time was that it couldn't really expand past a small niche audience. But then, you see, they did a really smart thing: a soft reboot between Books One and Two that retconned out of existence a lot of the stranger and more confusing aspects of the continuity that had prevented new readers from jumping onboard.

"And I get that original-series fans had a problem with it, and the next-generation addicts can give them a really hard time, but overall I think the renumbering really expanded the franchise's appeal. After all, the new guy, the son who inherits the mantle of the father? I mean, that's just real hero's journey stuff, it's Storytelling 101. It's like Dick Grayson becoming Batman, or Bucky Barnes becoming Captain America. I have always been a sucker for a legacy hero."

The faithful nodded vigorously at my impromptu speech. I was running my mouth so that I could thoroughly look around the tent; fortunately at the end of my sermon, my eyes found what I had been hoping to find. Behind a table on which an array of crackers and popcorn and sports drinks had been scattered was a desktop computer with a flatscreen monitor and one of the small body cameras attached via USB. Sitting at the station was a black woman with a round, Campbell's Soup Kid face and glasses and a glorious heap of dreadlocks piled on top of her scalp. When the senior manning the grill announced that the burgers were ready and everyone pretty much lost interest in me, I wandered over to the computer table. Before I could greet its guardian she said:

"*You're* Danny Rand."

"You heard?"

"*You're* Iron Fist." When she pushed her glasses back up on her nose I could see the entwined woman symbols tattooed on the inside of her right wrist.

"I can neither confirm nor deny my secret identity."

"*You* were raised in the mountains of Tibet among K'un-L'un, capital city of Heaven, where you were apprenticed to Lei Kung, the Thunderer, achieving the ability to channel your chi through your hands by defeating Shou-Lao the Undying and plunging your fists into the dragon's molten heart."

I frowned. "You can't tell that just by looking at me?"

The IT lady barked out a laugh. "Well, I'm Tasha." She shook my hand. "I don't know what kinda nonsense you're up to, but thank you for helping me get my nerd on and making my day slightly less tedious."

"My pleasure." I shook her hand. "I guess we should probably leave it at Danny for now. I take it . . . " I looked back at the Baptists, who were paying us no mind. "I take it you're not with these guys, huh?"

Tasha scowled. "Hell, no, I'm not with them. It's just a job. I'm local, and I am gonna give my boss hell on Monday for renting me out to the God-Hates-Fags people, don't think I won't. I been a geek all my life, but never got within sniffing distance of Comic-Con, so I got all excited when they said they wanted me to work it. But this was *not* what I had in mind."

"They give you a hard time because, uh . . . "

"Because I eat pussy? Naw, they're all right. In fact, they're really, really . . . *nice*. It's kind of freaking me out to be honest with you."

"I hear you."

"Now tell me what I can do for you before I have to send you home to Luke Cage."

I nodded at the bodycam hooked into the computer's USB port. "They keep you around just to manage bodycam footage?"

"Nah, man, their social media game is fierce. I shoot their videos for Instagram, I upload all their shit to Facebook, Twitter—half of these olds can't use a flip phone, so I'm their lifeline to the Internet. The bodycams are just in case somebody picks a fight. They use the raw feed later to identify the attacker—I don't need to tell you a lot of people try to kick these guys' asses. And sometimes they use the footage as content, too."

"How long do you keep the 'content'?"

"Gotta store it all at least until the end of the con. You don't know when it might come in handy. Thing is, though, video's a real data hog. An hour of it is like one gig, and there's only about twelve gigs' worth of storage on each one of these ancient cams, but that don't matter 'cause the batteries only last, like, four or five hours of continuous filming anyway."

"Pretend I have no idea what you just said."

"Point is, we gotta keep swapping the bodycams, dumping the footage on the hard drive, wiping the cameras, then sending them back out again."

"So you got it all on here?" I said, pointing at the computer.

"Yeah, I got it, I got it."

"Is there any way I can see what you captured from Wednesday night? Like, between eleven and midnight."

Tasha shrugged. "Sure." She sat down at the keyboard.

"Really? You're not going to ask me why?"

"Nah, man, you're Iron Fist. I assume you're tracking down some evil-ass ninjas."

"I'd like to tell you but I probably shouldn't, for your own safety."

Tasha awakened the monitor with a slap of the space bar, then called up a video viewer app that split the screen into sixteen rectangular squares, like a digital fly's multifaceted eyes. Each box was the view of a different Eastboro Church street preacher spaced about a thousand feet apart along the sidewalk in front of the convention center. The brake lights of cars passing on Harbor Avenue left long bloody pixel streaks across the screen. This late at night, groups of con-goers and cosplayers were small and infrequent—Hogwarts robes flying, plastic assault rifles dragging along the ground, weighed down by their enormous Atlas Entertainment branded swag bags. A Skeletor in a bone codpiece came right up to one of the cameras and blocked it briefly with his middle finger. A guy in sunglasses and no shirt walking with two women suddenly swerved and ran up to another, hocking and spitting a big old loogie over the lens, presumably aiming at the wearer's head; the view flailed wildly into a frozen, pixelated blur.

"What you got here is everything from like twenty-two thirty hours to midnight, when they pack it in," Tasha said. "You looking for anything in particular?"

"I'll know it when I see it," I said. "I hope."

Tasha clicked on the control bar at the bottom of the master screen and began fast-forwarding through all the videos at the same time. A Heath Ledger–style Joker and a Margot Robbie–style Harley Quinn practically skipped, arm in arm, across one end of the Harbor Drive sidewalk to the other at comical speed. A company of orcs with leather armor and battle axes quick-marched across the street to the Bayfront hotel bar. A Quicksilver (classic flavor, original green costume) lived up to his name by running, at 10x-speed, to the light-rail stop, but in Buster Keaton fashion he fell down, got up, and fell down again, then got to the station just as the train pulled away. Too slow, super-speedster: oh, the irony.

Around 23:22 on the ticking timestamp, the camera owned by the preacher positioned near the bottom of the staircase that led up to the Sails Pavilion began to register the arrival of the *Dante's Fire* cosplayers, gathering for their Guinness World Record photo op. By 23:36 they were completely filling the screen, multiplying in the speeded-up tape like horny rabbits until the Baptist's-eye view was surrounded and the only thing you could see other than anime characters was the trolley station across Harbor.

At 23:45, I saw it. "Wait, go back."

Tasha froze the images. "What am I looking for?"

"This guy, this . . . ninja? See him? As he goes past the camera?" I pointed to a figure heading up the steps; he was clad from head to toe in a plastic arm and a sort of modified black bicycle helmet with fins on it. He was completely ignoring the other cosplayers and plunging up the stairs, taking them two at a time.

"You mean Ulee-o?" Tasha said. "The tall one?"

"Yeah—oh, whoa, do you recognize that guy? Do you know what his name is?"

Tasha blinked in surprise. "Yeah, his name is Ulee-o. The archnemesis slash secret love interest of Dante. And I do mean slash, as in inspiring some of the steamiest slash fiction ever masturbated to."

"Once again: please assume I have no idea what you're talking about."

Tasha gasped in horror, as if I'd just confessed to war crimes. "You've never seen *Dante's Fire?*"

"I know, I know, I'm history's greatest monster. Just scroll back, okay? I want to see something."

She rolled back the footage. Ulee-o walked backward very quickly down the stairs and through the wall of cosplayers, then through the traffic on Harbor. He made it across the railroad tracks just as the trolley backed up in front of him, paused briefly, then reversed out of frame. Just barely I could see him walking backward, disappearing into the Gaslamp Quarter.

"Can you freeze just this screen here?"

"*Pffft,* don't insult me."

"Okay, great, do that and—let the other ones roll forward at normal speed. He goes up to the Sails Pavilion. Let's see if he pops up anywhere else."

Tasha did as I asked, and neither of us realized we were holding our breath.

"There," she said suddenly, rising halfway out of her seat. She paused the cornermost screen that seemed to depict the southeast corner of the convention center, the camera trained on my hotel, the Bayfront, across the street.

She froze the image on what appeared to be the same Ulee-o running from right to left across the screen, throwing his completely masked head around to look behind him. The listed time-stamp was 23:54.

"Yeah, that looks like him, all right," I said. Tasha rolled back the image until Ulee-o disappeared out of the frame. She then let it play at regular speed and Ulee-o ran past the camera and disappeared as fast as he could in the direction of the Gaslamp Quarter.

"Okay, okay, great," I said. "Now roll that back and freeze it—and give me that other one just as he's climbing the steps."

Tasha nodded. I had my sketchbook in my hand and captured the entire monitor in just a few minutes.

"You know you could just take a picture of the screen with your cell phone," Tasha said.

"I guess. But this is more second nature to me. I've been doing this since long before cell phones."

"Why is this so important to you?"

I talked as fast as I drew. "See how this guy shows up—at a run—from the Gaslamp? He goes up the steps and completely ignores the cosplayers. He wants people to think he's participating in the *Dante's Fire* picture, but he doesn't register with the Guinness judge who's standing over there in the kilt; he just goes right up to those steps. Those steps lead not just to the Sails Pavilion but to the harbor area that runs all the way along the back of the convention center. He's looking to waylay this guy—Danny Lieber—you hear about the murdered guy? Kills him, and by the time Danny staggers over to where the cosplayers are, this guy is running around the convention center at the other end, by the Bayfront—see?"

Tasha looked at me glassy-eyed.

I lifted my pencil off the page and looked back. "What?"

"You really *are* Iron Fist," she said, and snapped a photo of me with her cell phone.

– – – –

Dirtbag had been hanging back, watching me in the tent from afar, but texted to let me know he was headed to Petco to get his zombie on. It was just as well because I had to return to the con and be on a Comics to Film panel, where some guy spent the Q&A session chewing me out about the differences between *Gut Check* the movie and *Gut Check* the comic, as if I had any real control over the former. After the panel I signed a bunch of autographs and left the hall by a side entrance and that's when I saw them.

Down the long hallway, dressed in identical black jeans and leather jackets, came my pursuers from the other night. In the better light of day, the letters MEH in Gothic script stood out more vividly around their necks. They limped shoulder to shoulder—on opposite feet each wore a plastic orthopedic boot that reached to midcalf, protection for injuries I presumed they suffered at the *Cell Block Z* immersive last night that I may or may not have had something to do with.

"C'mere," the one on the left yelled, "we just want to talk."

Uh, no thank you. This was just too weird.

I held up a "not right now" hand and looked for the nearest exit:

And that's when I saw her.

Long blonde ponytail.

Sunglasses.

Archeologist khakis.

It was her.

The mystery pedicabbie.

My alibi.

And I let her walk just past me in the direction of the bikers, to whom she handed out a small, square flier like she was handing everyone else. The human juggernauts just ignored her and kept their beady eyes fixated on me.

I put my advantage of two functioning ankles to good use, skipping around the MEH twins as they tried to lunge for me. I called out to the back of the driver's head, "Hey—uh—stop!" But in the glass cavern of the upstairs meeting room every noise echoed into incoherence and she didn't budge or turn her braided head.

At that moment a pair of ceiling-high double doors opened and disgorged a torrent of humanity dressed as wolves—a wolf in a polka-dot bikini, a wolf in green fairy wings, a wolf in a monocle and top hat—with quite a number of young women, and one or two men, in crimson capes and scarlet fishnets. Using my keen powers of deduction, I reasoned that the *Red Riding Hood: Werewolf Hunter* YA novel trilogy/Freeform show/Telltale Games series/Dynamite comic book/scented candles/protein bar panel had just let out of Hall H, and I was now trapped in the outflow.

I wasn't the only one. The driver was embedded a bit farther down the slow-moving mass. I tried to push my way through the horde of furries to get to her, but it was like drowning in a bead of mercury: wolves and hoods kept shifting to block any avenue I might have to advance.

I looked behind me and my heart sank. The bikers plowed
directly into the mob, whatever disadvantage they had from their
giant boots now completely removed. They were able to cleave
the crowd like a snowplow, elbowing nerds without even raising
their elbows, just batting them aside with the meat bumpers that
were their corded arms.

We minced as a group to the escalators and the pedicabbie
got funneled downstairs, with me and the bikers right behind
her, albeit behind by ten or so werewolves each. The bikers tried
to push their way down the stairs but even they realized that any
rough stuff would send quite a few Big Bad Wolves and not-so-
little Red Riding Hoods flipping over the railings for a long drop
with a short stop. Their advance stopped to a crawl.

I could see the lobby floor of the main convention center,
similarly crammed with humanity. The pedicabbie got off the
escalator long before me, and the bikers were still inching in my
direction; they would catch up to me long before I caught up to
her. I was getting desperate as they squeezed down, a drip-drip-
drip of fleshy white dude.

Jesus. This was History's Slowest Chase Scene.

At the very bottom of the escalator passed a half dozen cosplayers, with a clever theme: they were all dressed in black suits
and ties like *Reservoir Dogs* but wore different colored Spider-
Man masks: Original Flavor, Venom, Carnage, Scarlet Spider,
Spider-Man 2099, and Spider-Man Noir.

The bikers were just one or two steps above me, reaching
for the back of my shirt.

That's when inspiration hit.

"Wow, you guys look great," I cried as soon as I stepped

off the escalator, pulling out my phone. "Can I take a picture?"

"Absolutely," Venom said. They all immediately stopped in their tracks and vogued, Charlie's Angels style, web-shooters pointing in various directions, as I held my phone to my face. Half the fans around me oohed and aahed and stopped dead in their tracks too.

Unfortunately, they stopped right in front of the escalator, and every human being on it was fed directly into them, including the bikers. Soon they were all on top of one another in a cursing, yelling mass on the floor.

Sometimes I impress me.

I put down my phone and dashed into the crowd. The downstairs lobby was much more spacious than the halls above, and I was able to duck and weave around eight girls dressed in Japanese schoolboys' uniforms sitting cross-legged in the middle of the floor for no discernible reason. I finally made it to the pedicabbie and I put my hand on her shoulder.

"I've been looking everywhere for you."

Surprised, she quickly pulled her shoulder out from under my hand and whirled around. I found myself looking at a tall, skinny Filipina wearing sunglasses and a braided blonde wig.

"Great," she said cheerily and handed me a flier. "Hope to see you on Saturday!"

She vanished back into the crowd.

I looked back at the escalator and made sure the peg-legging bikers were trapped underneath the Reservoir Spideys before losing my own damn self in the crowd.

Heading out to my hotel to get changed before the Kirbys, I was once again steeped in a flow of human molasses, so I looked

at the flier the not-pedicabbie had handed me: It depicted a Slave Leia, chin cocked sneeringly at the camera, holding Jabba the Hut's severed head on a platter in her left hand and her own chain in her right. The metal leash snaked down and around the neck of a hunky Han Solo kneeling at her side; he was clad in nothing but his black vest, pleading like an S&M client with his dick tucked tastefully between his thighs. "RULE 34 GEEK BURLESQUE," it said over the top. "Sex-Positive * All Genders/ Orientations Welcome * Pop-Up This Saturday Night Only Midnight."

There was something strange about the flyer that I couldn't quite put my finger on.

Until I realized that the woman dressed as Slave Leia was my mysterious pedicabbie.

- - - -

I was happy to finally have a lead on my alibi, but pursuing it would have to wait. Tonight was the Kirby Awards ceremony, the whole reason I came to this con in the first place: to give a now dead man a lifetime achievement award. I went back to my room and changed into a nice pink button-down shirt, then headed over to the Hyatt. The doors opened to the voluminous marble lobby, revealing Sam and Twitch standing there waiting for me.

"Fancy meeting you here," I said.

"Your name is on the website as a presenter," Twitch said.

"We have a few quick follow-up questions, if you wouldn't mind," Sam said.

"What if I did mind?"

"The questions, they would remain," Twitch said and spread his hands.

"That's what I thought. Let's find a place to talk."

The ground floor of the Hyatt was a labyrinth of high-ceilinged stores, coffee shops, and bars, similar to what you'd find inside a casino. We sat down at an empty table against the wall of one generically fancy drinkery, all mahogany paneling and those low-backed plush armchairs that made you feel like you were slumping no matter how you tried not to.

"Are you familiar with an individual named Pilar Hernandez?" Sam asked once we'd settled.

"No," I said.

"You're sure she doesn't follow you on Facebook?" Twitch said.

"And Twitter?" Sam said.

"It's possible. I have thirty-five thousand Twitter followers and maxed out my Facebook friends last year. I don't know the name of every single person who follows me."

"Uh-huh." Twitch scratched a few words in the Book of Special Thoughts. "She follows you on both those services, just so you know."

"If you say so."

"We say so," Sam said.

"And you haven't had any personal contact with Pilar Hernandez since you've been here in San Diego?" Twitch said.

"To my knowledge I've never had any personal contact with Pilar Hernandez, period," I said.

"To your knowledge," Sam said.

"Yes," I said, my jaw clenching. "I do not know a single

thing outside my knowledge."

"You don't remember her tagging you on a Facebook post seven months ago?" Twitch said.

I cast my memory memory as far back as I could but came up empty. "No, what post?"

"This one," Sam said. He produced a large Android phone and turned it toward me. On the screen was a young woman with purple-streaked hair leaning too far into the computer's mounted camera. Behind her could be seen partial elements of the rest of the room: the corner of an unmade bed, blinds covering a window, a faux travel poster for Hogwarts.

"This is a message for Danny Lieber and all the smug know-nothings at Atlas Comics," she said into the camera. "Here's my latest review of the current arc of *Mister Mystery*."

She stood up, wielding a large dull-gray automatic pistol, and walked out of the room.

"Holy shit," I croaked.

That was it, that was the whole video. But it wasn't really the gun I was reacting to.

"Ring any bells?" Sam said.

"Yeah," I said, and had to force a swallow down my dry throat before continuing. "She picked me up at the airport. She's been . . . volunteering at the con. She said her name was Violet."

– – – –

Sam and Twitch were understandably aroused by this comment and grilled me thoroughly over every interaction I'd had with Violent Violet slash Pilar Hernandez since my arrival in San Diego. I told them everything I could think of.

"It's just . . . the time I have spent with her . . . I have a hard time believing she was doing anything other than blowing off steam," I said. "Was she really serious?"

"Atlas Entertainment seemed to think so," Twitch said. "They took it pretty seriously. They didn't tell you about it?"

"No . . . Maybe the video got taken down before I could see it."

"This a pretty common thing for you—death threats?" Sam said.

"Death threats are uncommon but not unheard of. There's not a comics fan alive who doesn't think he can do his favorite characters better than the professionals. Some of them are more strident than others. I guess Violet—uh, Pilar—is reacting to a storyline Katie and Mod did where Mister Mystery gets brainwashed by the villains into becoming a fascist, and his longtime love interest gets knocked off. There was a big sales spike for a hot second. Happens all the time in comics. But then next year they'll bring her back and everyone will go nuts again and sales will go up one month. Why some fans act like it's the end of the freaking world every single time they temporarily change or kill off a character I'll never understand. But then I guess if they weren't emotional about it, they wouldn't be fans, right?"

"You're saying this is normal?" Sam said, arching an eyebrow.

"Reviewing a comic book series with a handgun? There is nowhere on Earth that would be normal. No way. Have you been able to find her?"

"Frankly, if we had Ms. Hernandez in our pocket we wouldn't be talking to you," Twitch said. "I don't think she is a real volunteer. If she has a badge and a volunteer shirt, we'll have to figure out where she got them."

"So if she contacts you or you spot her, call us immediately," Sam said, handing me his card again.

"Absolutely. And you're gonna warn Katie Poole too, right?" I said.

"And Mr., uh, Mod, yes."

"Oh, yeah, him. Yeah, I guess you should warn him too."

– – – –

By this point my brain had been pummeled by more shocks and reversals than I'd experienced in my entire life. I staggered into the Kirby Awards banquet in the main Hyatt ballroom and in something of a daze took my seat at my designated table of comics luminaries and publishing employees.

Which was maybe for the best. Fifteen years in the business have corroded my interest in industry awards; for one thing, there are so damn many of them, given out by every manner of institution and organization, that it's hard to keep track of who's up for what; and that kind of amortizes the value of each individual trophy. Furthermore, the same handful of currently popular It-Boys and -Girls won the vast bulk of them every year anyway. All the better-known awards were voted on by comics creators, who always went for their friends and their friends' books; most comics creators I know, myself included, don't have the time to actually read many comics anyway, so in categories where no friends are nominated they just vote for the most recognized title.

I mean, that's what I do.

I've long wondered where this compulsion to rank each other by merit and anoint a best in show comes from. Is it left

over from the brutal public art critiques we grew up with in college art school classes? Is it hardwired into the pack mentality
of the human animal, constantly jockeying for higher status toward the Alpha; or is it a psychological need to have your labor
and toil validated by somebody, somewhere, somehow, to calm
those nagging whispers in your head that you are no good, an
imposter?

I am fairly certain that if a plane full of comic book people
crashed on a desert island, the first thing we would do, before
securing food, water, and shelter, would be to start giving each
other awards, even if they were just coconut shells and bamboo
lashed together with vines, *Gilligan's Island*–style: Best Tourni-
quet, Best New Cannibal Deserving of Wider Recognition, Scur-
viest Gums, etc.

Hey, don't get me wrong, I love getting my ego stroked as
much as the next red-blooded American; I've been nominated a
few times. This year, flipping through the program while waiting
for the ceremony to begin, I was surprised to see my name listed
as something other than a presenter: the *Gut Check* omnibus
released last year in conjunction with the movie was up for Best
Domestic Reprint (Fiction). Did my publisher tell me about that?
I honestly couldn't remember.

As further proof of comics' elevated cultural cachet in our
current historical moment, the Kirbys rated getting an actual celebrity for its emcee; this year it was a well-known comic, Dante
Dupree, who I vaguely recalled seeing in a Comedy Central
showcase somewhere. Dupree established his "comics" bona-
fides by expressing his love for Star Wars, *Game of Thrones*, and
Harry Potter, the great unifying trifecta of modern pop culture,

then launched into a slightly geekier version of what I assumed
to be his regular act.

I couldn't follow any of it. I couldn't stop thinking about
what Sam showed me on his phone. I wasn't exactly an expert
in Violent Violet's—Pilar's—behavior, having known her only a
couple days, but the girl in the video did not seem at all like
the person who picked me up at the airport. She was odd, sure,
but . . . was she the sort of nutty fan who could kill an editor because she thought he was raping her childhood, as the kids say?
Was that what she had been spending the whole con trying to tell
me? But hadn't she started saying that to me before the murder
even happened?

My God—what if she was trying to tell me what she was
planning on doing, and I might have prevented all this madness
just by listening?

The Best Letterer and Best Foreign Language Reprint of
Nonfiction Material had been presented, passing totally unno-
ticed by me, when I felt a hand on my shoulder. I turned to see
a frizzy-haired geek girl in owl glasses with a headset and a clipboard leaning over me.

"We're ready for you in the Green Room, sir," she whispered. "If you would follow me, please?"

She led me out of the banquet hall through a side door that
connected with a small room to one side of the stage via a short
corridor. The presenters—a motley mix of comic book legends
and supporting cast members of CW superhero shows—milled
about in varying degrees of anxiousness, waiting to be called to
the lectern. Winners also exited this way after being called up on
stage, clutching their trophies, flushed faces all smiles.

Owl Lady immediately tried to dash off to some other task as soon as she dumped me in the room, but when I looked at the envelope and index cards of nominees that she had handed me, I touched her arm.

"Hey, sorry? I think there's been a mix-up. This says Best Writer, but I'm here to hand out the lifetime achievement award?"

"Yes. Sorry, I should have said. In light of current events, the awards committee has decided to not give out the lifetime achievement award this year. The intended recipient, Ben K, has been disqualified from receiving it on account of him, you know, dying. He'll be eligible for the Hall of Fame next year. We had Samuel L. Jackson cancel on us last minute—I think he got food poisoning?—so would you mind filling in for the Best Writer category?"

I blinked. "How can I say no to Sam?"

She might have said "thank you" but I wasn't sure because she turned away and moved on to her next mission so quickly that she left a mild sonic boom in her wake.

Once left alone, I noticed an extremely good-looking man in a camelhair blazer and turquoise V-neck making his way over to me. He had sandy blond hair and blue eyes and stubble so precisely trimmed it must have been measured off with a level.

I stepped out of the guy's path, but Mr. Handsome stuck a hand out at me. "Mike M, am I right? Pardon, mate, I don't mean to bother you, but I am a huge, huge fan." He had a thick Australian accent. "*Gut Check* is like one of my favorite series of all time, and your run on *Mister Mystery*—aces. I got 'em all, plus the variants."

I shook the guy's bronzed mitt. "That's very cool, thanks for saying so, man. You presenting too?"

"Yeah, they've got me doing Best American Edition of Foreign Material."

"And you are—sorry—"

"No worries, mate. You don't watch *Cell Block Z*?"

A dim recognition flickered through my brain, glimpses of his perfect jaw plastered across subway platforms and highway billboards. "Oh, yeah, sure—"

"Armond Delaine. I play Jack Jenkins. 'The Gentleman Rapist'?"

"That's very . . . edgy? I guess?"

"Yeah, cheers. We don't hold back from portraying what it would *really* be like to be in a maximum security prison during a zombie apocalypse."

I nodded vigorously. "Well, *somebody* has to."

"But at university I studied to be a cartoonist, you know, before I realized I was handsome. So listen, mate, I wanted to run something past you. I imagine you do a lot of these things, yeah?"

"Awards ceremonies?"

Armond laughed, exposing teeth you could make no-stick cookware out of. "No, comic cons. I didn't really know this before Z-Block took off and I started hitting the circuit hardcore, but people on what I guess you'd call geek-genre TV shows can really make a killing at these events. We're talking about featured performers pulling in two garbage bags full of $100 bills in one weekend in Buffalo or wherever. And the security at a lot of these venues—no offense to any of them—is downright dreadful."

I nodded for real this time. "No lie. I mean, usually I can fit what I make into my wallet, but it's still a lot more cash than I like to wander around with. And most banks close—"

"Saturday at noon, which isn't even halfway through most cons. You see what I'm saying, mate." Armond flicked a business card at me. "That's where we come in."

Across the card the words "MEATWALL—Pop Con Management • Representation • Security" were written in the form of vein-bulging muscles. The other side just had a close-up photo of bloody red ground chuck.

I pointed at the name above the phone number and email address. "Who's Terrence Lawson?"

"Oh, Terry is the best. He's got a background in this field. He's a huge fan of Z-Block and volunteered to help me out at a con in . . . Denver, I think it was? I started recommending him to my mates on other shows. Pretty soon we realized there was an untapped market for this sort of service, so we co-founded this firm."

The owl-eyed-glasses geek girl with the clipboard appeared by Armond's side wearing an expression that indicated she was planning to eat him. "Mr. Delaine, it's just about time."

"Right," Armond said, and shook my hand. "Anyway, if you have any need of our services, be sure and give us a ring. Oy, mate—great to meet you. Like I said, big fan."

"Thanks, same here," I lied as Armond turned away, hooking his handler's arm with his own. Her knees buckled slightly as her body rippled through a visible orgasm. Somehow, she maintained sufficient fortitude to put one foot in front of the other and lead him to the stage.

Burning with masculine jealousy, I put the Meatwall business card in my back pocket and promptly forgot all about it.

— — — —

I went to wait in the wings, beside an enormous table gleaming with trophies, for Best Writer to come up. Named, of course, after the legendary American comic book artist known for his bombastic fight scenes and otherworldly technology, the Kirby Award was a one-foot-tall silver Plasticine tower spawned from the unholy union of a SETI satellite dish, Frankensteinian lab equipment, and an alien warship, sprouting at the top a lush broccoli head of "Kirby Crackle" a/k/a "Kirby Dots," which he often used to indicate the presence of unfathomable cosmic power. It was the ugliest damn thing you had ever seen; my designer's eye immediately noted several simple tweaks that could've improved its unwieldiness and brought it more in line with Kirby's vision. But the perpetually cash-strapped not-for-profit that ran the Kirby Awards was as proud of its statuette as a second-grader bringing home a misshapen ashtray from the art class kiln for Mommy, so most of us cartoonists kept our mouths shut and just sniggered at its hideousness out of earshot of the ceremony's organizers.

The audience applauded politely when Dante Dupree introduced me, their spirits not yet entirely broken two hours into a five-hour ceremony. Animated 3D letters spelling BEST WRITER slammed with teeth-rattling force into a colorful splash-page collage on the large flatscreen rising behind me.

I stepped to the lectern and glanced down at the index cards that had been handed to me. "*Webster's Dictionary* defines writing as . . . ," I started to read until I couldn't stop laughing, then I decided to extemporize instead.

"Well, not plagiarizing the dictionary like an eighth grader, I'm pretty sure." The audience laughed with me. "At least I hope not." I've done enough guest-artist college teaching in my day that when it comes to public speaking, I do not entirely suck. "Anyway, here are the nominees for Best Writer. To qualify for this award you have to ask your poor artist to draw only one crowd scene per script, with special bonuses for no crowd scenes. Oh, and no horses. Horses are a pain in the ass to draw because no part of their anatomy makes any damn sense, particularly while they're running. Yet another reason to be angry at God."

The crowd chuckled at that, but then burst into real guffaws as the slides for the nominees began appearing behind me. I turned and saw a famous photo of Sebastian Mod that had made the rounds of the internet a year or so back, buck-naked and holding one of his comics over his crotch. In the photo Mod had the wiry physique of a high school freshman on the long-distance track team who had been dipped up to his scalp in a giant vat of Nair.

Oh, Jesus. "Sebastian Mod, for *Mister Mystery*," I read off the card. There were the names of four other slobs and their books spelled out phonetically on there also, and I read them dutifully, but my mind saw no point in registering what they actually were. They were just placeholders. The identity of the winner was as inevitable as a sunset. Sebastian Mod had long ago become the guy who won awards because he was the Guy You Gave Awards To.

Once I was done reading the other four nominees, I hesitated opening the envelope as if, Schrödinger's Cat–like, I could keep alive the possibility that Mod hadn't won simply by never lifting the lid.

But I'm a Grown-Ass Man, despite my best efforts otherwise, and that was not the Grown-Ass Option.

"And the Kirby goes to . . . " I tore open the envelope.

Without looking at the card first, I declared:

"Sebastian Mod, for *Mister Mystery*."

Only then did I look down at the card and see with no satisfaction at all that I was 100% right.

The audience erupted in applause, along with a smattering of cheers. The winner wasn't surprising enough to garner too extreme a reaction. I looked out over the crowd, mostly faceless blank blobs behind the stage lights in my face, looking for the gleaming dome of Sebastian Mod's pate rising from one of the banquet tables, but did not find it.

Instead, emerging from the gloom of the audience in a spectacular blue strapless gown, hair done up in a magnificent pile on her head speared with decorative sticks, came Christine. She had a small blue-and-diamond handbag hanging from the hand that hiked the hem of her dress just high enough for her to make her way between the tables and up onto the stage.

My first irrational impulse was that this was the glorious rom-com moment of triumph, when the one you love realizes what a fool she's been all along and at the last possible second makes a public declaration of permanent devotion.

But no, Christine took the stage and gently nudged me out of the way with her elbow and picked up the Kirby. She leaned into the microphone and said:

"I'm sorry that Sebastian couldn't be here tonight. On be-half of him I'd like to thank everyone who voted for *Mister Mys-tery*. He really loves doing this book and is so thrilled at how well the fans have responded to it. Thanks again."

The audience clapped politely and Christine immediately spun on her heel and marched into the wings. She was in the hallway outside the green room before I managed to catch up to her and grab her arm.

"Are you all right?" I said.

She spun toward me, backhanding rivulets of mascara from under her eyes. "Piece of shit," she said.

"Who? Me or Sebastian?"

"I have half a mind to smash this stupid trophy against the wall. SuicideGirls is having their event right now; I bet he's over there getting his perv on."

"SuicideGirls? Is that still a thing?"

Christine sniffed. "And you can't imagine the looks I've been getting. Geek Jezebel. The one who got Danny Lieber killed. Oh, why did I even come to this con in the first place? I am so freak-ing dumb. You're probably thrilled."

"No, not me," I lied. "I just hate to see you so upset." I handed her a cocktail napkin I'd shoved in my back pocket during the reception.

She wiped her eyes until the napkin was the color of a bruise. "Listen, I'm sorry I went so, you know, bitchcakes on you last night. That wasn't cool, but . . . I gotta be honest, being back here is way more stressful than I thought it was going to be."

"You're telling me."

"I can't sit through another second of this stupid ceremony.

You want to grab a drink somewhere?"

My heart started dribbling like a basketball into my throat. "Sure," I said, voice squeaking. Bringing it down to a more manly level, "I found this great dive bar on G Street that I guarantee you is the only place in the Gaslamp that has no con-goers in it whatsoever."

"Nah, I don't want to walk that far in these heels. Which hotel you staying at? The Marriott?"

Thump-thump-thump-thump-thump. "No, the Bayfront?"

"Why don't we go there and try and talk like normal humans."

"Absolutely. I can be an extremely normal human when I want to be, especially when plied with alcohol. Lead on."

Christine turned to go, and I stepped forward to follow her. I was vaguely aware of the door to the green room banging open behind me, but it didn't mean anything until the geek girl in the owl glasses managed to cut off Christine's advance, stopping us in our tracks.

"There you are! Come on, they need you onstage."

"What? Why? I already gave out that thing," I said, pointing to the unwieldy Kirby in Christine's arms.

"No, you won."

"I what?"

"*Gut Check Omnibus* won Best Reprint. Come on, they're waiting!"

The geek girl with the clipboard grabbed me by the arm and pulled me back toward the stage.

"You go," Christine said. "I'll meet you at the Bayfront bar."

"I'll keep my speech short!"

"And congratulations!" she called as I disappeared back inside.

– – – –

The audience had been waiting for me long enough that the applause was just dying down as I stepped on stage, but at my appearance the clapping reached a respectful new crescendo for a few seconds. The headshot from the front page of my website grinned down on me from the screen.

"There you are," said the presenter, avuncular *Thor* legend Walt Simonson. "You kept us waiting so long I was almost going to take this home myself, but it's too damn heavy." The crowd laughed as Simonson shook my hand, congratulated me, then quit the stage.

I hefted the Kirby in my hand. It was indeed heavier than it looked. "Thanks," I said into the microphone. "I mean, thank you very much, seriously. This is a real surprise. Like, so much so, I didn't even realize I had been nominated. So I don't have any words prepared, or anything . . . I guess I'm just surprised *Gut Check* won Best Reprint. I mean, you didn't nominate it for jack when it came out. What happened in the years since then? Did it just get better with age, like a fine wine or something? Or was it the only nominee you heard of on the ballot because of the movie?"

"*Yeah!*" somebody rebel-yelled from the back, but otherwise the audience sat frozen in awkward silence.

"Sorry—that sounds bitter, doesn't it? A bad attempt at a joke is all. In all seriousness, thanks to everyone who voted for me, I really appreciate it—it means a lot. Thanks."

I nodded and gave a short little half bow, and the crowd wearily applauded again as in enough already, and Dante Dupree started to climb the steps to the podium. But when he was not quite halfway to the wings I spun on my heel and returned to microphone.

"One—one more thing, actually. Sorry," I said to Dupree, who remained on the stage steps like a deer caught in the head-lights. "I just wanted to say that the thing that kind of bothers me about the whole Best Reprint thing is that we have a tenden-cy in this business to turn everything into nostalgia, that we're rewarding things not when they happen but after the fact, the memory of them. It's like we can't ever value what we have while we have it, you know? And I don't just mean awards for titles—I mean people. As most of you I'm sure know, we lost the Great One, Ben K, a couple days ago."

I acknowledged the smattering of clapping and cheers with a nod before continuing:

"Yeah, and he really was like a second father to me, no mat-ter how corny or cliché that sounds. And I just found out he was having serious health issues, and because of that, serious money problems. And yeah, Heroes 4 Heroes was gonna help him out, but the fact we need a nonprofit charity to help our greatest cre-ators in their golden years shows that we're not honoring them while they're still around. Not with awards but with, you know, money. Royalties. Option money. At least some of the millions others make off their characters. It's just not right."

The applause was now growing, and at every table at least one person near the rear was standing up and clapping hard, Charles-Foster-Kane-at-the-Opera-House hard. This was basically the speech I had written when I was planning on giving the award to Ben K, alive, on this very stage, and so the words just kept spilling out of my mouth:

"But partially we have ourselves to blame. We, the members of the comics community, and not just because we sign bad contracts and constantly undervalue ourselves at every turn. No, we're as bad as the fans sometimes, in the sense that we don't shout from the rooftops that these characters don't just spring out of nowhere, you know, like Athena from the head of Zeus or whatever. I know that's a weird classical reference, but my parents are college professors and it just popped into my head.

"Comic books and superheroes *aren't* mythology. They didn't just spring out of the ether, out of some collective cultural unconscious. And they aren't cranked out in some nameless factory by a bunch of anonymous drones, either. Every single hero or villain up there on Hollywood's screens came from someone. This isn't a product of corporations. This is art made by human beings. Every image on every booth and cosplayer out there came from people, and until we make sure everyone knows their names, not just the names of Batman or Wolverine or whoever, there's no point in us handing out awards to each other every year, because we're all still gonna have to beg for handouts when we're old and gray. I'm probably just rambling at this point, but I just had to say it: honor people now the way they deserve it, not just here in this ceremony but out there, in the world, everywhere, before it's too late."

By now I could barely hear myself over the applause. Everyone was on their feet and clapping. I hefted the Kirby Award over my head and said, "And thank you again for this cosmic broccoli. Good night!"

If there was a mic in my hand I would have dropped it. But it was mounted to the podium, so I just walked off the stage to a thunderous ovation.

– – – –

As I returned to the green room, I was vaguely aware of cartoonists and celebrities thumbs-upping me from the peripheries of my vision, but all I was really thinking about was joining Christine at the Bayfront bar.

I almost made it to the door before a human roadblock blocked my path. The man, if that's what it was, wore a dark blue suit and a white button-down shirt and no tie. His head looked like it was the prototype from which the Madballs were cast, those foam toys from my eighties childhood in the shape of heads of mummies and skulls and aliens and things, basically spherical but with bumpy protuberances to suggest eyes and ears and nose and such. The best way I can describe him is that he looked as if an Irish rabbi had animated a golem made entirely out of corned beef. His expression projected profound boredom with the world's myriad horrors. He didn't have a giant neon sign on his massive forehead flashing COP over and over, but maybe that was because it was so completely unnecessary.

Its mouth opened and said in a distinct Noo Yawk accent, "I really liked your speech, sir."

"I'm not sure it made any sense at all, but thanks." I tried to walk around him but he simply stepped sideways to cut off my escape, giving truth to the oft-uttered superhero comic cliche: *How can something so big move so fast?*

"My name is Brendan McCool," the apparent human said. "I'm head of security for Atlas Entertainment."

"Security? I didn't know Atlas had a security department."

"I know, that's how I like it," he said. "It's more of an informal position, really." McCool shifted, one foot to the other. I couldn't be sure I didn't feel the ground move with him. "I'd like to request that you come with me."

I gaped at this giant cracked Liberty Bell of a man, who could squash me by accident and not realize it until he looked at the bottom of his shoes. "And if I turn down your request?"

McCool's expression didn't change. "Then I'll keep making the request until it's granted."

I sighed. "Yeah, okay, sure. Let's get it over with. Where we headed?"

"You'll see." He reached out with his pylon arms to lead me to the door. "I promise not to take very much of your time. In fact, I think you'll be back before the ceremony is over."

"Then could you just throw me in the ocean instead?" I asked, following behind him.

– – – –

McCool opened a series of fire doors that led into the hidden burrows of the hotel where busboys dashed past with trays and maids pushed laundry carts. A large, bald, human male in a suit with an earpiece nodded at McCool as he passed, speaking the wordless cant of former law enforcement.

Ultimately we emerged in the parking lot, where palm trees swayed and you could hear the boats in the marina creak. A limousine idled at the end of the sidewalk, and McCool opened the passenger side for me. I looked suspiciously into the purple-lit interior: no one was in there.

"Where are you taking me?" I asked.

"Not far," McCool said in the monotone of a man who doesn't care if you believe him or not.

My curiosity was piqued, I will admit, and that overcame my initial survival instinct to bolt the hell out of there. Besides, I was pretty sure McCool could run me down and trample me like a rhino. So I climbed inside, snapped on my seatbelt, and held my Kirby Award in my lap. McCool followed me laboriously, with much huffing and grunting and groaning, and that was just from the car's shocks.

The limousine barely whispered as it pulled away from the hotel and turned onto Pacific Highway. I wasn't sure where we were going until I saw signs for San Diego International Airport.

"Whoa," I said, sitting up straight. The Kirby nearly fell out of my lap. "Whoa, whoa, whoa. What are you trying to pull here?"

"Cool your jets," McCool said.

"The cops—San Diego PD—they told me not to get on a plane."

McCool shook his head. "No, they didn't."

"Were you there?" I said. I practically stood out of my seat as if I was going to open the car door and jump out. "They explicitly said not to get on a flight—"

The big man reached out and flicked me back in my seat like I was a booger on his fingernail. "Sir, I served in the New York City Police Department for twenty-five years, and I can guarantee you that they did not tell you not to get on a plane."

"I—"

"What they *told* you to do was not to leave town. Which you are not."

McCool poked a meaty finger in my direction:

"But you *are* getting on a plane."

— — — —

The limo did not turn into the arrivals entrance to the airport, or the departures, or even long-term parking. Instead, after a couple right turns away from the harbor, it drove down a deserted unlit access road alongside a tall chain-link fence surrounding the runways. Planes took off so close the limo's windows rattled from the force.

The road took us farther and farther from the gleaming terminal in the distance until the limo slowed in front of a gate in the fence. Inside a small blockhouse a uniformed police officer watched a movie on his iPad until the headlights panned into his vision. He got out, said something to the driver, then unlocked and opened the gate by hand and waved us through.

I could only look out the side windows, not through the windshield because of the opaque screen separating me from the driver, so all I saw was an isolated runway surrounded by grass. Then the car turned and parked. Looming before me was a white private jet with a gangway leading up to the door near the cockpit. Running down its side were Chinese characters and some kind of part-elephant, part-squid, part-cat-chibi thing grinning down from the tail wing. XI'AN INDUSTRIAL ENTERPRISE CO., LTD ran in smaller letters underneath the Mandarin.

McCool rocked forward and back once, twice, a third time,

propelling himself out of the seat and through the open door without tipping the limo onto its side. For the first time, he was talking and moving at once.

"We won't waste your time, so we'd ask you to do the same for us, please. We will be short and direct, and if you respond in kind we will have you back at the con before you know it."

The big man motioned for me to get out of the car and follow; I left the Kirby trophy on the seat. I saw there was a second limo parked on the tarmac, and before I could walk over to the gangway a second bruiser descended the stairs, followed by a somewhat baffled-looking Saudi man in a white linen thobe. By the time McCool led me up the gangway and into the jet, the Arab guy and his minder had climbed in the other limo and driven away.

The plane's main cabin was dimly lit, with about a dozen seats arranged around small tables; a small man with white hair and a thin gray beard clicked through emails on a laptop; when we entered he glanced up to register our presence before flicking his eyes back down to the screen.

This was the not the first time I had laid eyes on the multi-billionaire owner of Atlas Entertainment, Ira Pearl. This was not even the first time we had been in the same room together.

The first time had been in the Mister Mystery Room in Atlas Comics headquarters in Manhattan. The conference room was named after Ben K's most famous creation and had acrylic pictures of the hero plastered over every wall; fittingly, me and Danny Lieber and a few other editors and writers were hunched over notes and laptops plotting out the next few story arcs of the *Mister Mystery* comics series.

Danny was in the middle of issuing some directive, looking down at the printout of an Excel spreadsheet publishing plan; I was looking at Danny, so when he looked up and fell silent, I followed his gaze to see someone standing in the doorway.

Dirtbag had told me innumerable stories about Ira Pearl's legendary cheapness: that he went from cubicle to cubicle berating employees for buying Post-its when they could just rip scrap paper into squares and write notes on the blank side; that one of the biggest entertainment companies in the world didn't have its logo on the elevator floor designations because Ira refused to pay the $200 to have the Plasticine block installed. His frugality bordered on OCD mania and his attention to the slightest minutiae of his company's expenditures was married to slightly darker stories—that he never allowed himself to be photographed or interviewed, that he never went anywhere unarmed, that he had a shadowy cabal of ex-NYPD running interference and favors for him (this part apparently was true).

But when I looked into the doorway of the Mister Mystery Room in Atlas Comics HQ that day, all I saw was a diminutive gnome, white-haired with bushy eyebrows, wearing a tie with no jacket and slacks hiked up above his waist.

"Oh," the gnome said. "You're using this room?"

Dead silence. Nothing about the gnome's appearance led me to believe this was one of the richest men in the world, and therefore one of the most powerful. For one thing, contrary to legend, no holster hung at his waist.

Nevertheless, next to me every muscle in Daniel Lieber's body tensed. He didn't even breathe. Lieber was a purely corporate creature. He owed his very existence to his facility for hegemony; he existed only to curry the favor of those above him and secure the obedience of those below him; he had no discernible skills other than the maintenance of whatever hierarchy he found himself in. Lieber's expression didn't change, he didn't move, he didn't say a word, but in the most primitive part of my brain, unevolved from its tiniest mammallian ancestors whose lives hinged on microsecond observations and subsequent reactions, I read the silent vibrations from the other man's body that signaled we were in the presence of an Apex Predator.

It was the fear radiating off Danny that made me realize I was looking for the first time at the oft-whispered about, never-photographed Ira Pearl.

"You're using this room?" Ira said. At the table half a dozen people were working, hunched over legal pads and laptops, so you could almost call it a dumb question. But there were no dumb questions, really, when you surrounded yourself with underlings who would answer any query that dribbled out of your mouth.

"Yeah?" Danny Lieber said quietly, cautiously, clearly floating it only as an option.

Pearl just looked at us for a second.

"Okay," he said, and turned and left.

Everyone in the room started breathing again.

Now, in the cabin of the private jet, I couldn't help but notice that the mug from which Ira Pearl sipped coffee was marked with the logo of Home Lots, the big box store specializing in heavily discounted merchandise damaged in other companies' warehouses; this was the company Ira had first made his fortune on, reselling the broken stuff that other retailers refused to sell—the slightly stained mattresses, the bureau that got a hole punctured in it while in the back of the truck on the way to a Poughkeepsie store. Ira specialized in taking other people's junk and making it a treasure, the business equivalent of "You gonna finish that?"

Thus it was with Atlas Comics, which had crawled, gasping, out of the primordial ooze of Depression-era pulp publishing with all its other four-color brethren. But after stumbling into cultural relevance in the hip and ironic sixties, it had suffered through a series of neglectful corporate parents, each more incompetent than the last, until the once-proud producer of childhood visions filed for bankruptcy in the 1990s. Ira was already doing business with Atlas anyway through one of his other companies, Toyetic. Action figures were a business tailor-made for the Ira Pearls of the world, in which Chinese wage slaves cranked out violent plastic boys' dolls for pennies that wound up on big-box shelves for twenty bucks a pop, the kind of ridiculously imbalanced profit margin that made the Iras of the world tumescent with desire.

Atlas owed Toyetic an obscene amount of money for making action figures of their superhero characters, and Ira used that debt to buy the publisher and its catalog of beloved characters for peanuts. ("You gonna finish that?") The company acquired funding to produce a series of ludicrously popular Hollywood movies based on those characters and turned Atlas Comics into Atlas Entertainment, a branding behemoth inspiring almost as much confusion and terror in its competitors as Ira Pearl inspired in his employees.

"Mac here tells me you're having some trouble with the San

Diego Police Department," Ira said, his face largely disguised behind the open clamshell of the computer.

"You could say that," I said.

Ira slammed the laptop shut with one hand. The frozen Hokusai waves masquerading as his eyebrows unfurled like the collar of a frilled lizard confronting a foe. "Listen, don't try and play me, guy. I don't play games. I don't have time for it. You either have trouble with the law or you don't, which is it?"

I had no idea where any of this was going. "They're a little confused. They think I might have killed Danny Lieber."

"And who is Danny Lieber?"

"He—he works—*worked*—for you."

Ira's eyebrows flapped hard this time, as though his face was trying to fly off his head. He looked to McCool.

"Yes, sir. He was an editor."

"A film editor? With the studio?"

"No, the dead-tree kind. In our comics business."

"Comics? We still make those?"

McCool nodded apologetically.

Ira's eyes rolled back to Mike. "Now, tell me honestly, did you kill what's-his-name?"

"I did not."

"Okay. I believe you. I feel for your situation. I get accused of garbage all the time. That's why I don't give interviews. I don't allow my picture to be taken. They just use it as grist for more lies. The way the press talks, you'd think I was personally there at the Crucifixion, that it was me who handed out the nails. When I'm nothing more than a small-business owner, just like you."

I arched an eyebrow at that. Is it that the richer you get, the more you believe your own bullshit? Or is believing your own bullshit a prerequisite to becoming rich in the first place? I can't help feeling out of luck either way.

"And I say that because you should know I have many close friends in the San Diego Police Department, and in the government of California. Well, not me personally, but I have friends of friends. What I'm saying is, they do favors for me from time to time, as friends do for friends, and friends of friends, and I might be able to help you with this predicament you find yourself in. But because we're both small businessmen, you would understand I am not in the position to simply do this favor for free. I don't do charity. I don't believe in it. It's unearned life support for the weak, it doesn't do them or us any good, you see."

"Uh-huh."

"Mac tells me that you were close with the late Mr. Benjamin Kurtz."

"That's . . . true."

"And you're still in contact with his widow, uh, uh, uh, uh."

Ira started snapping his fingers and kept snapping them until McCool realized on his own that it was he for whom the boss snapped and blurted out, "Rebecca."

"Rebecca Kurtz, is it? Am I right?"

Before I even really realized I was doing it, I started to laugh.

The eyebrows flexed. "Yes or no. I'm just in San Diego to refuel. I have to be wheels-up in twenty minutes to inspect my factory in Xi'an on time and I have two more meetings to get to after you."

"Fuck you," I said with a smile.

Ira looked to McCool, who covered my entire shoulder

with his expansive hand. "Let's keep it civil, hanh?"

I flinched off the ex-cop's mitt. "Don't touch me."

"Why don't you tell me what the problem is, guy," Ira said.

"The problem is Ben K died before finalizing your settlement with him over the Mister Mystery rights and you want me to lean on Becca to make sure she signs where her husband was supposed to."

"Yes. Exactly. And what's the problem with that again?"

"He *created* Mister Mystery!"

"For Atlas! It's called work-for-hire, read a law book. We own that I.P., no matter how his shysters have convinced some liberal activist judge to rewrite copyright laws in his favor."

"He deserves way more than whatever pittance you're going to give him."

"You have no idea what pittance we're giving him!"

"Let's all take a deep breath," McCool said, but both Ira and I ignored him.

"All you care about is the billions you're going to make off the movies and toys and whatever."

Ira blinked, puzzled. "Yes. Again: Exactly. You display a staggering command of the obvious." Baffled, Ira looked again at McCool. "Is this guy for real?"

"I'm afraid so," McCool said.

"Clean the wax out of your ears, guy," Ira said. "In addition to the very generous settlement package my lawyers negotiated—over my objections, I might add, that *trombenik* didn't deserve a single red cent. I'm supposed to lose money over his inability to read a contract? In addition to the profits I earned that he is taking out of my pocket, we also agreed to help him get his original artwork back, artwork that is worth more than the ink staining the pages only because of the effort I and my people and my company put into promoting his childish characters. Furthermore—"

I could feel the rage building inside of me until it lifted me out of my chair like a balloon. I took a step toward Ira—

—and was abruptly unable to breathe. Gasping, I fell back to the narrow aisle of the private plane, slamming my side on the edge of my seat as I dropped.

McCool stood over me, lowering the arm that he'd just used to clothesline me in the neck. "Sorry about that, sir."

"Well, that was a complete waste of my time," Ira said. "Get him out here."

"I thought it was worth a shot at least." McCool reached down and hauled me to my feet one-handed. "C'mon, buddy, time to go."

"Wrong again, Mac," Ira said. "I need you to do better on that."

"I will, moving forward, sir. I promise." McCool still had his hand on my shoulder and practically carried me toward the front of the plane. Before I was hauled all the way to the hatch, I kicked a foot out and braced it against the wall, managing to wriggle from McCool's vise-like grip.

"Let me ask you a question, Mr. Pearl," I said.

"If it gets you out of my hair faster, please, I beg of you, ask," the billionaire said.

"Did *you* have Danny Lieber killed?"

I swear, the man's white eyebrows flared directly upward like a Chrysler hood ornament.

"Why the hell would I bother with that?" Ira said. "Murder is for the poor."

– – – –

The limo was waiting when we descended the gangway. McCool didn't say anything until the car turned out of the airport.

"Are you mentally retarded?"

I scowled. "That's a pretty offensive term."

McCool leaned forward, tomato red in the face, and roared: *"I know it is. I was trying to offend you. That's why I said it!"*

He leaned back in his seat and wiped his brow with his lapel handkerchief. "I don't have enough fingers to count how many kinds of stupid that was. That's a guy you want on your side, not the other way around."

"I've had it with sucking corporate dick, sorry. He wants me to pat him on the back for helping get Ben's artwork back? That artwork was always Ben's to begin with. It was thanks to Atlas the artwork got stolen in the first place."

"That was long before Ira acquired the company. Long before his time. And just now the art started surfacing on the dealers' market. It's going for tens of thousands of dollars. Ira was going to use his resources to help get it back, to see that Ben K got as much of that money as possible."

"You know, this is bullshit, this strong-arming. People have to know about it. This may just become an anonymous sourced item in *Bleeding Cool*—'Billionaire Leans on Grieving Widow.'"

"You're too dumb to know who's trying to help you. Here's what's going to happen if you blab. Some people will believe you. Mostly the ones who want to believe all the bad stuff about Atlas

Comics anyway. And there aren't enough of them to save you.

"Because—and no disrespect—you seem like a nice guy, but who do you think you are? What did you ever do for people? We've been letting them escape their boring nowhere lives since they were four years old. Where does this superhero stuff come from? Who makes it? Nobody gives a flying fig so long as it keeps on coming. That's all the fans see from this lawsuit is stonewalling. They're terrified Atlas will lose custody of Mister Mystery and they won't get their monthly fix. And they don't need to hear that they're being cut off by some guy they never even heard of before.

"Who is this Mike M? Who is he to speak out? He's just another wannabe has-been never-was. Disgruntled that the company never treated him the way he thought he deserved, replaced him with someone else they thought was more promising, never put him on the big-name books like he wanted. He never got to be in the room when the big boys were making the real decisions or I would've heard of him before now. So what does he know anyway? He's trying to make us feel bad. He's trying to make us feel guilty. He should be lucky Atlas let him work on those characters at all. Screw him, that entitled so-and-so. His art wasn't that great anyway, that's why he never got big. How dare he try to make us feel bad for enjoying something we love."

"That's what you'll tell them," I said, with not as much force as I would have liked.

"We won't need to tell them," McCool said. "That's what they'll tell themselves."

I looked out the window as the lights of the city once again became visible on the other side of the harbor. "Your generous offer of help is a little late. The cops aren't even really on me anymore. They think this girl, this fan did it."

McCool laughed hollowly. "My God. You really are the biggest dumbbell that ever put on a pair of trousers."

I turned back to him.

"Who do you think turned SDPD onto that crazy one-armed chick in the first place?" he said.

My brow lowered but I didn't feel like giving him the satisfaction of voicing an answer.

"It's my policy to personally follow up on all such direct threats of violence to company assets. My people paid a visit to her dorm room after she posted that video on Facebook and we had a little chat. Talked to her parents. That was a while ago. Is she harmless? Maybe. Who knows? I do know this, though: I can suggest the cops take a different path whenever I feel like it. One that might not make you feel so cocky and comfortable."

McCool leaned back in his seat, satisfied, as if he could see my stomach tightening through my shirt and my skin and my bones.

"What you should console yourself with is this: in the end, you never really had a choice."

We sat in silence for the rest of the drive back to the Bayfront. As the car turned into the pull-around, I said, "I'm surprised Ira doesn't have guys to do his threatening for him."

"We used to have a guy who handled sensitive situations like this on the comics side," McCool said as I got of the limo.

"What happened to that guy?"

"You killed him," McCool said, closed the car door, and signaled for the driver to leave.

－ － － －

The limo rolled away about the length of the drive, then rocked to a stop with a screech. I tensed, braced for flight—*now what?*—but the rear passenger door popped open and McCool's catch-er-mitt hands emerged to place my Plasticine Kirby trophy on the curb. Then the door shut and the long black car pulled away into traffic.

A passing group of teenagers wearing cat ears and tails spotted it lying unclaimed on the sidewalk. "Look at the Shiny!" one yelled in a sudden fit of possessiveness.

I ran over and snatched the award away, hissing at the kids like Gollum until they ran away.

I went inside the Bayfront and made a beeline for the Space Bar. Ian Smallwood and a cloud of Brits tried to wave me over, mock-applauding the Kirby trophy in my hands, but I held up a hand. The bar was wall-to-wall humanity, and the two bartenders on call had the desperate, panicked look of hunted animals. I didn't see Christine anywhere.

I stepped outside to the ocean-side coolness of the back patio overlooking the harbor and called her. No response. I texted:

"Sorry I just got here."

I waited a couple seconds without an answer, then added:

"I am really sorry I basically got kidnapped. It was crazy." Nothing.

"I'll be at Bayfront for a couple of hours if you still wanna join," I texted for the third and final time.

I put the phone in my pocket then went back inside to join the boisterous Englishmen. I put the Kirby trophy in the center of the table and we spent the remainder of the night toasting it like it was the translucent idol of some pagan god.

SATURDAY

The portfolio.

The word was waiting in my brain when I woke up the next morning, blasting away any vague memories of the dream I'd had: Violent Violet was pedaling me through the desert, except the pedicab was shaped like the rocket ship that took Baby Superman to Earth, and I was inside, an adult but wearing a diaper—

Come to think of it, the less I tell you about this particular dream, the better I'll feel.

The abrupt memory of Danny's portfolio arrived with the sudden clarity of the just-waking hours, when thought could be as present and corporeal as matter. I leapt out of bed and wrestled my sketchbook from my pocket and flipped through the pages, finding the sketch of the crime scene.

Ben K used to say that the true magic of comic art was what happened between the panels. The "gutters," they used to be called, with comic creators' mordant immigrant street humor: The magic happened in the gutters. Not in what was drawn, but in what *wasn't*—you let the reader's imagination fill in the blanks between the panels to create the illusion of seamless life.

In other words, what you *didn't* see was just as important

as what you did.

And what did I not see in either of these drawings?

The portfolio.

The portfolio I had seen Dan the Man carrying that night in the Marriott bar. The cops never mentioned it or asked me about it. So I never drew it in my depiction of the crime scene. And Yu-Gi-Oh, or whatever his name was, the steampunk ninja cosplayer in the Baptists' bodycam footage, wasn't carrying it either as he was approaching or leaving the convention center.

I'm not sure my subconscious mind would have drifted toward the portfolio had Ira and McCool not brought up Ben K's stolen art the night before.

And Becca Kurtz told me she thought Ben K's apartment had been ransacked around the time of his death.

I sat at the writing desk in my underwear and stared out the window at the Dole banana port. A pair of quad-propped camo-green tilt-rotor aircraft chopped across blue sky with inscrutable purpose. What was the link between Danny Lieber's portfolio and Sebastian Mod? Or Violent Pilar? And if no one had found it yet, where was it?

Waves of nausea and heartburn hit me all at once, and I was running to the bathroom.

"I swear, I am *not* drinking tonight," I said out loud.

– – – –

I skipped breakfast and elbowed my way into the con instead. On my way to Artists' Alley I got the idea to head over to the original art dealers section. I discovered my first Ben K original at a booth with the obviously highly focus-grouped name "Buddy's Art."

It was gingerly binder-clipped on a metal truss behind the tables with the longboxes. On one side was a minor Kirby *Mighty Thor* page, inked by the much-maligned Vince Colletta, which depicted not the titular Thunder God but a mounted Lady Sif as a leering hag spied upon her in the shimmering waters of an enchanted pool. The price tag said $4,500.

To the right of the Ben K was an extremely rare Wally Wood splash from *Tales from the Crypt.* A man screamed as the Crypt-Keeper's head, looming over the hysteric in the upper-right corner, declared, "It was a diabolical plot! Ralph was sure Cora would be . . . SCARED TO DEATH!" I was a little surprised Buddy even deigned to allow it onto the show floor, because he wanted $15,000 for it.

The Ben K page was from the late 1960s, which I knew because of the stylized Atlas "A" in the upper left-hand corner of the art board. One of the only things the comics publishers ever bothered to do for their artists was to give them free paper, because it gave them one less excuse for missing their deadlines. The board had the active art area, where the page would be printed for the finished book, demarcated with a solid blue line invisible in the photostatting process. You had to make sure to draw anything you wanted the reader to see—characters, dialogue, props, action—within that solid blue line. A dotted blue line a half inch or so outside the perimeter of the live-art line showed the trim, or where the finished piece would be cut off by the printing press. A third and final dashed blue line a half inch from the trim showed the bleed, so if the artist wanted to extend the art all the way beyond where the page would be cut off, she knew how far to go.

Exploding all the way to the bleed line on this particular Atlas art board was a spectacular fight scene, with Mister Mystery singlehandedly taking on the thuggish troops of a madman's private army. With his trademark design virtuosity, Ben K had used the hero's swinging limbs and dancing feet to create the boundaries of each panel; then he shrank each subsequent image as Mister Mystery dispatched his attackers, with the borders diminishing along with the number of baddies, decreasing from a dozen to eight to six to four to two. In the lower right-hand corner, the hero's fist crashed across the last enemy's jaw, bringing the fight and the page to a close on a single point. It was beautiful. It was amazing.

It was $10,000.

Buddy had a floppy silver mane of aging California surfer's hair atop an aging body semi-gracefully succumbing to the drag of gravity. His personal style could be described as Grandpa at the Flea Market: 1980 TV-screen glasses, blue-and-white Hawaiian shirt, khaki shorts, socks with sandals.

Before I had lifted my portfolio on top of the row of longboxes Buddy was walking over with a hand extended. "Good to see you again. How's Christine?"

People at cons have a disturbing tendency to greet everyone as if the conversation we had had at the last con was just a few hours ago instead of twelve months or even years. I've learned to respond with the cool, placid gaze of an Alzheimer's patient desperately trying to disguise the fact she's losing her marbles by feigning total comprehension: "I'm great, how's your, uh, family?"

"Flown the coop, we're empty nesters now. College tuition is killing me, so that just means I am even more motivated to

sell your pages for absolutely as much money as I possibly can."
Buddy of Buddy's Art had a gleam in his eyes like a camel dealer
in a medieval casbah. "Did you give any more thought to what
we discussed last year?"

I had no idea what this guy was talking about. I unzipped
my portfolio with a grin anyway. "*Have* I? I know I'm looking
for a new art rep, that's for sure."

Buddy rubbed his hands together. "Then you, sir, you have
come to the right place. Who was handling your original art
sales before, if you don't mind me asking?"

"Ah . . . " I blinked. "My wife, Christine, handled that, but
she, uh, is maybe looking to hang up her hat, move into another
part of the industry."

"Really? She's sold a couple pages to me in the past year
from her other clients."

"Yeah, exactly, that's what I mean. She wants to separate
business from family."

"Smart woman. For years I had my wife helping me at
shows, but we had to stop or else by Sunday, never fail, we'd turn
into *Who's Afraid of Virginia Woolf?* You ever see that movie?
Taylor and Burton. Things are much quieter with just Burton."

"Depends on the Taylor, I imagine. And the Burton, for that
matter."

"Ain't it the truth. But yeah, show me what you got here."
Buddy of Buddy's Art flipped through the pages in my portfolio, which I had carefully selected to front the most spectacular
splash pages and covers, followed by heavy-action pages with famous characters, followed by the less valuable, more introspec-
tive conversational scenes toward the back. "You got *Fantastic*

Four, Detective, Mister Mystery, even some *Gut Check* in here. Nice, nice. These pin-ups new?"

"Yeah, they were for the *Gut Check* omnibus IDW did."

"Awesome. Hey, congrats on the Kirby win last night, I almost forgot."

"Thanks. Yeah, it was a real surprise, especially to me. Say," I nodded at the *Mister Mystery* page behind him, "that's a great Ben K you've got there."

Buddy of Buddy's Art didn't look up from my portfolio. "I know, isn't it? Such a shame. And before he could resolve the lawsuit. Sad. I almost regret marking up the prices."

"What do you mean?"

Buddy spread his hands. "Dead artist, higher price. I hate doing it, but that's the market. If I show respect for the dead, I'm at the mercy of those who won't. It's disgusting but it's the world we live in."

I did my best to nod slowly, even as my guts boiled. "Mind if I ask you where you got it?"

"Where I got what?"

"The page. The Ben K page."

Buddy looked at me. "You don't know?"

"Why would I know?"

"Well, for one thing, the two of you were tight I heard."

"We are—were. But I don't know every detail of his business life."

Buddy grinned. "You interested in buying it? I can give you a slight discount if we do business together, but I can only knock 5 percent, 10 percent off. I told you about the college tuition, right?"

"I might be interested if I knew the provenance."

"Look at you, the *artiste* with the big fancy words."

"It seems like a simple question, am I wrong?" My smile never wavered.

Neither did Buddy's. "You're not wrong. But I don't lug all my records to every con."

I arched an eyebrow, remaining coy. "You don't remember where you got a five-figure piece of art?"

"It's only been five figures since Wednesday," Buddy said.

I was somehow able to grit my teeth and maintain my grin at the same time, but I didn't say anything. Buddy of Buddy's Art closed my portfolio with a loud *thwap* and leaned over the long-boxes. "I get a flat fifteen percent commission for anything I sell, in person, online, or over the phone. Let me give you a business card. You think about it and give me a ring after the show is over . . . that is, if you think this relationship is for you."

His breath smelled like Tic Tacs and cigarettes.

– – – –

There were only a half dozen original art dealers on the con floor, and only half of those had a Ben K piece, including one spectacular cover I went ahead and sketched. None of the dealers were all that forthcoming about where they'd gotten the art. I couldn't tell whether it was because they were worried I'd figure out it was stolen or that I was planning on cutting them out and going to their source to sell my own art. Clearly I had some kind of gland in my body, previously unknown to science, that secreted a narc pheromone.

Fortunately, I knew someone who could play art dealers like a harpsichord; unfortunately, I had stood up this person at the Bayfront Space Bar the night before. I'd dreaded pulling the trigger on this particular option since thinking of it not long after waking up this morning, but now I saw no way to avoid it.

I reopened the text chain with Christine and typed:

"Again, really sorry about last night."

Then added:

"I really need Hyper-Competent Spouse help."

As soon as I sent it I winced, realizing I should have thought the phrasing through a little bit better, so I quickly followed up:

"Not the Spouse part, the Hyper-Competent part."

No response for a bit, so I added:

"It's helping me with art dealers, and I can pay you $$$, no worries. Text me back."

I been wandering across the crammed con floor while concentrating on my thumb; when I looked up, I was across from the Shire set of the upcoming *Lord of the Rings* sequel, *Sauron's Revenge* (the first of seven films).

Then the crowd of hobbits and orcs parted, and the MEH bikers in the orthopedic boots were clomping straight at me, and I had nowhere to run.

– – – –

I turned to escape and found the door to an exact replica of Doctor Who's TARDIS behind me. Instinctively imagining the cavernous console room inside, I threw it open and ran in, immediately banging my nose on the wall on the opposite side. Impossibly, the empty booth was smaller inside than it looked on the outside, proving that whoever built it had screwed up the single most important aspect of TARDIS design.

I managed to flip myself around like a rotisserie chicken but it was too late: the bikers in their giant plastic boots tried to squeeze inside with me. They got stuck in the tiny doorway shoulder to shoulder, so I had no way out either.

"What's your problem, man?" MEH One asked.

"Yeah, what's your problem?" seconded MEH Two.

"*My* problem?" I cried. "Why the hell are you guys after me?"

"We wouldn't have to track you down if you were ever at your Artists' Alley table," MEH One frowned.

"Yeah, why the hell don't you spend any time at your table?" MEH Two scowled.

"I spend plenty of time at my table. Maybe your timing is terrible."

"The flier for that charity party said you would be there, so we went there," MEH One said.

"The program said you'd be speaking on that movie panel, so we went there too," MEH Two said.

I threw up my hands. "Okay, but why?"

"Disco Money," said MEH One.

"Yeah, Disco Money," said MEH Two.

"Disco Money? Wha—huh?"

MEH One reached inside his leather jacket and I flinched, but he brought out not a weapon but a thin white envelope. He handed it to me.

"Our client commissioned a drawing from you but forgot to give you the money up front."

"Yeah, and he was really worried you wouldn't do it, so he asked us to give it to you."

Inside the envelope were five crisp one hundred dollar bills, so new they static-clung to each other.

"Oh," I said. "Disco *Mummy*."

I stuck the money inside my jeans. "I didn't realize I didn't charge him, so that's on me. Tell him not to worry, I've been working on the sketch on and off. He'll have it by Sunday."

MEH One breathed a sigh of relief. "Thank God that's over with."

"Can I ask you a question, though?"

"Yeah?"

"What's, uh . . ." I smiled nervously. "What's with the MEH tattoo? I don't get it. Is that a reference to something or . . . ?"

The two bikers looked at each other and when they looked back, I saw four blue eyes brimming with tears. "You look like you had a nice upbringing," MEH One said. "Strong family life. Am I right?"

"Well . . . yeah, it's true, I did."

"Well I didn't. Did some dumb things. Went away for a while for armed robbery. You can't do your time alone. The Aryan Brand, they looked out for me."

"Me too," MEH Two said. "This ink, it's like armor. Means other cons can't mess with you. But you think I actually believe in any of that racist shit? My baby mama's Mexican, bro."

"We got jobs now, we're trying to earn enough money for laser surgery to get these tats taken off," MEH One said, pointing to his neck. "But it's expensive, and painful, so we can only zap a little off at a time." So close up I could vaguely see less tan and pinker skin in the form of a "T." So "MEH" was actually supposed to be "MEHT."

"Yeah, you never done anything in your life you regret before, bro?" MEHT Two said, wiping his eyes.

My mouth just gaped in stupefaction. Did I just hurt a Nazi's feelings?

"But we gotta fix these ankles before we pay for more tattoo removal."

"Were you guys, uh, in the same car crash or what?" I said once they stepped out of the mini-TARDIS so I could too.

"No, we were chasing *your* dumb ass through that zombie prison thing." MEHT One poked me in the chest with a finger that would definitely leave a mark.

"Some idiot moved this laundry bin thing where we were supposed land out of a tube," MEHT Two said, shaking his head.

"Fractured an ankle when we landed."

"And we are so totally gonna sue their asses."

"Oh my God, that's awful," I said in what I hoped would be a convincing way.

"Not gonna lie," MEHT One said, "we wanted to sue your ass, but Terry talked us out of it, said it would be bad for business."

"Who's Terry?" I said.

MEHT Two produced a business card. "In all seriousness, you should check out our website. We help actors, artists, too. Porn stars. Fans. Any of the big whales at these things."

"Though, no offense bro, I hope I never see your face again," MEHT One said.

As they limped away, I looked down at the card. One side was a close-up image of bloody ground beef. The other side had the same MEATWALL copy, and the same contact info for Terrence Lawson, that Armond Delaine had given me at the Kirbys the night before.

I did a quick internet search for "MEHT" and was just delighted to discover that it was an acronym for *Meine Ehre Heisst Treue*, "My Honor Is Called Loyalty," the motto of the S.S. It became the signature of the largest white supremacist gang in the federal prison system when a particularly strict warden in Colorado banned overt Nazi symbolism like swastikas in body art in the 1990s, so the Aryan Brand adopted something (very, very) slightly more subtle as its official tat.

So Meatwall, the pop-culture con security and management firm cofounded by the star of *Cell Block Z*, America's favorite TV show about prison, had been co-opted by America's most feared real-life prison gang.

Lovely.

– – – –

The con crowds even this early on Saturday made my fight to Artists' Alley slow going. "If you are not on the red carpet please keep it moving!" roared security guards to no avail. By the time I got to my table I had five people in line. Katie's line stretched halfway to the cubical Funko fortress.

"Yo," she said, drawing Elsa from *Frozen* in some kind of badass superhero pose. "You seen your little helper around?"

"Who?"

"Your—you know. Your volunteer. Your groupie. Whoever she is. The one with, uh, you know. The one thing. That most everyone else has two of."

"Pilar?"

Katie frowned. "I thought you said her name was Violet." Clearly the police put as much urgency into warning the artist

and writer of *Mister Mystery* about Pilar's Facebook video as
they did running down my pedicab alibi.

"Violet, right. What about her?"

"I was hoping she could sit at my table while I go to the
ladies' room. Every time I lean forward to draw, I feel like I have
to pee. It's one of the great miracles of human pregnancy."

"You haven't seen her yet?"

"Nope."

"Me, neither. Maybe . . . " Maybe she's not coming. I hoped
she'd stay far away from the convention center. I imagined the
security guards and cops I saw patrolling everywhere were looking for her.

Assuming, of course, they hadn't caught her already.

– – – –

I did my best to escape the utter insanity my life had devolved
into inside the Zone, knocking out as many commissions as I
could, even starting on Disco Mummy Guy's. I found the Disco
Mummy episode of the 1979 Filmation *Plastic Man* cartoon online. Watching it on my phone, I could sort of see how someone
would be fascinated by this figure. She was an Aztec mummy
with an outrageously bad Mexican accent whose primary fixa-
tions in life were "stealing all the world's treasures" (her words),
disco dancing to a jukebox in her jungle ziggurat headquarters,
and making Plastic Man fall in love with her. The whole thing
was lovingly gonzo the way the best kids' entertainment is, with
just enough insanity to bring a smile to adults' faces too. Also,
the sight of Disco Mummy gyrating to disco music in her subter-
ranean Mayan temple headquarters was enough to inflame the

nascent hormones of many an impressionable youth.

It was a pleasant enough distraction, and I made Katie re-watch it with me and we shared a laugh, particularly when Disco Mummy attacked the Mexican army in a giant gold sarcopha-gus. But the fact that Christine continued to not text me back made me increasingly nervous. By the time I showed up for my prearranged meet with Dirtbag outside Petco Park at the end of his Dead Men Running shift, I had formulated a plan involving him using his pull with Atlas to get me into the company soiree that night.

The ritualized nature of comic-con parties had remained largely unchanged for the last decade, a Nōh play with three dis-tinct acts: the charity party was on Thursday night, the awards ceremony was on Friday night, and the big industry parties were on Saturday night. All the big entertainment corporations, and the media organizations that reported on them, tried to out-cool one another with ever-more-spectacular bashes.

But here's the thing: if seventh grade taught us anything, it's that *trying* to be cool is in fact the exact opposite of *being* cool. In fact, the very act of trying anything at all is the epitome of lameness. So all these parties, no matter how high the rooftop or how expensive the cash bar, all universally suck. They're filled with wannabe social climbers and pros trying to suck up to cre-ators and low-level Hollywood talent just hoping to be seen by anyone at all. If anything, it was cooler these days to skip a com-pany party than to be caught dead attending one.

That said, Atlas had significantly upped its game. Or more accurately, Xi'an Industrial Enterprise Co., Ltd., seeking to curry favor with the boss, had sponsored the Atlas Entertainment party this year and rented out the Cold War–era aircraft carrier USS *Midway* as its locale. The ship was lit up like a militant Christmas tree in a thousand twinkling lights, and the innumerable fighter jets and helicopters on its several-stories-high deck were underlit by flood spots. The Xi'an elephant-turtle-dingo spokesthing fluttered on a flag beside the modern (whole-word) Atlas logo and the Stars and Stripes. As Dirtbag and I rolled up to valet parking in his SUV, we felt like we had arrived for the glitzy opening night premiere of *War: The Concept.*

Dirtbag's status as Atlas bullpen royalty got us past security and across the gangplank to the ship. Soon we were on the flight deck, dazzled by spotlights and a laser show dancing across the side of the control tower and bridge superstructure, rising above them, the words BEWARE OF JET BLAST PROPS AND MOTORS big on its side, surrounded by the brutal geometry of warcraft. A DJ with glowing paint outlining his fingers and facial features manned what appeared to be the bridge, busting out mad tracks of remixed superhero theme songs. ("In your satin tight-tight-tights, fighting for your right-right-rights, and the old red white-white-white and blue," etc.)

Everyone at the party was dressed better than the usual con-goers, and Grey Goose vodka had sponsored the creation of several Mister Mystery–themed cocktails, which were handed out by models in Spandex goose costumes. But every member of every conversational cluster, even the ones in midsentence, had one eye turned away from their current clutch, looking to see if someone more famous or better connected might be found. Nobody wanted to be with the people they were with; there was always the tantalizing possibility of leveling up.

"My work as sidekick is done here," Dirtbag said, breathing in the cool night air. From up here you could see pretty much every locale in the city—the Bayfront, with its Mister Mystery facade, the convention center, and so on.

"What's your party plan?"

"I got my ex to take the spawn off my hands until tomorrow afternoon, so I am going to get my drank on, yeeeeeeeah boyeeeeeee! If I have to, I'll take an Uber home and come back for the Dadmobile in the morning."

"You don't want come say hi to Christine? I'm sure she'd be thrilled to see you."

Dirtbag threw his hands up and laughed. "I *know* she'll be thrilled to see *me*. You, however, are a very different story. Awkward! I do not want to be caught in the crossfire when she starts laying into you for your many selfish acts of dumbassery over the weekend, no thanks."

"Probably wise. Thanks for getting me this far, brother."

"No problemo, brah. Good luck." We shared a manly one-armed bro-hug and then he went to chase down the nearest cocktail-carrying goose lady.

I turned to look for Sebastian Mod and his girlfriend, strongly suspecting they'd show up at some point, and found myself face-to-face with a large poster on an easel depicting a smiling Daniel Lieber. Flowers were heaped at the base, and multichromatic markers rested on the easel's tray so people could write some expression of remembrance or condolence right on the poster. Adding my own inscription would have been the nadir of bad taste. Nobody was congratulating me for murder at this party, filled with Lieber's coworkers and allies at Atlas Comics.

Many recognized me and were giving me the eat-shit side-eye while wondering how the hell I got in here in the first place.

Fortunately, I soon spotted my reason for being here. Christine stood in a white dress, see-through from the knees down, underlit next to a skinny, blunt-nose Sikorsky H-5 copter, surrounding her fluttering hair in a nimbus of gold. She had one hand on the chain-link fence surrounding the edge of the deck; she was looking over the ship at something I couldn't see. Not unless I got closer, that is.

Girding my proverbial loins and clearing my throat, I did just that.

— — — —

I wasn't quite at the edge of the *Midway*'s deck before I could see over the fence and realized she was looking at *Embracing Peace*, the giant statue of the sailor kissing the nurse. It looked much smaller from up here, but still huge compared to the tiny specks posing for selfies on the embarcadero below. It was odd to see the landmark from so high up, at such a radically removed perspective, as if to remind me of how distant I was from the person who began this quote-unquote "adventure" down there, from that point, not even four days ago.

"What do you think it means?" I said without greeting.

She barely glanced my way. "It's that famous photo from the end of World War Two."

I laughed. "When I first saw it I thought you'd think it was a monument to lack of consent. It's not like these two know each other. She's not resisting, but she's not exactly embracing him. It does kind of look like he's putting her in a chokehold."

"Really?" She frowned. "I think you're missing the point."

"And what is the point?"

"It's a *statue*. It's not *real*. So it can be what you *want* it to be."

"Okay, Christine. I am an artist, you know. I understand the concept of interpretation."

"You're not acting like it." She turned to look at me, her expression serene. "If you want it to be about peace, an expression of love, then it's about that. If you want it to be a permanent celebration of lack of consent, then it's about that. I would ask, what inside of you makes you *need* it to be about lack of consent?" She pointed at the statue. "That thing is made out of metal. It doesn't have any darkness in it. The only darkness it has comes from you."

I'd had enough bullshit college coursework in my life to keep arguing with her, but I didn't see the point, particularly since I preferred her perspective anyway and the last thing I wanted was round number infinity of me versus Christine, so I dropped it.

She turned her slight smile on me. "But it's more interesting that you think that's the first thought that would go into *my* head. You sure you know me as well as you think you do?"

"Probably not." I let the breeze wash over me. "Where's Sebastian?"

"Who cares?" she said, much to my surprise, then added quickly, "I think he's at the Ice Bar at the *Absolute Zero* immersive thing down the street. He said he might join me later."

Making a point to look contritely at my feet, I said, "I'm really sorry that last night—"

"I know," she said, cutting me off.

"No, seriously, what happened to me was crazy, but still—"

"Really, it's all right." She took a deep breath. "It's just . . . I don't know what the point is of us continuing to talk. I love you. I really do. I always have and I always will. And just the little bit I've seen of you this week, all these feelings come rushing back of all the amazing things we did together, and what a great life we had. But the truth is, when you stood me up last night it just . . . reminded me that for us, no matter how good the times were, they'd always get overwhelmed by the bad."

"Jesus, Christine," I murmured.

"Just hear me out. And I'm not just putting it on you. I give you a hard time but I'm not a total fool. I know a lot of the blame is on me too. You just spent all your time at the drawing table, it made me feel like a second-class citizen in my own house. But I, you know, I think I expected you to give me some purpose . . . I was expecting you and your career to give meaning to mine. I never . . . ." She squinted past me, as if she was trying to bring something in the distant past into focus. "I never figured out what that was while I was with you. It's almost like your success was throwing shade onto me. To the point where I couldn't see my way to my own life."

"And now?"

"Now—I just kind of fell into this thing with Sebastian in L.A., you know? And it feels like another start. So I'm going to try and make it work. I know that must be a little hard to take. You've never been his biggest fan."

Stab, stab, stab in my heart. "Who, me? No, Sebastian's great. Really. I'd put him easily in my top three Toxic Narcissists."

"Yeah, okay, I get the point. Anyway. In your texts you said you had something you wanted my help with? I hope it's more Mike M comics. We need more Mike M comics. I wish you hadn't stopped. It's one thing you walked out on me when you caught me and Danny. It's another that you never came back home. But comics . . . if I thought you had given that up because of me . . . well, then, for that I really couldn't forgive myself."

"Don't beat yourself up about it. I just haven't felt inspired is all. I've just been . . . numb. In some kind of in-between state. I can't muster the effort to draw anything other than what people tell me to. Con commissions are good for that."

"So what do you need me for?"

"It's about Ben K's stolen art. I could use some advice."

She looked at me for what seemed like a long time.

"Okay. I think I can help you. Let's get the hell out of here."

"Absolutely! Where to?"

"Someplace quiet. How about your room?"

Pound, pound, pound in my heart. "Seriously?"

"Yeah, why not. Let Sebastian chase me around for once. I may go so far as to admit that as a boyfriend, he's only slightly less terrible than you."

"Damning with faint praise, but I'll take it."

"Wait here, I just need to say goodbye to some people."

"You got it."

She strode away in her high heels, past a pregnant woman waddling toward me in a truly retina-melting one-piece orange plaid dress: Katie Poole.

I hailed her over even though she was headed my way anyway. "You want to sneak onto the bridge and figure out a way to sail this thing to Mexico? We're close enough, I guess we can just drift—"

Giddy with the conviction that I was about to score a decisive victory for the forces of good against the forces of Mod, I didn't register her dour Greek-tragedian mask until she threw her drink in my face.

– – – –

An ice cube bounced off my left eyeball and the lid jammed shut. I was half-blind, sputtering and confused, when she hissed:

"*I know.*"

"You—know what? What do you know? Makes one of us. Katie, what's wrong?" I was rubbing my eye trying to get the Sprite out of it.

"*Katie, what's wrong?*" she said in a mocking singsong. "Sitting next to me the whole con, laughing and telling jokes, being all ally-y, when I should have known . . ." Her voice stuck in her throat and she tried to blink away tears. "Goddamn hormones. You don't deserve to see me cry."

I could finally open both eyes. "Katie, I swear to God, I have no idea what you're talking about."

She paced around in a circle, her face getting redder and redder. "It's just so fucking *tiring*. Defending yourself every minute of every day. You get so sick of taking it in the ass from everyone, online, in person, all the time, and you hope that just one day you can stop looking over your shoulder, and *wham!* That's when they get you, the minute you let your guard down. I should just duct-tape my asshole shut! That's the only way to guarantee protection."

"Look," I said, spreading my hands. "Even if you don't believe me, could you just tell me what it is that got you so upset?

I need to—"

"They're replacing me," Katie exploded. "They're taking me off *Mister Mystery* because I'm not"—she stabbed at the air with bunny ears—"'moving the needle.' And you're moving in before the corpse is even cold!"

"No, no, I swear to God, Katie, no one in Editorial has approached me about this, and I will turn them down if they do."

She shook her head. "It doesn't matter. Once they slot you into their little boxes in their heads, once they stick that label on you, you never get it off. It might as well have already happened."

"Wait a minute," I said, risking a step toward her. "Did Sebastian tell you this?"

Katie sniffled. "It doesn't matter who told me. I heard it from someone who knows. I'm sworn to secrecy. I already knew Sebastian wasn't happy with me. Ironically, I think that sexually harassing garbage person Danny Lieber was the only person protecting me from him. Thanks a lot for murdering him."

"I didn't!" I took a breath. People were staring. This was, after all, a pretty boring party, and we were the most interesting thing here not in Spandex. "Just—look, can we talk?"

I led her by the crook of the arm inside a CH-46 Sea Knight, a transport copter with a rotor on each end. Inside, a red bench with a dozen seatbelts lined either side. A couple was necking on one but fled when I killed the romance by giving them my best worst look.

It was impossibly hot inside the helicopter, but at least it was semi-private. "I don't think they've actually made a decision yet, Katie. Particularly not so soon after Danny's gone. There's still time to make this right." I put my hands on her shoulders.

"I will do everything I can to help you. I swear."

"Okay." She swallowed and looked at me sideways. "You really didn't know anything about this?"

I put my hand over my heart. "Scout's honor."

"Aw, geez, I am such an ass." She hugged me. "I threw my drink on you and everything. I'm so sorry."

"Don't worry about it."

"I get these awful mood swings from the Rosemary's Baby inside me. And you know Javier is out of work too. Both of us going down at the same time—"

"I totally get it, I've been there. Don't you worry. I am on the case."

"Thanks, man. I can't tell you what this means to me."

"Hey, it's cool. You'd do the same for me."

"Actually, I probably wouldn't. But then you don't need the job as bad as me, Mister Hollywood."

Katie and I hopped out the back of the Sea Knight and parted ways, and I hurried to intercept Christine. She saw my face and asked, "Is everything all right?"

"Yeah—well. Sort-of-not-really. Here, take my key. The room number's written on the little paper sleeve. Head to the Bayfront, and I'll meet you there. I have to run an errand. I'll be back as soon as I can."

"Are you freaking kidding me? You're going to stand me up in your own room? That's cold even by your standards."

"I suck, it is true. But this is really important. It shouldn't take long."

"What are you going to do?"

"I am going to go actually murder someone!" I probably

shouldn't have yelled so loudly as I ran for the stairs to the gang-plank, but that's exactly what I did.

– – – –

The *Absolute Zero* Nuclear Winter Experience sprawled across a vacant lot on the other side of the train tracks, just behind a large reflecting fountain pool that Cartoon Network had rented. Over its shimmering surface floated large balloons of Jake, Finn, Robin, Starfire, a Powerpuff Girl (do they have names?), all your favorites.

The line was thinning out as it snaked up to the entrance of the large half-toppled casino covered in snow that was, I guess, a central setting of the Syfy show and graphic novel, which is set in a postapocalyptic Las Vegas Strip smothered in subarctic con-ditions. The main attraction was a 3D VR amusement park ride thing that dumped you in a re-creation of the Lion Clan's Emer-ald City home, a nod to the MGM Grand presumably, complete with actors dressed in saber-tooth tiger furs.

I was more interested in the adjacent Ice Bar—a rather lit-eral expression of the show's nuclear winter setting, in which a building made entirely of ice maintained its structural integrity at a brisk 23 degrees Fahrenheit. The queue here was even shorter than the one for the Experience; it led to rows of lockers where attendants dressed as Lion Clan tribespeople handed me a heavy faux-fur parka and a furry hat in the shape of some mutant beast's decapitated snout.

I could see my breath as soon as I stepped inside the bar, and the sudden sharp frigidness of the air stung my cheeks. Through the vapor I could see the network wasn't messing around: Everything in the room was made of ice. The walls were translucent ice, the tables were hewn blocks of ice, the chairs and benches were roughly hewn ice with furs thrown over them for butt protection. Frozen into the walls were tin signs advertising the fictional *Absolute Zero* casinos on the irradiated strip and the various postapocalyptic tribes they housed. A dozen or so revelers wrapped in big shaggy coats like hopeful singles at a Sasquatch-themed furries mixer carried around blue cocktails in octagon-shaped glasses made of ice. The only real lighting was an ice chandelier flickering with orange and green lights, and the speakers frozen into the ceiling around it throbbed generically terrible trance music.

It didn't take long for me to identify Sebastian, with his red-and-blue fogged-up shades, tucked away in a secluded alcove that was mostly out of the bar's sightline. He sat on the furs of a throne made entirely of ice and fawned over a shag carpet with legs that I assumed was a woman. I took a seat at a fur-covered ice slab where I had a pretty good view of the two of them. When she excused herself by carefully stepping across the slippery floor in the direction of ladies' room, I moved in.

Sebastian had somehow liberated his phone from the layer of pelts heaped on his body and was flipping through his Twitter mentions as I approached. He didn't see me until I was almost on top of him, and he didn't recognize me until I stuck my face in his, which in my defense was the only way to make myself heard over the bad dance tracks.

"Don't—" Sebastian said. He backed up and his different-colored shades slid down his nose so I could see the fear shining in his eyes. "Don't!"

He slipped on the frigid floor and dropped to his knees. At that moment I sort of realized what was happening. I could have retreated, I could have stepped back, but here's the thing:

I didn't want to.

I balled my hands into fists and did not retreat. Instead, I moved forward.

"Don't *what*?" I hissed.

"Don't," Sebastian croaked again. Was he tearing up?

I leaned in real close to the trembling Mod.

"I need to hear you say it," I whispered.

"Don't," Sebastian croaked again.

"I'm going to need to *hear* you say the whole thing."

Sebastian swallowed and licked his lips before whispering:

"Please don't kill me."

For the first time I didn't have the impulse to protest when someone accused me of murder. Instead, I peered down on Sebastian as a hawk might consider a field mouse:

"Why not? What's in it for me?"

Sebastian's tongue loosened, and the words started spilling out of his mouth. "Look, if you want me to break up with Christine, I totally will. The thing between her and me, it's not a big deal, it's just a—you know, we're just dating, it's not serious, yet. I don't mean to say I'm using her, but if I had known you felt, well, that's why, you know . . . I've been ghosting her a little bit this week. It's awkward, seeing you two together, you know? So you give the word, and it's over. I will kick her to the curb, I swear."

I was less delighted than I thought I would be: Mod was just a little kid, always craving validation, desperate to please.

He had a big black hole where his self-esteem ought to be. His imposter syndrome had imposter syndrome: It thought maybe it was genuine victimhood.

"Don't break up with her if you don't want to," I said.

"Well, yeah, thanks, except I kind of really do. It's not—I don't know. It's not her, it's me. I have ADHD when it comes to women. Lord, I was born a rambling man, you know?"

"And you're not going to fire Katie Poole off *Mister Mystery*. Got it? That's the price you have to pay for never worrying about me again."

"You're sleeping with Katie now? Oh my God, *are you the father of her baby?*"

"No, I'm not—we're just friends, okay? Can't you just be friends with a woman?"

Sebastian Mod looked baffled. "Why would I *want* to?"

"What were you doing before you showed up at Christine's birthday karaoke party on preview night?"

His brow furrowed. "What do you care?"

"I've added it to my list of reasons not to kick your ass."

"Wait a minute." Sebastian wiped his eyes. "You—you think *I* killed Danny?"

I looked at him.

Sebastian stood up and straightened his coat. "That means *you* didn't. Nice try. I'm not telling you shit. And your baby mama can kiss her ass goodbye."

Comics nerds, bullied and abused, subjected to slights both imagined and all too real, do what all victims do, in one degree or another, whether they resist or not: They internalize the brutal logic of their oppressors and look for opportunities to revisit abuse on others. The most sectarian fanatic in the terror camps of the Middle East has nothing on the comics fan, who is constantly hunting for the Other, purging the unworthy, the unproven, those who love the wrong things too much or don't love the right things enough. Exclusion from the group is as defining as inclusion. Schoolyard bullies grow up and move on because the blows they landed were on soft targets and thus did not bruise their knuckles overmuch; the subjects of the bullied have lasting scars. They grow up and apply the experience of adults onto what the bullies taught them: Find weakness. Attack. Attack. Never apologize.

So I punched Mod in the nose.

As I said earlier, I'd never gotten into a real fight before. For one thing, as a person who literally earns his living with his hands—well, my right hand, specifically—I can't afford shattered fingers or busted wrists. But I had spent my entire adult life drawing people punching other people, so it was all but effortless to inform my fist to ball up and my arm to snap forward. It surprised us both—the punch—and with the thoughtless exactitude of beginner's luck, I found my target perfectly. My fist caught the connecting piece between Sebastian's duochrome lenses, and the cheap strip of metal snapped in half. Then Mod's nose collapsed with a satisfying pop, like bubble wrap being flattened, and he reeled away with a cry. Though he tried to wrap his arms around a column to keep from falling, that too was made of ice, so he just slid all the way down with a comically painful squeak.

"Everyone already thinks I'm a murderer," I said, "so why not start now? And if you get Katie Poole fired, I promise I *will* fucking kill you."

"I don't negotiate with terrorists!" Sebastian said. He spit the blood streaming across his mouth onto the floor.

Whatever self-image I'd imagined—that I was a nonviolent person—seemed very ten minutes ago. Despite the difficulty getting traction on this skating rink of a floor, I managed to pick up Sebastian by the now-bloody lapels of his now-bloody pelt and slam him into the icy wall. He flopped around on impact like a crash-test dummy. Though I'm about two or three inches shorter I had twenty pounds more muscle, thanks to a year living out of hotels with nothing better to do than hit the fitness center ever day. It was dark and loud and no one paid us the slightest attention. From a distance we probably looked like two giant chest-bumping Tribbles; whether we were scuffling or making out was a total mystery.

"Why'd you show up at Christine's party past midnight? Where were you before that?"

"I—I don't think I did," Sebastian said, pulling away from me. He yanked some wadded-up napkins out of his pocket and pinched them over his gushing nose. "No, I didn't. I had Indian food with my agents from UTA, then I went straight to the Gaslighter. I couldn't have been there later than eleven forty-five."

"That's not what Christine said."

"How the hell would she know? She wasn't there when I showed up."

I blinked. "What?"

"I couldn't find her. Everyone said she was in the bathroom, but I didn't see her for a good twenty minutes. When she showed

up, she was out of breath. I thought maybe she had a quickee
with you. Why do you think I've been avoiding her this whole
weekend?" He let go of the napkins to gesticulate for effect but
the wad remained stuck, soaked through with crimson, like the
nose of a horror-movie clown.

I turned away and headed for the Bayfront. An enormous
cloud of roaring darkness was billowing over me, and even
though I knew I couldn't outrun it, I was still going to try.

I could hear Mod's croaking defiance behind me. "You've
screwed yourself, man! You hear me? I'm gonna make sure no
one in this business hires you! No con will book you! *By the time
I'm finished, you'll be sketching caricatures of tourists at fucking
Sea World!"*

– – – –

The Beastie Boys' "Intergalactic" thrummed through the hallway of the eleventh floor when I stepped off the Bayfront's Space
Elevator and headed to my room.

Another-Dimension-Another-Dimension-Another-Dimension

Three doors down from mine the walls erupted with
high-pitched teen laughter and the steady beat of retro hip-
hop that had debuted five years before anyone inside the room
was born. Nerds always rightly exercise their right to cherish
the just-new and the never-old. As I passed by, I could hear
the clink of beer bottles and sped-up chipmunk conversation
and a brief scream. It was easy to picture the party: Half a
dozen high school students in a room with a single queen bed,
sleeping ass-to-elbow on the floor like illegal migrant workers, happy to be out of the house, dropped off by Mom and

Dad, wearing their costumes like their one, true skins, getting drunk and high, not to deaden the edge of life but to sharpen it. Every few cons I would get a room next to the biggest, loudest fan party on the floor, but about halfway through my rootless odyssey of show appearances I stopped huffily stomping to the front desk to ask to be relocated. I stopped hearing in their revelries a personal annoyance and instead started to understand the joy as it was; it reminded me that the humdrum for me was a reason to celebrate for them. Their youthful ecstasy renewed my vigor, like a proud mentor passing the torch. Or maybe more like a vampire leeching off youthful vigor. I knew which interpretation I preferred.

Another-Dimension-Another-Dimension-Another-Dimension

In this specific instance I was grateful for the cacophony because even I couldn't hear myself sliding my extra key card through the lock and opening my hotel room door. I wanted to take Christine by surprise, and more importantly to catch me by surprise. I wasn't sure which question I wanted to ask first because I wasn't sure which answer I wanted to hear least.

Hey babe, did you know your current boyfriend sees you as little more than a disposable receptacle for his dick, and so in light of these new revelations what do you say we fly to Newark and rip up those divorce papers together and P.S. I love you?

Or:

Why did you lie to me about when you were at your own party?

I chose to table the decision until I was looking Christine in the eyes. She wasn't in the short hallway that led from the door past the bathroom; its door was open, lights off. I didn't see her on the bed watching TV or checking email at the open laptop on the writing desk, and for a second my heart sank. She had given up waiting for me, again, and left, again, and I had missed her, again.

Then I saw her foot sticking off the end of the bed and my brain told me it must be at that angle because she was falling off. I took one step forward to help her but then stopped because that didn't make any sense at all, because that couldn't be her foot, because a live human foot wouldn't ever be twisted that way.

I knew. Even before I knew, I knew. My stomach twisted like it was wringing all the bile out of itself. Spots swarmed at the edges of my vision, along with some kind of static blizzard in my brain, but not enough to block my view before I reached the edge of the bed and saw the bloody pile heaped on the narrow strip of floor. Something that used to be a woman I had laughed with and thrilled to her kisses and held while she cried. Someone who sat with me in a hospital emergency room and fell asleep on my shoulder while flying across the Atlantic, someone who screamed at me in fury and made love with me outside in the rain.

She used to be a human being but now she was a just a thing, a facsimile in the same basic shape as my wife. Except no one bothered to finish her face, to put bone and skin on it—instead there was just a sloppy purple-reddish mush where all of that should be.

It was then that I saw the bloody stump on the bed. It was the Kirby trophy, that lumpy monolith of cosmic ephemera. On the base, where my name and the name of my comic book were engraved, glistened crimson of various darkening stages.

Nope, nada, nyet, no thank you, that's enough for us, I'm outta here my consciousness decided, and the brain static was quickly accompanied by a high-pitched whine and the swarming black dots shrouded my vision. My knees failed and I sat backward, into air, my back crashing into the writing desk and dragging half of what was in it onto the floor with me.

I did not lose consciousness, not entirely. I didn't throw up, either; my throat constricted like a fist, too tight for that. My chest heaved painfully and my ragged breaths drowned out all other sounds. Then a girl screamed in the party across the hall, not in fear but delighted surprise, and it was enough to jar me back into myself.

Hey, Sam and Twitch, it's me. No, no, not calling to turn myself in. I just want to report that my estranged ex-wife—yeah, the lover of the guy you think I killed, yeah, funny thing that— she was just murdered too, in my hotel room, with my Kirby that has my fingerprints all over it.

Nope, no, it wasn't me, wrong again, stop jumping to conclusions, you guys.

Good news, though! I actually have a real alibi this time: I couldn't have done this murder because I was on the other side of the tracks physically assaulting the most famous comic book writer in the world.

Oh, Sebastian Mod is definitely pressing charges? So even if you believed me about Christine you have to take me into custody anyway and therefore there's no way I can help find info that will prove my own innocence? Okay, got it, here's my wrists. Cuff 'em.

I went back over the scenario a couple times, trying to find a way out of this maze of Being Completely Screwed, but failed. The best thing that had ever happened to me in the past was lying dead on the floor, and the future looked to be a giant leaden cube, an obstacle there was no path around.

Another-Dimension-Another-Dimension-Another-Dimension

My eyes regained focus and alighted on the black rectangle of an iPhone lying among the various desktop detritus scattered on the floor.

I picked it up in its Paul Frank monkey-skull case and punched the Home bottom. The phone vibrated irritably and presented me with a keypad. "Try Again."

I punched in four random numbers and it shuddered again: "Touch ID or Enter Passcode."

I took a deep breath.

Touch ID.

I looked at Christine's shoe sticking out from the bed, as inert and lifeless as the foot inside it.

I knew I had to make a decision. Either option could easily lead to my personal destruction. But only one involved me giving up my freedom, to sit and stew in a cell while entrusting others to help me. People who, let's face it, had very little motivation to help me at all, and in fact could help themselves by making sure I never saw the outside of a prison again.

So my decision was simple. But that didn't make it easy.

The bottom line was, I just couldn't trust anyone to do this but me. And I was going to take this thing, whatever it was, as far as I could on my own before someone stopped me. I owed it to Christine, to Ben K, hell, even to Danny Lieber. But most of all I owed it to myself. I had drifted for the last three years on a stagnant stream of self-pity and apathy. It was time to get out of the goddamn pool.

I stood up on knees still uncertain, and swallowed. I forced myself to go back over to what used to be Christine, looking at her still form out of the corner of my eye, nausea building.

When I reached down for her hand, a stifled "no" audibly escaped my lips. Mouth, nose, brain, knees, stomach—all individual body parts cried out in protest.

It wasn't until I touched her that I had to choke back tears. Her fingers so limp, her skin so cold.

But her thumb was still warm enough for me to unlock her iPhone.

— — — —

I walked out of my room and down the corridor and even managed to nod politely at the desk clerk I passed in the hall, who I correctly guessed was heading to the Beastie Boys fans' room to ask them to turn down the music.

I punched the call button for the Space Elevator and waited for it and got in it when it arrived and rode it to the Space Mezzanine, where I smiled at the two teenaged girls who got in dressed as Sherlock (Cumberbatch) and Watson (Freeman) and rode the rest of the way down to the Space Lobby.

I walked through the Space Lobby and the Space Restaurant and the Space Bar and outside to the Space Patio, and once the salty sea air of the harbor surrounded me there was something anciently maternal about its embrace that gave me the freedom to cry.

It was an excessively manly cry, short and silent, mouth

closed and mostly swallowed in the throat, to not draw the attention of the con-goers and unaffiliated lovers strolling along the harbor walk; likewise tears were allowed to roll down my face and dry in the ocean breeze in case one too many reached my cheeks.

Then a police siren, and then another, pierced the unseen horizon behind me, and with a sniffle and a backhand across my eyes I was walking not-too-fast-hopefully along the water, just another face in the night.

I took Christine's phone out of my pocket and had the presence of mind to go into Settings to tell it to never go into sleep mode; this would mean I would not be challenged again for the password. Unfortunately, that would also mean a constant drain on the battery, which currently stood at 36 percent and was dropping fast.

Nevertheless, I curiously thumbed through a few apps just to see what was there to be seen, and my heart quickly sank: Not because of what I found, but because I found nothing at all. Christine had meticulously erased the browser history on Safari and the recent call traffic on her phone; her Maps location notifications had been turned off, so it wasn't keeping an ambient record of her movements. Just as she had no reason to lie to me about the party, she had no reason to purge her phone of a data trail unless she was trying to hide something. Not Christine, the original Hyper-Competent Spouse who kept track of our taxes in a baffling color-coded folder system that separated home-office expenses from expenses for the whole house for which you could claim only a partial deduction based on the percentage of the house taken up by your home office. To call Christine anal

retentive would be an insult to her and to Freud. She wasn't retentive; she was hermetically sealed.

I went into her email. Based on what I had already seen I
was not surprised to find the Inbox empty, but it occurred to me
to look in the Trash: the app only deleted discarded messages
every thirty days.

I found a bunch of polite rejection letters from various entertainment companies not hiring her and some coupons for that
week's deal on running pants at Lululemon (Christine was a
huge runner), a cancellation for a pistol range class three months
ago (pistol range?) and a few messages from artist clients asking
about sales and queries from prospective buyers. I also found an
entire genre of deleted emails that were quite interesting: A doz-
en or so listing songs and bands, all replying to the same initial
missive appended at the bottom:

>>On July 16, 8:45 AM, Christine Black wrote:

>>Hey guys, just a quick reminder I'd like to get as many of
your karaoke songs (artists names too please!!) before we all arrive at Gaslighter Wednesday night so A) I can make sure the bar
has them and B) we can get this party rolling IMMEDIATELY
before jetlag sets in for any of us.

>>I know most of you are going to think this is my OCD
acting up again (and you're totally right) but I miss so many of
you and I want this night to go off without a hitch!!

>>Thx in advance xxxooo cb

The set list. She knew the set list for her karaoke party.

That set list, from beginning to end, ran about twenty-five
minutes. The Gaslighter guy's printout was still folded in half in
my sketchbook. I compared it to the timestamps on the draw-

ing I'd made of the image captures from the Baptist's body-cam footage. There was just a few minutes' difference between the two captures of the Ulee-o running to the convention center and back again. It would only take fifteen, twenty minutes for someone to run from here to the Gaslighter and back.

An experienced runner.

All I needed to do was thumbnail-sketch it in my head, the way I would rough out a sequence of comics pages.

Panel 1: Christine greets guests as they arrive, makes sure everyone sees her.

Panel 2: Sings the Pretenders' "Back on the Chain Gang," waits for everyone else to sing too. People are getting drunker and drunker, having a great time. Does anyone notice Christine isn't drinking? She says it's a rum and Coke but really it's a diet soda with nothing in it.

Panel 3: Now it's time. She's just belted her second number—"My Shot" from *Hamilton*, according to the set list. The next person leaps up—the marketing guy at Boom Studios, what's his name. Everyone is focused on him. She slips out the back. Or maybe even just to the ladies' room because she knows there's a side door that leads to the alley.

Panel 4: She changes into her *Dante's Fire* costume.

Panel 5: She runs from the Gaslighter to the convention center. A person of ambiguous gender completely covered in black ninja gear would look startling anywhere else except in San Diego during con week. It looks like she's hustling to make the Guinness World Records shoot.

Panel 6: She's halfway there. No more than ten minutes have passed. She has time, but not a lot. Back at the Gaslighter, everyone is still singing. Everyone is paying attention to the stage. It's doubtless anyone has noticed she's left. If they did, no one told the cops about it.

Here, I have to start a new page. Six panels, while once the standard number on a page in, say, the Silver Age, have fallen out of fashion. But I've always been a traditionalist.

This is a good place to end the page to build suspense though. The big reveal is coming and you want it to surprise the reader, that's why you put the cliffhanger as the last panel on the right-facing page, so they have to turn it over to see what happens next:

Panel 1: Danny fidgets nervously behind the Marriott, where he waits with his portfolio.

Panel 2: Whoever he was planning on meeting, it was probably not a runner in full body costume. Here she comes into frame, emerging suddenly out of the darkness, illuminated by a streetlamp. Does she approach stealthily or run right up to him? One thing is obvious: She does not have much time. Her identity is completely covered. So there is only one conclusion:

Panel 3: Christine shoots Danny. She's not there to chat or to argue. Presumably this is where her shooting-range classes come in.

But still. I was with this woman for over a decade. Sure, she could be a little tightly wound, and she knew how to nurse a grudge, or five. But was she really capable of blasting another person to death? This was the only part of the evidence that didn't fit: Christine herself, and what I knew about her.

Or . . . did I really not know her at all? And was that the possibility I didn't want to believe?

Panel 4: The same thing as the first page, but spooled backward. (Combined, this grouping could make a pretty good double-page spread.) This panel is the same as the second shot from the Baptist's bodycam: Ulee-o running back toward the Gaslighter.

Panel 5: Christine whips off the costume in the alley. But where does she put it and the gun? Somewhere no one would look. Simply throwing it out is too risky . . . Ah, yes. In the Instagram pictures of the party you can see all those oversized con bags. Just stuff it in there, carry it back into the bar.

Panel 6: Forty minutes have passed. You can hear the staccato synth beats as you push into the club. The DJ is calling your name. Christine? Christine? Where is she? Oh, there she is—she's walking to the stage, maybe a little out of breath, maybe a little glassy-eyed. She could have had one too many rum and Cokes. Or she's churning with adrenaline and nausea because she just killed someone. But she still blasts her way through A-ha's "Take on Me."

It was a strong sequence, solid. An elegant meld of action and character beats. But there was something wrong. It took me a few minutes of turning it over and over in my mind to realize what it was.

The portfolio in Danny's hand while he was waiting—was that correct? Because the police never mentioned it, so they didn't find it, and Danny couldn't have had it in his hand when he died. And "Ulee-o" didn't have it in the the bodycam footage, either.

So I was wrong about who the killer was.

Or the killer snatched it and stashed it somewhere before fleeing.

Or some other random person stumbled across it and swiped it after the murder . . .

But there was one other possibility.

— — — —

Danny Lieber's trail of blood ended on the steps of the Sails Pavilion at the San Diego Convention Center—and I was determined to trace it back to where it started. I walked down to the marina and past the row of yachts rented by various entertainment websites. Beneath the sodium lamps, the traces of Danny's blood were long gone, cleaned away by whoever's job that was.

I eventually wound up in the back parking lot of the Marriott Marquis. Most every space was occupied by massive trailers belonging to various news and media organizations, which hummed with internally generated power. A few bored Teamsters sat around under tents guarding recharging banks of walkie-talkies and A/V crates with their Sharpie-on-masking-tape labels and banks of monitors. A long narrow alley led from the rear of the lot toward the parking garage and the front entrance of the pool bar. Danny could have gotten here after he left me. At the front of the lot, facing the marina, was a small brick building housing restrooms, with a pair of eucalyptus swaying in the ocean breeze.

Boxwood hedges studded small islands between sets of parking spaces. While I was looking in them, finding nothing more than the usual candy wrappers and cigarette butts, my phone buzzed with a text from Dirtbag:

"Where r u r u & Christine alright"

I could feel myself spinning downward on a crash course.

Instead of trying to pull out of it, I had chosen the certainty of control. I leaned hard on the stick, only increasing the death spiral. I insisted on my right to see the ground as it rushed up to meet me. A roar filled my ears and I could feel life racing past, nearing the end of its course, even though I was standing completely still.

The last thing my conscience needed was allowing anyone not already involved in this mess to blunder into my wake and get dragged down with me.

"Dude there are cop cars all around the Bayfront," Dirtbag texted next. "U can see it from the Midway deck."

I closed my eyes, exhaled, and returned the phone to my pocket without answering.

I looked across the asphalt expanse, rapidly running out of reasons to cling to my current theory, when my eyes alighted on a small white picket fence that formed a corral smack dab in the center of the lot. A swivel office chair with a missing wheel lay atop a heap of white garbage bags. The Dumpster inside the corral was stuffed to capacity; I'd bet the odds of any garbage truck getting here through teeming comic-con crowds before Monday were all but nonexistent.

The fence gate was secured with a chain and combo lock, but it listed on its hinges wide enough that I was able to squeeze inside without popping off any shirt buttons. I took down the broken office chair and used it as a springboard to vault up to the bin.

My shins immediately sank into amorphous trash and my shoes ruptured plastic, spilling wads of used paper towels, pizza crusts, and bits of broken light bulb. I tried to be subtle but my

search rapidly became a race between my arms and my gag re-
flex. I started picking up bags and chucking them to the ground.

I excavated half a dozen bags and was close to despair until
I hit on the idea of searching along the edge of the Dumpster. I
ran my hands all the way around, starting at the far end; when I
reached the side of the trash container closest to the fence gate,
my fingers closed upon a hard plastic handle. I yanked upward
and up came Danny Lieber's sticker-covered portfolio.

I grinned—and then immediately shut my mouth as the
overwhelming miasma of used diaper washed over me. I scram-
bled out as quickly as I could and returned to the darkness of the
marina.

The way the portfolio had been shoved sideways at the edge
of the bin suggested that whoever put it there meant to come
back later and retrieve it. The obvious image sketched in my
mind was of Danny, nervous, still sweating from a near-fight
with me, emerging from the garden alley, looking around, not
seeing his rendezvous anywhere, and, making sure he wasn't being watched, shoving the portfolio into the Dumpster. He clearly thought some negotiating would be going on: for guys like
Danny, there was always a negotiation. He wanted something
from the person he was meeting before he would turn over the
desired goods. He thought the meeting was about the one thing
when really it was about the other thing. Or perhaps the killer
was interested in both things, but the murdering part was more
important; she had not allotted enough time to search for the
portfolio, so she had to return to the Gaslighter empty-handed,
a partial failure.

I walked to Seaport Village and found a park bench beneath

a coral tree, its muscular trunks corded like anatomical drawings of severed limbs. I sat down, put the portfolio in my lap, and unzipped it.

"Of course," I said out loud.

SUNDAY

Clutching the cheap plastic handle of Danny Lieber's portfolio in my cold, clammy palm, I queued up to enter the Rule 34 Nerdlesque Club. The line snaked around the corner of Fifth Avenue and Market, comprising a healthy gender mix of con-goers in Pikachu hats and Link caps, waving Harry Potter wands and Sonic Screwdrivers.

I could see the spinning police lights bathe the stories-tall Mister Mystery on the front of the Bayfront in a red and blue strobe. Standing out on the sidewalk, watching my pursuers without them being able to see me, I felt weirdly comforted. A bicycle cop in his dark blue uniform and almost-black helmet coasted down the street. I met his eyes with a level gaze and no fear. He looked away without comment and disappeared into the honking, shouting night.

What's funny—not ha-ha funny but the other kind—is that this was the first time I had ever waited in a line to see anything at Comic-Con. I was experiencing the event the way the majority of con-goers did, the way I was watching them now: reading the books and comics they'd scored that day, arguing with friends, raving about the movie clips they'd seen.

"Top Five MCU movies. Go."

"Man, I have so many shows in my DVR queue right now, it's honestly contributing to my anxiety. I should just wipe the slate clean and start fresh, but that makes me anxious too."

"I hate it when they dress like just one part of the character and then they expect you to know who it is."

"Well if I *knew* where Lou Ferrigno was signing we'd *be* there right *now*!"

"Anakin! Come back here!" A red-haired mom chased a three-year-old escapee down the sidewalk.

At twenty minutes past midnight the queue shambled forward, slouching toward a storefront in the middle of the block that had been transformed into a temporary DIY nightclub. In the large window where the shop's wares had once been displayed was an easel bearing a blown-up version of the Dominatrix Leia from the club flyer. How many times had I walked past this sign over the weekend without recognizing my mystery woman in a different costume? Dumb, dumb, dumb.

The bouncer was a huge white dude with the body of an eggplant and Gene Simmons's haircut. He wore a black T-shirt that said ASK ME ABOUT MY FEMINIST AGENDA in big white letters. He was checking driver's licenses with a handheld light, then wrapping pink wristbands on those who qualified for booze.

When I handed over my I.D., I asked, "Do you know if there's an outlet in there I might be able to hook my phone up to?"

"No," the bouncer said.

"No you don't know if there's an outlet, or no there isn't one?"

"No," the bouncer said, beckoning the woman in cheetah facepaint behind me, "because this conversation is already over."

The waitresses were all in Harley Quinn facepaint and

PROPERTY OF JOKER half-jackets. As each new patron shuffled inside, we were directed to sit at the nearest tall bar seat beside tiny circular tables facing the stage. There was a two-drink minimum. I absentmindedly ordered a Blue Moon and wondered how I was going to figure out if the pedicabbie was even here. But that was a problem for after the show, and at present I was living minute to minute.

I pulled out my sketchbook and roughed in the scene of Christine's murder as it had been laser-etched into my brain. Physically drained and emotionally spent, I was becoming anesthetized to horrors; previous methods of coping were no longer useful. When I drew the last line, the image remained as vivid as it had been before I started drawing. Defiantly unpurged, the drawing was a Dorian Gray–like reflection of the torment in my psyche.

The Harley Quinns had deposited a guy in a ponytail and a ThunderCats shirt on the seat next to me. When he happened to glance down at the image in my sketchbook, he scootched his chair a couple inches farther away.

An emcee in a soul patch and a suit made entirely of laminated comic book pages bounded onstage and announced himself as Daddy Longboxes. After some mercifully brief pseudo-stand-up, made up mostly of rapid-fire geek culture references and bad sexual double entendres that really made you appreciate the comedy stylings of a true professional like Dante Dupree, he quit the stage so the real show could begin.

The lights dimmed briefly, then came up white-hot on the rear curtains, which parted with a hydraulic hiss on the speakers and an ankle-deep outpouring from a fog machine.

I closed my sketchbook and looked up when the cheering crowd practically rose to its feet. Clomping out of the dry-ice cloud, looming like a giant shadow, its thunderous footsteps provided by a prerecorded soundtrack, was an enormous cardboard and PVC exoskeleton painted Caterpillar yellow streaked with the mud and rust highlights of a working bulldozer. The operator was visible only in silhouette, her identity shrouded by backlights. She stood at the edge of the stage for just a second, claw arms outstretched as if preparing for an embrace, to allow the crowd to properly scream homage.

Then a familiar guitar and violin riff began to thrum and the audience clapped along with it. With a whir of pistons and gears, the exoskeleton extended its left arm; then with a similar grinding and clanking its right claw stretched out and mechanically yanked off the left claw, letting it drop to the stage in a crumple of papier-mâché and cardboard paper-towel tubes. The claw then flew out to the right, the exposed human left hand reached out, and with the clanking of a turned ratchet on the soundtrack it pulled off the right claw too in the precise industrial movements one would expect from a robo-stripper.

Off came the legs and the PVC helmet encompassing the operator's head, the crowd clapping encouragement and two Swedish blondes on the soundtrack from the seventies phonetically chanting "Gimme gimme gimme a man (after midnight)." Ultimately, out of the shell emerged a curly-haired brunette in a beige jumpsuit with RIPLEY stitched over her heart.

The audience went bananas. I felt my mouth widen into a grin despite myself and I started clapping rhythmically along with the audience as Ripley jumped and danced around the stage. She

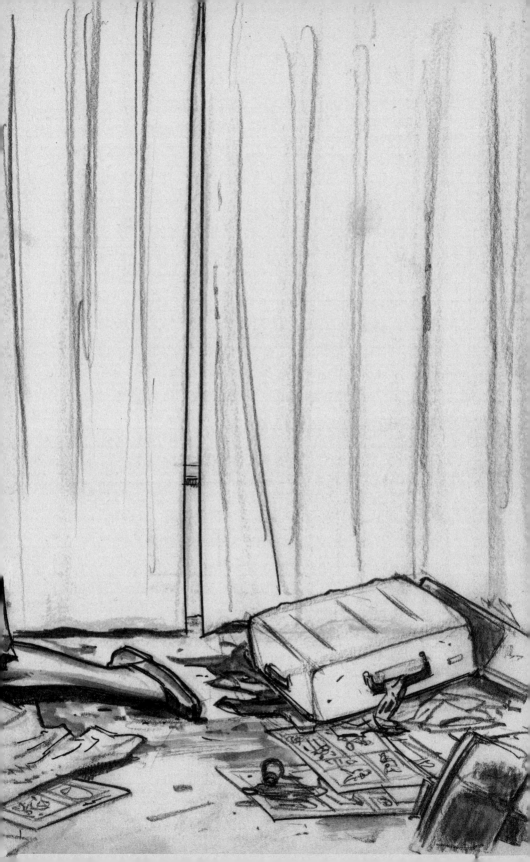

did a split in the center, unzipping the front of her space onesie and revealing a white tank top beneath. Behind her you could see where the back curtains had been replaced by a round aperture, some kind of porthole to the stars.

When her butt hit the ground, a shiny black dildo-shaped mass flashed past the opening. The audience gasped. Hearing something, Ripley cocked her head, but when she looked behind her the intruder was gone. She scissored off the floor and out of the jumpsuit at the same time, ending up in a tank top and white panties. The crowd hooted and *yeah*ed their appreciation.

Ripley made a great show of crossing her hands and gripping the hem of her tank top. She was starting to pull it up when the Xenomorph alien dashed behind her in all its spiny, scuttling majesty, and the crowd screamed and laughed.

Ripley stopped, and turned, and looked around, and saw nothing. She turned her back to the audience, grabbed the hem again, and started to pull the tank up, her foot pumping and butt wriggling, keeping time with ABBA. Just as she pulled it over her breasts, the alien ran across the stage again—this time in front of her. The audience yelped and she dropped her shirt; but when she turned to look for the source of the noise, nothing was to be seen.

Once again Ripley wriggled the tank top up her chest, and the audience started yelling "Go! Go! Go!" and I found myself yelling too. The third time was the charm—she whipped off the top and threw it to the stage, the crowd roaring.

Ripley whirled around to reveal little crablike Facehugger alien pasties over her nipples, and lo, how the people cheered. She rolled her shoulders and made the tassles twirl in the air, which sufficiently distracted the audience from the Xenomorph's reappearance at the edge of the stage. It remained there, unseen, camouflaged among the pipes and lights and microphone stands, until a spotlight pointed it out with a music sting and a hiss of dry ice, and I genuinely yelped out loud in surprise.

ABBA faded to silence and in its place the tense piano lead-in from James Horner's *Aliens* soundtrack began to build—the omnipresent trailer theme of "Bishop's Countdown"—as Ripley retreated into a defensive crouch on the other side of the stage. The Xenomorph pursued her warily, hissing and drooling.

Suddenly the alien stopped—it turned toward the audience and ripped off its vinyl bodice, revealing a black leather bikini top and assless chaps beneath. The crowd went absolutely batshit crazy.

Ripley and the alien did a dance together, spinning around and taking turns dipping each other while the audience hummed along to "Bishop's Countdown" until the act ended. It was ridiculous and sexy and subversive and creative and fun and cool and amateurish and weirdly vulnerable but fearless all at once. Ripley and the Xenomorph clasped hands and took their bows. She gestured at the alien and took off her giant phallic mask, underneath which, I now saw, was the pedicab driver from Wednesday night.

The two dancers disappeared behind the back curtain. I couldn't help noticing that more and more faces around me were turning away from the stage and to the entrance behind us. Daddy Longboxes mounted the stage but didn't speak right away because he too was trying to get a look at whatever was happening behind us.

I turned toward the doorway and my mouth went dry. Outside were Sam and Twitch and two or three uniformed police officers arguing with the bouncer, who had planted his bulk solidly in front of the entrance. While many people stood around in timid confusion, at least a third of the crowd surged in the direction of the San Diego PD to make their displeasure known.

"*Ghuy'cha'!*" yelled the ponytailed ThunderCats dude to my left. "It's a raid! They're trying to shut us down!"

"This is bullshit!" A large woman with a lime-green diamond rising out of a spring attached to her head rose to her feet and shook her fist at the cops. "Anti-sex bullshit!"

"Stonewall!" somebody yelled, apropos of nothing, and soon the chant rose up from the crowd:

"WE'RE GEEK! AND WE'RE PROUD! WE'RE GEEK! AND WE'RE—"

"Hey—hey, guys?" Daddy Longboxes tried to call from the stage, but even through the microphone his voice couldn't be heard over the din. "Maybe we should just chill out. When you block the aisles like that, it's a fire hazard . . ."

Enough of the crowd had relocated near the entrance that I had a clear path to the stage. Daddy Longboxes had hopped off to move to the front of the throng and try to disperse it. I dashed past him, leapt onstage, and pushed through the curtain. Four dancers in skin-tight costumes who had been peering out to the main room stumbled back as I blundered in. They were dressed as Poison Ivy, Scarlet Witch, some kind of sexy archer elf, and the segmented blue neck-to-toes leotard of *Metroid*'s Samus.

"You're not supposed to be back here," Samus said.

"I know, sorry." The backstage area was a hastily jumbled

collection of painted foamcore backdrops—the S.H.I.E.L.D. helicarrier, Castle Grayskull, et cetera—and freestanding wheeled racks of hanging costumes. A makeshift screen made from several safety-pinned bedsheets bisected the space; judging by the hourglass shadows cast against it from light on the other side, it appeared to be the changing area.

"Hell's going on out there?" asked a Rule 63 (google it) Punisher whose black bikini top formed the eye sockets of the skull emblem on her chest. "Are we really getting busted?"

"No way, Preston said he got all the permits," Poison Ivy said.

"Oh, like that would be the first thing he's ever fucked up?"

Samus held a large hand-cannon prop and pressed it against my chest. "Dude, you gotta get out of here. Rules are rules."

"I know, I'll be quick, I'm just looking for—" A tiny green light emerging from behind the changing room partition caught my eye. The pedicab driver appeared, sucking on an e-cigarette. She had changed into a gunmetal-gray hoodie and black hose.

"Hey! Hey!" I started waving my arms and pushing through the dancers, nearly clocking Samus in the head with Lieber's portfolio. The pedicabbie didn't move an inch as I stumbled over; she just looked at me from beneath her eyebrows. "Do you remember me?"

She looked me over. "No."

"Get Preston," Samus snapped at Scarlet Witch, who had resumed her post peering between the curtains.

"Preston's busy," Scarlet Witch said. "And not, like, in a good way."

I floundered desperately for words. "You told me about the forest—in Poland. At the kiss statue. On Wednesday night?"

"Its title is *Embracing Peace*." Her expression didn't change. "Right, you're sketch guy. You were flirting with me."

"Maybe a little. But that's not important right now. I really need your help—"

"We got a strict no-stalker rule here, dude. Out, *now*," Samus said, walking over and reaching for my shoulder.

"Oh, shit!" Scarlet Witch said from the curtain. "The cops are making the audience line up along the wall . . . and Preston is bringing the plainclothes guys over here."

"Cops?" the ex-Xenomorph said.

"What do we do?" one of the dancers said.

"Put a shirt on!" someone yelled behind the changing curtain.

I did a doubletake as the pedicab driver dashed behind the sheets separating the changing area from the rest of the space. She reached a flimsy wooden door and threw it open to a short connecting hallway that ran the length of the building. She opened a door on the opposite wall and entered some kind of bar storage room, packed high with kegs and cases of Bud Light tallboys, fitfully illuminated by buzzing fluorescent lights.

She sensed movement and realized someone was following her—me. She stopped, turned, and stuck out her chin. "Listen, buddy, you know you're not getting laid tonight, right?"

"Not my motivation. I swear. I just really need to talk to you. Super quick. But away from here. Obviously." I told her my name and extended a hand.

She stuck her arm out straight and shook mine. "Christina."

I nearly yanked my hand back like I'd been shocked. "What did you say?"

"Krystyna. With a K and two Ys." She raised a brow. "You

got a problem with that?"

"No," I said, "not at all. Not in the least."

"Look, I can't stop you from following me. But you don't want to be anywhere near me if they catch up."

"Why's that?"

"Because I'm in this country on a student visa that expired six years ago." She opened the storeroom door and we were in the loud, crowded sports bar next to Rule 34, with two hundred TVs all tuned to the same Padres away game. She made a beeline to the side exit, and I had to dodge tray-carrying waitresses and roaming drunks to keep up.

Part of me thought I should tell her that it wasn't ICE busting the club but SDPD looking for me. But another, much larger part of me concluded it was unwise to make her any less inclined to let me tag along than she already was.

————

" . . . and so, because I was with you when this guy was being killed, you're my alibi."

For *that* murder, I didn't say out loud.

We were making our way as far from Rule 34 as possible, down a deserted stretch of Eighth Avenue. A cockroach scuttled brazenly down the sidewalk with us, so big that at first I took it for a cigar with legs. A tall homeless guy with Einstein hair admonished an empty Dasani bottle with his finger, shaming it in front of the heaping trash bags filled with its recyclable brethren lashed to a nearby shopping cart.

"It's not like I looked at my watch or anything," Krystyna said. "So?"

"You say we were together at the same time this guy was getting shot, but I don't know that for a fact."

"You don't keep, like, a log for fares or—"

"Are you crazy? As long as they get their cut at the end of the week, Super Rickshaw could care less who we take where. They don't even let us accept credit cards. Nothing written down. All cash. Makes it easier for them to cheat on their taxes."

"Crap."

"It would be our word against the cops' is what I'm saying."

"Still . . . "

"Cops don't care about anyone's word but their own."

"Look. I can't do nothing because it all seems hopeless. I can't think that way, I'm not wired to—"

"I didn't say I wouldn't help you just because it's hopeless. Hopeless causes are kind of my whole thing."

"Seriously? Oh, wow. Thank you. I mean, don't get me wrong, I have no desire to get you in trouble with Immigration."

"But you don't want me to talk to Immigration, right? I don't have any problem with San Diego PD. My California driver's license is legal. I mean, so far as they know."

"That's great. I have just one more favor to ask you."

Krystyna arched an eyebrow. "You want me to open a vein?"

"That won't be necessary. I was wondering if you could find me a charger to juice up my phone and uh . . . I need a place to crash?"

"The cops are really coming after you that hard, huh?"

"I'm afraid so. I want to come to them on my own terms."

"You're going to turn yourself in and what, I'm coming with you as a witness?"

"Something like that. But not, I don't think, until . . . "

"What?"

"I don't want to walk in there with just an alibi. I need the story. The real story. Who the killer is. And I think I'm very close to being able to do that."

One end of Krystyna's e-cig glowed as she sucked on the other. "You're real lucky my life just happens to be super boring right now."

－－－－

They were going to hang me. That much was certain.

I could hear the murmur of their anger and the crackle of their torches through the shades I had pulled over the windows in a futile attempt to keep them from knowing I was inside.

But I wasn't fooling anybody. They knew. In my mind's eye I could see them throwing the noose over the thickest branch of the half-dead sycamore in the front lawn outside. I heard the sputtering protest of the horse they led beneath the tree. They'd sit me in his saddle as the rope was placed around my neck.

Dad was in the room with me while I feverishly drew by lantern light, worry permanently etched on his face.

My dad was doing his clucking and sighing, his where-did-I-go-wrong-with-him routine. I had an entire issue of *Mister Mystery* laid out across the dining room table—twenty pieces of art board with the Atlas Comics logo in the corner, one for each page of the final printed book. I was desperately making corrections to the inks before the mob got inside. I had my Wacom tablet propped up on the kitchen counter where the Ben K originals were displayed as reference. I was doing my best to fix my drawings so they looked exactly like the great master's. I was breathing heavily, sweat dripping from my brow; I worked as quickly as I could so no perspiration would fall on the pages and smudge or spot them. Still, I was pleased with what I'd drawn. I could convince the mob outside, I knew I could.

I could convince them that I was more valuable alive than dead.

Dad shook his head. "I told you you had no talent for this. I mean, you have talent. Pure aesthetic talent. But not the temperament. Entertainment is all about telling others what they want to hear. You're too stubborn for that. I've always told you, your mind is better suited for academia."

"Like yours?"

Dad laughed. "They're not after *me*, now, are they?"

"You're too pessimistic. You've been a pessimist my whole life. I know I can do this."

"You don't get it. They're never going to love you the way you want them to love you. And they're never going to love you as much as they love Ben K."

I stood back, chest heaving, and surveyed my work.

Then I nearly cried out loud.

The amazing adjustments I thought I had been making were, in fact, ugly scrawls that looked like graffiti, or like the scribbles of an emotionally disturbed child. I looked down at my hand and dropped my drawing implement with a shout. In the darkness I hadn't grabbed a thin Copic marker but a thick crayon from a toddler's oversized box. Too late I realized I'd been defacing my artwork like the wall of a men's room.

I turned to the corner where Dad was sitting, planning to

head off his inevitable snide comment with one of my own, but he was gone.

With a deafening roar the door to the house imploded and the mob poured in, all grasping hands and screaming mouths, backlit by the dancing orange of all the effigies of me on poles outside. My time was up: there was no way to placate them, no room in their rage for mercy. Then they were upon me.

I didn't sit upright with a gasp when I woke, like in the movies; muscle groups don't work that way (try it sometime). But my eyes flew open and I breathed heavily and listened to my heart thump for a good four minutes before I finally was able to move.

The Padres promotional blanket that served as my bedding slid off my body as I sat up on the black leather Ikea couch. The sliding glass doors that faced Imperial Beach had no curtains, so frosted sunlight, inert in an early-morning Southern California gloom, owned the room. My chest heaved as I surveyed my surroundings, a squatters' delight of overflowing ashtrays, half-eaten take-out cartons, a last-generation television hooked up to a duct-taped Playstation 3, and whatever furniture the occupiers had reclaimed from the streets.

The Uber driver that Krystyna (I still can't get over that) hailed to take us here turned out to be one of her housemates. Their six-bedroom McMansion was among numerous casualties of the most recent housing collapse, a flipped property that had flopped. The owner, some international real estate consortium, calculated that it was cheaper to leave it and the other sprawling homes in the development empty and take the tax write-off rather than absorb the massive loss to unload it at current market value. One of Krystyna's other housemates was sleeping with the guy whose job it was to check in once a month and chase squatters like her out. As long as she could put up with his chronic bad breath and questionable taste in gold chains, she and her likeminded misfit friends could live here rent free.

Adrenaline still drummed through my veins from the nightmare. I got up and went to the glass doors to look out at the surf patting the white sand with its eternal rhythms of there-there-there-there. I checked Christine's phone, which I had plugged into the wall with Krystyna's charger: 100%.

I dropped back down onto the couch. In the distance, one of Krystyna's innumerable housemates—a United Nations of illegal immigrants and runaways recovering from or very much succumbing to significant drug problems—snored high and loud, almost proudly.

All at once, the acute terror of the unreal dream faded, replaced with the chronic dread fostered by the sheer shittiness of my actual real-life situation. I groaned and rubbed my eyes.

I am going to *have* to get drunk tonight.

— — — —

So, it looked like I was going to miss all of Sunday at the convention. Oh, well. If any of the organizers discovered my Artists' Alley spot unstaffed it would not augur well for the continued grandfathering of my table. But prison was probably worse, so *c'est la vie.*

Fortunately, Sunday is always the deadest day at any con, even capital-C Comic-Con. It's invariably Family Day, when parents are encouraged to bring their kids, often at a reduced ticket price, and kids notoriously do not have much money. The diehards empty their wallets the first few days, so business is pretty slow—just kids pawing at everything on your table, assuming it's all free. I usually spend con Sundays hunched over my Bristol, banging out commissions.

Hiding out in Krystyna's squatter beach mansion, there was no reason for me not to do the same. Fans had given me good money for an original artwork; since I had their email addresses, I could track them down from any Undisclosed Location and snail-mail their finished piece. So I took my pencils and my markers and my Bristol, went out onto the sand-scattered porch facing the Pacific, found an unbroken beach chair, and went to work.

I also had one comission for myself, something inspired by my dream, something I suspected would serve me especially well in the near future.

I was halfway through this personal commission when Krystyna emerged from the house in a cloud of pot smoke. She was wearing overall shorts and a white shirt with a sunflower on it.

"So, how long have you lived like this?" I was in the zone and perhaps not as circumspect as I could have been.

Krystyna's brow lowered. "What do you mean, like this?"

"Sorry, I didn't mean it like—no judgment, I swear!" I held up my hands defensively. "Like, you know . . . " I could feel myself digging my grave deeper and deeper. "Like squatters. Beach bums."

"We *are* beach bums."

"You don't have any family back in Poland? With your illegal status, I bet it's hard to go home to visit."

"You don't know anything about me. You don't know anything about my family. What's your problem, man?"

"I know I don't. That's why I'm asking. I guess . . ." I swallowed. "You said you've been doing this a long time, right? Five or six years?"

"Yeah?"

"And, I mean, is it worth it? The wandering?"

"What do you mean, is it worth it?"

"What . . . " Even I knew I wasn't talking about her anymore. "Do you see an end to it? A purpose?"

"Are those the same thing?"

"I'm asking you."

She thought about it, sipping her coffee, smoking a cigarette, looking at the beach. "We're not moving toward anything. When I was a stupid kid I thought I had a purpose I wasn't fulfilling. At first I wanted to be a painter, and one day sophomore year I saw a sketch Picasso did when he was seventeen. I wasn't that good yet so I dropped out of the program. I felt I was so far behind already. What was the point? I had a boyfriend who was in a band, so I had that going for me. It's so cliché, but I thought that was so hot. He came here and I followed, because I didn't think I had a purpose without him. I think that scared him. He didn't want the responsibility. But he didn't have the guts to break up with me, so he just started cheating. It wasn't hard for him. He was in a band, after all."

I thought of Christine and Danny. "Is that why they cheat? To make you break up with them?"

"He did. He sure as hell wasn't going to break up with me. Change scared him too much. God knows it scared the shit out of me. So he just tried to . . . layer onto our relationship. By, you know, adding sluts." She chortled. "When I found out and said

I'd forgive, oh man. You should have seen the look on his face. Pure fear."

I smiled. "So he did break up with you, in the end?"

"No, not in so many words. He was such a pussy. God. I don't know which one of us was the bigger coward. The best he could do was keep me from going with them on their next tour, up to San Francisco, Portland, Seattle—"

"Where they hit it big?"

"Are you kidding? They never made it back from that tour. I mean, the band didn't. A few of the members did. I don't know what happened. Probably nothing happened. They decided it was time for new lives. My guy never came back from Vancouver. I think he's an illegal immigrant in Canada now."

"But you stayed here."

"I did. I had made friends, the crash happened, this place opened up, and . . . " She made her signature shrug. "It's home. What can I tell you? It's home. A good life is its own purpose. That's all you need. I know it sounds stupid but it's true."

"You don't have a vagabond life. This place is the end of your wandering."

She laughed, snarfing on the butt. "Man!"

"What?"

"Don't sound so happy for me."

"It's not you I'm worried about."

————

The texts from Dirtbag started around ten o'clock in the morning.

"Dude, where r u"

10:25 AM.

"Did u here about Christine?"

11:15 AM.

"Just let me know you're OK"

12:05 PM.

"I'm going to con, swinging by your table, let me know if you want me to get anything"

12:45 PM.

"Dude cops were at your table. Asked if I seen you. Watch yr ass."

Krystyna popped out at lunchtime to run errands and I went into the kitchen, winding my way around the surfboards and drying wetsuits lying on the dining room table and chairs to the haphazardly stocked fridge. In addition to doggie bags with various housemates' names written on them I found an open packet of bologna and Miracle Whip Light that passed the smell test. There wasn't any bread so I just spread mayo on a stack of deli meat, which I then rolled into the most Caucasian burrito ever. I ate it with a smile of Caligula-like decadence.

Not long after one o'clock I unplugged Christine's iPhone from the wall. As I did, I noticed a piece of paper stuck between the phone and its hard plastic monkey case. I wriggled it out with my meager fingernails:

"MEATWALL—Pop Con Management • Representation • Security"

My blood ran cold. I remembered what Buddy from Buddy's Art had said when I asked him where he got the Ben K piece:

"*You* don't know?"

Possible translation:

You don't know your own wife sold it to me?

I opened Christine's contacts and in the Search field typed the number of Meatwall co-owner Terrence Lawson from the business card.

One contact found:

"Terry."

One past text in her old queue, from him:

"Hit me back once you have it in hand, darling."

Whoop, there it is, etc.

On Christina's phone, I texted Terry:

"I've got it."

On my phone, I texted Dirtbag:

"Sorry for radio silence. Things got bad."

Terry wrote back:

"Finally. thought maybe was never gonna hear from you girl"

Dirtbag wrote back:

"Where u at bro"

I wrote back to Terry, as Christine:

"Complications. You heard about Danny"

"You heard about Christine," Dirtbag texted.

Terry texted, "Yeah thats fucked up. Almost makes me want to call it off"

"I've got the portfolio," I texted to Dirtbag.

"WTF get out where," Dirtbag texted back.

"You want or not," Christine's phone texted to Terry.

"Dumpster behind Marriott," my phone texted to Dirtbag.

"Yeah girl let's meet tonite after the show alrite," Terry said.

"Holy shit your fucking kidding me," Dirtbag said.

"I'm gonna need your help for this last part," I texted back.

"When and where," I texted Terry.

"When and where," Dirtbag texted me.

"Get you at the marina, tiki bar in Seaport Village, 9pm sound good?" Terry texted to Christine.

"Seaport Village marina, there's a tiki bar there, 8:30 sound good?" I texted to Dirtbag.

"You got it," I texted to Terry.

"You got it," Dirtbag texted to me.

The clock on the top of my phone screen read 1:35 PM.

I had seven hours to finish my personal commission.

– – – –

Dirtbag met me at the bar of this cute Hawaiian-themed restaurant with Beach Boys–era posters and albums lining the walls, featuring blonde white people running toward the surf, boards under their arms, ivory smiles unburdened by doubt. I told D-Bag what I planned and to his credit he didn't immediately stand up and walk out the door, which I found slightly heartening except for the fact that he was the one person I knew who was more irresponsible than I was.

Around nine we left the joint. It was just a few short steps to the marina entrance. A big metal gate blocked the dock; you couldn't get through it without a key card. We'd been waiting only a few minutes when the gate creaked open; it was held by a short, older white guy in a black T-shirt and jeans who didn't seem so much a skinhead as just plain bald. He did have more tattoos than visible skin, one of which was the second most popular Aryan Brand tat, a red-hot dagger carving out a reverse SS symbol. Around his neck in florid Teutonic calligraphy was *"Meine Ehre Heisst Treue."* This guy was perfectly happy with all his life choices.

When the Brand member saw me and Dirtbag, he did the aggro short guy thing of marching right up to D-Bag, stopping just short of bumping into him, and jutting his chin upward like the tip of a spear.

"I was expecting a lady person. Alone."

I tried to step between them, but only got one foot in. "Yeah, sorry, Christine can't make it. I'm her husband." I held out my hand, which the Nazi made a great show of ignoring. "She said she texted Terry and he was cool with it." This was true in the sense that I had texted Terry from Christine's phone forty minutes before arriving and got an affirmative response back.

"Who's your boyfriend?"

"Moral support."

"You scared of us?" The Brander actually looked offended. I was beginning to think that white supremacists were a much more sensitive bunch than I had previously been led to believe.

"Should I be?"

"Nah. We're adorable." The skinhead looked at both of us again. "This wasn't the plan. I don't like it."

I shrugged and raised the portfolio. "I brought the stuff. Tell Terry. He'll want to see us."

The Aryan Brander pointed a finger at us. "Stay."

"Woof woof," Dirtbag said.

The sentry walked down to the end of the slip, where a yellow speedboat with a stylized marlin on the side was waiting. He hunt-and-pecked a text message into his flip-phone's keypad. It only took a minute to receive what must have been a favorable response. He reached into his vessel, removed a metal detecting wand, and walked back to us.

"Up with the hands," he said. He wanded me and then patted down my pockets and checked my waistband. When the wand buzzed around my jacket, he made me take out and hold my wallet and phone and then buzzed them again. He did the same thing to Dirtbag.

While Dirtbag took his keys and cell phone out of his pockets and held them in his fists, the Nazi found something lumpy in the left cargo pocket of his shorts. "What's this? Take it out."

Dirtbag produced a box for a Millennium Falcon LEGO mini-kit just bigger than his hand. "Comic-Con exclusive," he said. "For my kid," he added unconvincingly.

"Uh-huh. Sure it is. Get in the boat, nerds."

The three of us boarded the boat. Dirtbag and I sat while the bullet-headed Nazi commandeered the throttle and roared away from the dock. We just kind of kept going, out of the bay, past the moored warships, beyond the dozens of small sails bobbing like floating petals, beneath the high roller-coaster swoosh of the Coronado Bridge. Well out of range of the Navy's channel a few large pleasure boats rocked in an endless swath of ocean. I'd heard Hollywood types had resorted to living offshore during Comic-Con once hotel rooms in San Diego became a more precious resource than unobtainium.

The aging skinhead eased off the throttle as a triple-decker yacht cruised closer and closer. "VALHALLA • Bodega Bay" declared the bow. It was the exact same model, as far as I could tell, as the boat Christine had rented for our wedding reception. After we'd exchanged vows on the parade grounds of Governors Island, we all piled on the yacht at Yankee Pier and sailed it around Manhattan. It began to rain, so we had to retreat inside for the dancing, but the sight of the Statue of Liberty looming nearby, torchlight refracting through the rivulets of water on the window glass, made the droplets sparkle.

With the fresh reminder of what I'd lost, my mouth set into a grim line. By the time we boarded the bigger boat, where we found ourselves surrounded by biker-looking Aryan Brand members drinking beer and listening to the banal synthetic twang of country pop, I could return their hard looks with one of my own. I scanned around and didn't see my friends from the TARDIS, which made things a little easier. It stood to reason they wouldn't be here—getting in and out of boats couldn't be the easiest thing in orthopedic boots.

Terry, their leader, rose off the divan. The sides of his skull had been shaved and the landing strip of hair across his scalp was swept back into a long braided ponytail that didn't stop until the small of his back. He wore leather pants and a leather vest and leather wrist bands and I guessed a leather thong, currently not visible. "M-E" was tattooed on his neck. He must have been further along on the public rehabilitation front than anyone else. As he stepped closer, I saw little pewter skull-shaped beads tied at the ends of his red beard.

"Terry, right?" I shook his hand. It didn't so much crush mine as apply just enough pressure to make it clear it could totally crush mine if I gave him half an excuse.

"Yeah. Christine's old man, right? She feeling better? She said she was under the weather."

"Nah." My expression didn't change. "She's the same."

"That's too bad. Do you and your friend—"

"Dirtbag."

Terry's eyes twinkled. "Now that sounds like an earned nickname. Respect. You and Dirtbag want a beer?"

"No, thanks," Dirtbag said, his voice cracking. At the same time I said, "Absolutely."

"Awesome. Let's party." Terry nodded to one of his underlings, who busted out two Coors Light tallboys from a voluminous ice-filled cooler.

When I set down Danny's portfolio to accept the beer and pop open the can, Terry's eyes were drawn to it as though it glittered. "Gotta say, when I heard Danny got greased, I assumed that was the end of our arrangement. Too bad about him. He a friend of yours?"

"You could say that."

"This used to be a nice town till the left let the goddamn mud people run wild," said one of the Nazis, and the others bobbed their heads at this sage wisdom. "They'll carve your ass for a ham sandwich."

"We don't need to build a wall, we need a tactical nuclear strike," one of the women said. Then she looked at me as if daring me to disagree with her, testing me to see if I was One of the Good Ones.

I sipped my beer and didn't say anything, hazarding a sideways glance at Dirtbag. His eyes were as wide as Pepe the Frog's and his skin the same color. I was beginning to worry more about him than the Branders.

"Well, he was still a Jewboy, so let's not go too crazy with the crocodile tears," Terry said, and the two Branders who spoke up found other directions to point their eyes. "He probably died trying to hold on to his last nickel." Terry turned his attention back to me. "But he was our Jew, our middleman, and his untimely demise leaves us in something of a bind."

I just sucked on my beer. After the silence continued for a second or two, I cocked my head. "You're gonna have to be more specific."

Terry cracked a slight smile. "Danny wasn't just the guy giving us the pages Atlas Comics stole from Ben K, he was the guy verifying the shit was authentic. We've been turning this shit around at the high fours, low fives. But now that Ben K has gone to Hebe Heaven, we're gonna be able to triple, quadruple our prices. And you know Meatwall knows the high rollers. We know where to find the money. But our whales aren't completely stupid. They know the shit is hot but they're willing to overlook that part in order to get their hands on a piece of history. They do need some assurances what they're buying is the real deal, *and* what the standard market prices might be."

Then he held up a finger. "I only needed to explain this to your old lady once, but in case she didn't pass it along I'm gonna tell you too. The big spenders trust Meatwall because they know who's behind us. Bitches who try and fuck us over know who they have to answer to. The people above me? They know how to deal with cucks and potheads who try to get smart with the money they're owed. Am I making myself clear?"

I could feel Dirtbag tensing beside me, straining to say something, so I quickly cut in:

"Crystal. And your concerns, they're totally valid. Believe me. So I've got good news for you: when it comes to appraising Ben K art, you've actually leveled up."

Terry crossed his arms over his prodigious chest. "Convince me."

"The reason I brought Dirtbag with me," I said, nodding at my friend, "is because he wasn't just the main Atlas Comics production artist for many years. He started out as Ben K's art assistant."

"Is that right?" Terry nodded appreciatively. "No shit?"

"Yes shit," I said, even though Dirtbag blinked WTF at me in Morse Code. He clearly didn't appreciate that I hadn't bothered to warn him about this wrinkle in our cover story. I would have happily done so if I hadn't come up with the idea halfway through Terry's monologue of threats. "So you see, we're sitting pretty in that regard, even though Mr. Lieber, may he rest in peace, is no longer with us."

"Well, then." Terry clapped Dirtbag heartily on the shoulder, staggering him a bit. "Welcome to the team, amigo."

"Thanks," Dirtbag said, and attempted a smile for the first time since stepping onto the yacht. "Can I use your bathroom? I, uh . . . "

"Haven't quite got your sea legs, huh?"

"Yeah, no, I should've taken something before coming to the docks. Stupid."

"Nah, happens to a bunch of guys. Doesn't mean you're a total pussy or anything." Terry grinned and winked at his gaggle of scumbags to make it clear he absolutely believed that it did. They didn't bother to conceal their smiles. "Torque, show our new appraiser to the head and give 'im some of those antiseasick pills or patches or whatever from the first aid kit."

"Sure thing." Torque turned out to be the little bullet-headed dude who fetched us from the docks. "Follow me." Swaying on uncertain feet, Dirtbag followed Torque inside the main cabin. I wondered if Dirtbag's problem was the seasickness drugs he didn't take or the recreational drugs he did take before he got here.

"Armond renting this boat is the smartest thing he ever did for us," Terry said. "He used to try and get us rooms just outside the Gaslamp but we can party a little loud for the locals."

"Trying to deal with the Comic-Con hotel website is a nightmare, right?" I said.

"Tell me about it! It crashes constantly. That's why the hashtag is #hotelpocalypse."

"Preach it, brother." I held up Lieber's portfolio. "Would you like to inspect the merchandise?"

"Absolutely." Terry rubbed his hands together. "Show me what you got, Hoss."

I unzipped the case. "Does big-time TV star Armond Delaine know he's in a business partnership with the Aryan Brand?"

My question did not spoil Terry's good mood. "Armond Delaine is not in a business partnership with the Aryan Brand. Armond Delaine is in a business partnership with me. He is helping out ex-cons, which is a very good thing for society and the world and blah blah blah. Believe me, a lot of ex-cons, not to mention a shit-ton of current cons, love *Cell Block Z*. I mean, it really tries to show what life would be like in a maximum-security prison during the zombie apocalypse."

"Well, *somebody* has to." Prison inmates like shows where prison inmates are the heroes; one-armed women like Pilar Hernandez like Violent Violet; big bearlike dudes like Marvel's Hercules or Valiant's Armstrong; Muslim kids like Ms. Marvel;

people in wheelchairs like Oracle; black women like Storm; white guys like everything because everything is made for white guys. The emotional politics of identification and representation ain't rocket science.

But even though I've never seen *Cell Block Z*, I highly doubt it is a white supremacist jeremiad, yet these dunderheads accept it with open prison-tatted arms. Fans devour comics about superheroes selflessly devoting their lives to helping others but have no problem bullying women and POC creators online. Fandom has a nasty tendency to absorb the surface appearances of a thing without ever bothering to internalize its underlying message.

Huh. I guess it *is* just like religion.

Terry continued, "But here's something my good friend Armond Delaine can't really appreciate: when you join the Aryan Brand, it's for life. They keep your head above water in the human sewer that is the American penal system, and if you somehow do make it back out into the real world, you owe them. You owe the Brand the remainder of your days because you would not otherwise have them. So they expect their cut, outside as well as inside the stir. If they don't get that, what the fuck reason did they keep you alive for in the first place?

"But to answer your question, no, my friend Armond does not know this. He does not need to know this, because it's got nothing to do with him." Terry grabbed my shoulder with the meat claw he called a hand and made sure I looked him right in the eye:

"And if anyone tells him, I'll kill 'em myself."

"Fair enough," I said cheerily, then opened the portfolio on the table in front of him.

"Yeah, yeah, show me what you got," he said, and then leaned over the single pencilled page he found inside.

"Holy crap," he said, eyes dancing. "Is that what I think it is?"

"I believe it is," I said.

"Amazing," Terry breathed, reaching out to pick up the page. The other Nazis gathered around, all *ooh*-ing and *ahh*-ing. One graying Brander said, "I totally remember these from when I was a kid." Even these, the hardest of hard cases, were carried back on the tides of nostalgia along the sea of time.

"Um . . . " Miss Nuclear Strike, who couldn't have been a day older than twenty-five, squinted at the page with a blank look of non-understanding. "What are you dummies all jizzing over? I don't get it."

"Of course you don't, Barb, you dumb bitch," Terry said. "You're so young you barely know you're alive. I remember these like it was yesterday."

Torque had wandered over to admire the page, leaving his post guarding the bathroom that Dirtbag had disappeared into. "Christ on a crutch. Is that a Mister Mystery Hostess Fruit Pie ad?"

"That it is," I said.

Beginning in 1977, the Hostess company, proud makers of such fine shrink-wrapped baked treats as Twinkies, Cup-Cakes, Ding Dongs, Sno Balls, Fruit Pies, Ho Hos, and the oft-neglected Suzy Qs, began running single-page ads in superhero comic books that took the form of comics pages themselves. In these short strips, a marquee superhero such as a Batman or a Spider-Man would be confronted by some unstoppable villain, alien, monster, or giant robot that, all other options having been exhausted, had its mission of rapine and destruction halted by the hero throwing a Twinkie or a Ho Ho in its path. The miscreant would be so enraptured by the taste of the Hostess product that it was then easily apprehended by the superhero and turned over to the authorities.

On this particular board—drawn on the old Atlas Comics paper with the stylized big-A logo stamped in the corner, just like the other Ben K originals I'd seen on the show floor—Mister Mystery looked down through the skylight into a museum where a villainess sat upon an Aztec throne, having liberated an ancient scepter of vast Mesoamerican magicks she would use for world domination.

Fortuitously, Mister Mystery never went on patrol without a healthy supply of Hostess Fruit Pies stuffed in his trenchcoat pockets to satisfy those inconvenient midnight cravings. The mere sight of the flaky sugar-coated packets injected with apple-flavored goo dangling on the end of a fishing line made the villainess forget all about her nefarious plans as well as basic common sense. She leapt off the throne, throwing the rod of power aside, and grasped at said fruit pie—and that's when Mister Mystery lowered the boom.

"They never actually ended up running this ad," I said, "so I don't know if that will affect the price. But they did get Ben K to pencil the only Hostess ad featuring his most famous creation, so that's gotta be worth something."

"Hell, yeah," Terry said. He was practically drooling.

"I know who Mister Mystery is," Torque said, "but who's the chick in all the bandages he's fighting."

"Oh," I said, "that's Disco Mummy."

Terry and one of his lieutenants exchanged delighted looks.

To fans and creators there was the dream of creation and the art that made it at least partially real, and then there was the money that allowed for the transition between the two. Guys like Terry didn't see the dream or the art, or didn't care about them. All they saw was the money. Or maybe for them making money was both art and dream. They would have been equally happy selling meth or Toyotas or child pornography. The widget, whatever it was, was irrelevant. Organized crime was a giant sucking chest wound and what it sucked in was profit, and that wound would never and could never be healed. Each poor mope up the food chain had to answer to the one above him. It wasn't that much different from regular capitalism, really, except it was disreputable because the exploitation was so much harder to hide. Crime doesn't have the common decency to lie.

"Perfect," Terry said. "One of our clients—you know Kevin Dumont, the Warriors star? This kid, he's his cousin and he's got money to burn. He's soft in the head and has a hard-on for this Disco Mummy chick. He will absolutely lose his mind when he sees this. We can spear him for some serious, serious bank."

Torque shot me a suspicious look. "And Pigpen can confirm this is legit?"

"Dirtbag. And I wouldn't have brought him here if he couldn't."

"Fantastic. Fantastic." Terry looked down into the empty portfolio. He blinked. "Where's the rest of it?"

"What do you mean?" I said. "That's all there is."

"Fuck that," Terry said, handing Torque the art board I had spent all afternoon drawing so he could swivel the full might of his pectoral muscles in my direction. "Two weeks ago Christine said she'd have half a dozen pieces ready to roll. I already started lining up buyers. You're gonna make me look like an asshole."

There were so many things I could say to that, but I stuck with, "This is all I've got right now."

The Branders, absorbing and enhancing the increasing agitation of their leader, began to circle me with hard looks. The armor of anger and bravado I had constructed around my fear was beginning to crack.

"This," Terry said, "is bullshit." He pulled out a largish Android and began dialing. "I smelled a rat as soon as you showed your ugly fucking face. We're gonna get to the bottom of this or you're going to the bottom of the goddamn harbor."

The phone in my pocket, the pocket I thought it would be unwise to make a sudden move for, began to ring—Christine's phone, that is.

Terry heard the ring, looked at his own phone, and then pulled a revolver out of his waistband and pointed it in my face.

"What? The? *Fuck?* What are you up to, man? Start talking or start dying!"

When the shot rang out, I stumbled back a few feet and almost fell over in the somatic assumption that it had been aimed at me. A couple skinheads hit the deck, literally, hands over their heads. But it was Terry who dropped his pistol, his knees giving way under him, his eyes wide with shock.

"*Nobody move, motherfuckers!*" Standing in the doorway leading to the cabin was a glassy-eyed Dirtbag, holding something that didn't look anything at all like a gun. But when Torque went for his pistol, the white plastic cylinder kicked back and so did Torque, in the opposite direction, clutching his chest as he cried out an incoherent curse.

Dirtbag moved closer into the fray, pointing his weapon at the Branders. "Nobody on your knees! I mean—wait—nobody move and—I mean everybody—on your knees! Let's go!"

I started to lower to my haunches with the others, but Dirtbag yelled at me, "No, man, you get the money!"

I blinked, not comprehending. Money? What was this abstract concept called money? It wasn't until Dirtbag kicked something across the deck—the gym bag that had been lying where Terry once stood—that it clicked what he wanted. I grabbed it by both straps.

"To the boat! To the boat, man! Go!" Dirtbag followed me as I jumped down into the speedboat. He turned and pointed the gun to each kneeling Nazi as he went.

Clutching his shoulder, Terry screamed out, "You know who you're stealing from? You are the dumbest motherfucker who ever lived!"

"And you just got robbed by him!" Dirtbag yelled back, and then he let out a crazed, high-pitched laugh. "So what does that make you?"

He jumped in next to me and took the wheel. "Here, point this at them."

Dirtbag handed me what looked like a starter pistol but was in fact a completely solid white piece on one end with what seemed to be a metal handle. It was so scaldingly hot I could barely wrap my hand around it. "I don't know how to fire this."

The speedboat roared away from *Valhalla* and Dirtbag had to yell over the engine to be heard. "Don't worry about it, I doubt it fires anymore. I'm surprised I got two shots off, even though it's got a couple metal parts. There's no way the rest of the thermoplastics aren't melted by now. Just point and wave— and Jesus, keep your head low."

I saw a couple Nazis popping over the rail of the yacht and I crouched low, pointing the pseudo-pistol in their direction. The hairless heads quickly disappeared.

I remembered the small Millennium Falcon box that had been in Dirtbag's pocket. "Dude, did you seriously make a gun out of LEGOs?"

"No, dummy, I 3D-printed a gun and put the parts in the LEGO box. The metal parts and bullets are small enough that I palmed them along with my keys when he wanded us. I assembled it in the can as soon as I got my hands to stop shaking."

I tested the trigger of the plastic gun and it just snapped off and fell into the water. "You just ripped off the largest white supremacist prison gang in the country with what is essentially a toy."

"I know." Dirtbag grinned. "Isn't it beautiful?"

"It's bananas, is what it is."

"What? C'mon. They're Nazis. It's practically a moral imperative to rip them off."

— — — —

Dirtbag pointed the speedboat back the way we came. I couldn't help feeling like the U.S. Navy warships lining the bay were watching us. Apparently no one heard the gunshots because we arrived at the Seaport Village dock without being waylaid by SEAL Team 6. I didn't see the *Valhalla* following us; perhaps the Branders determined the wiser move was to take Terry and

Torque to the hospital.

We brought the boat up to our still-vacated spot on the dock. Dirtbag grabbed the duffel bag and then we fled through the gate to the parking lot where his Dadmobile was parked.

Once we were safely seated inside, seatbelts clicked, Dirtbag erupted in a high-pitched yell and high-fived me. "Fucking-A, man! Am I right? That was badass. Like something out of *Grand Theft Auto*." He drove out of the lot. "And it was so *easy* too, that's the craziest part, right?"

"I don't think so," I said. "The craziest part is . . . "

"What?"

"I feel like you knew the money was going to be there."

"What do you mean? I saw the bag lying right there on the deck. It was logical what was in it."

"Yeah, but you planned ahead. And life planning is not what you're really known for."

Dirtbag said nothing for a bit, then chuckled, shaking his head at the road in front us. "You know what, man? Fuck you."

"Fuck *me*?"

"Yeah, you always thought I was a loser."

"No."

"Yeah, you went on to be a big swinging dick, a *Wizard* magazine Top Ten kind of guy, one of the hot artists, the ones who always got a Kirby nomination, a movie deal, you're practically a brand name."

"Give me a break. I'm comics-famous. That's like being the world's smartest cockroach."

"It's more than I ever got. I studied with Ben K, just like you. I got torn a new asshole by him, just like you. Except I never grew beyond his shadow. I could ghost him and swipe him to the point where no one could tell us apart. But you took the foundation and you built on it. While I toiled away in the bullpen, touching up crappy inkers' lines and fixing typos in the lettering until Adobe Creative Suite replaced me."

"There's another thing that bothers me."

"Sure, sure, let it all hang out. Open up the heavens and let the shitstorm rain down on top of ol' D-Bag, go right ahead."

"You never asked me what was in the portfolio."

"What? Sure I did. You said it was, uh . . . "

"Go ahead."

"How the hell should I know what was in Danny's portfolio?"

"Yeah, how the hell should you?"

"Man." Dirtbag shook his head. "You expect me to keep chasing you in this merry-go-round of a conversation? Or you ever gonna find your own way off?"

"I texted Katie Poole. I asked her who said she was getting fired off *Mister Mystery*."

Dirtbag stiffened.

"She wouldn't tell me. But guess what? She would tell a girlfriend. So I texted her from Christine's phone."

Dirtbag's expression didn't change. "So what, man?"

"So you told her on the *Midway*, sending her to me, thinking it'd be a pretty good bet I'd get hot enough to go after Sebastian. Then you could finally corner Christine, alone, in my room.

"Problem is, I don't know if it fell out of your pocket or what, but that photocopy I gave you of pedicab places in the Yellow Pages, it was there in the room. I didn't notice it until I looked at my sketch of the scene, but you were there, Dirtbag.

Weren't you?"

We were stopped at a light, which turned green, but the Dadmobile didn't move. The streets of San Diego were deserted. Comic-Con had been over for only five or six hours, but reality had returned to the city—dull, everyday life, same after same, like water filling a broken boat when you stop bailing it, like gravity once you let go of the edge of the cliff.

"She was no good, man," Dirtbag said.

"You really think you're the best judge of that?"

"She killed Danny."

"I know."

"She set the whole thing up with Meatwall. I mean, she met them through Danny because they used to do security for the Atlas parties and they'd show up with their actor clients and everything, so he was the go-between. But using them as the dealers of Ben K's artwork, that was all her, man, from the very beginning."

I bit my lower lip. "I think I believe you."

"It's the truth, man! I didn't mean to . . . " Dirtbag licked his lips. "She just really pissed me off. She didn't tell me that she was planning on getting rid of Danny. She didn't ask my input at all. She just fucking did it! I mean, we both knew Danny was talking about backing out, he was starting to get cold feet."

"Because of the lawsuit, right?"

"Right, the Eye of fucking Sauron that is Ira Pearl all of a sudden gave a shit where Ben K's stolen artwork was, and Danny was basically a company man at heart. All he's good at is defending his own job anyway. His position at Atlas is literally all he's got. He and Christine had really been fighting like cats and dogs about it. This drop-off, this was going to be the last one and he was out."

"Of the portfolio, you mean."

"Yeah, and she wouldn't even tell me what she did with it. She said she was out too. Whole thing had gotten too hot, she said, it was time for all of us to walk away. She was just so smug and matter-of-fact about it. The look on her face . . . just like yours now, man. Like she was so much better than me. And she wouldn't tell me shit. Like it wasn't important. I grabbed your Kirby off the table and waved it in her face and she just smirked at me, like I didn't have the balls.

"You know, now that I think of it, she still had that look on her face when I smacked her the first time. She didn't even lose it until I hit her a few more times, like the idea of being wrong about something was so fucking impossible for her to fathom. But by then I was cranked up and I couldn't even stop myself. Not until she didn't have no more face at all."

My throat clenched. My extremities felt all numb and tingly. I had no word for the emotion I was feeling, if it was an emotion at all, or just some kind of vacuum where emotions would ordinarily be.

"Did Danny know?"

"Did Danny know what?"

"That the Ben Ks were fake. That you were the one who drew them."

Dirtbag blinked, breathing heavily, like he had just been awakened from a dream. "Yeah. He knew."

"But Danny didn't know that Meatwall is essentially a money-laundering front for the Aryan Brand. And if he told Ira and

McCool and Atlas Entertainment that the Ben Ks were fake to save his own ass, the Aryan Brand would find out Christine had ripped them off and her life wouldn't be worth shit, *particularly* if her ass went to jail for fraud. So she cleaned up the mess. You take out Danny, he was the weak link. Now nobody can trace the fakes back to her. She was always really good at that. Hyper Competent."

Dirtbag rubbed his face. "Aw, man. You—you left the portfolio on the Meatwall boat didn't you?"

"Yeah. It's fine."

"Fine? You think it's *fine*? Do you know what's in that portfolio?"

"Yes, a fake Ben K that I drew myself. I may not be as good at aping his style as you, but I can still copy the Great One pretty well when I have to. I made up a Hostess ad with Disco Mummy."

"With who?"

"A villain from the 1979 Filmation *Plastic Man* cartoon I've been kind of obsessed with lately. But don't worry about that, it's not important. Honestly, I just had to make sure my theories were right. They mostly were."

"So . . . you have the rest of it."

I exhaled before answering. "Yeah. It's in a safe place."

Dirtbag sat straight up. "Which is where?"

"I'm not really inclined to tell the murderer of my wife jack shit about anything."

During our conversation the Dadmobile was still sitting at the light, which continued to cycle from red to green to red.

When it turned green again, somebody behind us finally honked. Startled, I turned to see a Mini Coop roar around us, its driver giving us the finger. When I looked back, Dirtbag had pulled out a revolver from under his seat. In the dim light it shone like a dull star. He held the gun but rested it on one knee.

"What?" he said on seeing my expression. "I live in a shitty neighborhood. Now. Please tell me where what was in Danny Lieber's portfolio is."

I met his stare and somehow didn't stare at the gun.

"Okay," I said.

– – – –

The TV-show immersive environments had been taken down and boxed up; the stars had flown private jets back to their celebrity compounds, walled up and gated away from the masses; the playful second skins on the buildings had been stripped away, leaving behind the brutal truth of glass and steel. The middle finger of reality raised high in gloating vengeance: Suck it, nerds. Playtime's over. We now return you to your regularly scheduled programming of a tale told by an idiot, full of sound and fury, signifying yadda yadda yadda.

The A1 U-Store facility, just off the exit before the airport, was almost cruelly real, a labyrinth of low concrete not-garages with corrugated doors. The staff had long since gone home on a Sunday night, but as a customer I had the four-digit code to unlock the front gate. I rented storage units in half a dozen locations around the country, which allowed me to travel light; I just swung by and grabbed extra prints and clothes from my cache whenever I needed them.

The Dadmobile crawled through the aisles, headlights peering for my unit. Dirtbag had one hand on the wheel and one hand on the gun and would not stop fucking talking.

"Christine, she overreacted. I can still do this. Now that Ben's dead, the price of his stuff is gonna go through the roof. That Meatwall guy is a racist dick, but that doesn't make him wrong. I can still ghost Ben K like nobody's business. I think maybe you're right, maybe people will figure out the pages are fake, but I can still turn around a few more first, make something in the low sixes. But first I need what's in that portfolio. I knew Christine screwed me as soon as I heard Danny had been killed, but she stopped answering her phone, I didn't know where she was, so I started following you around San Diego on Thursday, thinking maybe you could lead me to her. It was a stroke of luck you dove into Petco that night, where I had that crappy part-time zombie job. Easiest way to keep tabs on your quote-unquote 'investigation' was become a part of it."

I had stopped listening to him long before we came upon number 616, my unit. Dirtbag parked the car but left the brights on, pointed at the door. He made sure we got out of the car at the same time, revolver in hand.

"Look, I know you got every right to be mad at me."

"Gee, thanks for validating my feelings."

"But what's done is done. I'm not proud of it, but I got re- sponsibilities. I got kids. I got to think about them—"

"Fuck your kids," I said.

Dirtbag stepped back as if I'd shoved him. His face hard- ened and he advanced a stride or two, strengthening his grip on the gun. "What did you just say to me?"

"I said fuck your kids. For one thing, nobody gives a shit about your shitty kids except you. Stop blaming every terrible, selfish thing you've ever done on them. Don't drag them into this and use them as human shields for the fact that you have the ethics of a fucking swamp rat."

Dirtbag emitted an animal-like roar that had me practically bracing for the impact of the bullet. "You know why my wife left me? Because all my dreams, which she found so inspiring and different when we were first together, turned out to be a pile of shit. I couldn't provide for our family the way they needed to be. I can't get mad at her for that. Because you know what? She's right. We bust our asses, day in and day out, cranking out pages, twisting our fingers into dead sticks, so rich guys can pocket the royalties from our books and Hollywood douchebags can make them into movies and stars can be so so so hip listing all the graphic novels they read on Twitter while we have to crowdfund our fucking medical expenses or go begging to charities like H4H. When do we get to feed at the money trough, Mikey, huh? When is it my turn? *When do I start living the dream instead of just dreaming it?*"

I licked my lips, which didn't do me any good. There wasn't a part of my mouth that wasn't bone dry. I had planned for all of this, for us to come here, but I was expecting to lead Dirtbag into a trap. Krystyna was supposed to be here with the cops, but she wasn't. Maybe there were a slew of police cruisers hiding in the darkness, waiting to flip their lights on and scream, *Freeze you're under arrest*, but looking around A1 there didn't seem to be any corners to hide cops in. I couldn't hear anything except the dull hiss of tires on the Pacific Highway.

This looked to be the end of the road. I had overthought myself into a corner. Oh, well. I was pretty much tired of wandering. In a way, I was glad it was coming to a close. Time to rest my weary head.

Dirtbag put the barrel of the pistol on my forehead. "And I can't help but think that the only thing connecting me to the Aryan Brand now . . . is you."

I'm not going to lie. I was pretty damn low at this point. Part of me wanted him to do it. The November was in my soul and I kind of wanted to knock my own goddamn hat off.

"So stop talking shit about my family, okay? I have every motivation to reunite you and your piece of shit ex-wife, okay? Now open this thing."

I unlocked the padlock and threw open the door with a deafening rattle.

I would like to be able to say I was expecting Violent Violet to be standing there in the middle of my storage unit surrounded by a sleeping bag and McDonald's wrappers, eyes wide and gleaming in the headlights of the Dadmobile.

But I was as dumbfounded as Dirtbag to see her. Unlike Dirtbag, though, I was unarmed, so when he cried out and pointed his gun at her, she shot him first. The same pistol she had been holding in her Facebook video roared off the tiny walls of the storage unit and drowned out Dirtbag's curse as he dropped to the ground. The revolver came loose in his hand and on instinct I kicked it as hard as I could, punting it into the darkness, where it skidded into invisibility.

I turned back to Violent Violet and she had the gun pointed at my face. I thought then that maybe I should have taken Dirtbag's pistol for myself instead.

"Hey, Pilar," I croaked. Her hand was shaking and her big eyes were blinking in rapid-fire succession, like she was undergoing some kind of electrical shortage. "What, uh, what are you doing here?"

"I'm sorry, okay?" she said. "I'm sorry I'm sorry I'm sorry. I didn't mean to take the key you gave me to this place but I forgot to give it back and when I heard the cops were after me I thought I could hide out here until the con was over and now . . . and now . . . " She could barely bring herself to look at Dirtbag. "Is he dead?"

I kicked Dirtbag. "Dirtbag, are you dead?"

"Eat a bowl of dicks, brah," he said through gritted teeth. Blood seeped through the fingers of the hand he was pressing against the left side of his torso.

"See? He's fine."

Pilar Hernandez sniffled back tears and shook her head like she was trying to throw it off. "No no no I've screwed it all up again. I did it again. Just like when I posted that stupid video. That was dumb, I was in a really bad place and I'd fallen behind on my medication and I just—I just went off. And then that huge Irish dude came to my dorm room and they sent guys to my mom and—and—now this. Oh geez, oh geez."

Sirens screamed in the distance. Pilar looked like she was going to swallow her tongue. She pointed her gun at me again.

"You called the cops on me?" she screeched.

"Absolutely not," I said, hands raised. "I called the cops on *him*. He's the one they're after, not you. You're innocent!"

"No," she said, shaking her head. "I'm not. Atlas Comics sent that huge Irish dude to my mom's house! My mom! The look on her face after she called me home, it looked like I'd died. I couldn't stay in school after that, everything was just noise, just nothing. I couldn't stay there, everyone saw that guy come in. I've been living in my car for a month. A month! Do you know what's that like?"

"I think you know I do."

The sirens grew louder and tires began to screech as the cruisers started lining up at the gate to the U-Store compound.

"I just wanted to tell you, I wanted you to know, you mean so much to me, and Violent Violet means so much to me, and when I saw on the message boards you were going to come to Comic-Con I just went and camped out at the airport and waited for you to show up because I just wanted to tell you, I wanted you to know when I made that stupid video, I didn't mean you. I didn't want you to think I meant you. I shouldn't have tagged you and I shouldn't have made it in the first place—"

"I know you don't, Pilar, and now you've told me and everything's cool—"

"No, it isn't." She put the gun to her head. "Fuck it, I just can't take it anymore—"

"*No!*" I took a step toward her and surprised us both with the vehemence of my shout. I got her to take the gun off herself, which was a good thing, but then she aimed it back at me, which was considerably less good.

"What do you care?" she said. "I don't really matter you. I'm just a stupid rando chick to you."

"Shut up!" Tears and words welled out of me in equal measure. "Look, you're being really selfish here, Pilar, really fucking selfish, okay?"

"Stop yelling at me, man!"

"*No!* I can't screw this up too, I just can't, all right? If you shoot yourself I'm going to throw myself in front of that bullet!

Because I've already lost my career and my marriage and my house and I really really hate that stupid movie they made out of my comic book, okay? But I can't say that out loud without sounding like a whiner! And I can't lose you too, all right?"

Pilar blinked through her tears but didn't lower the gun. "What does it matter?"

"Don't you get it? Don't you get why dummies like me put up with the bullshit and bad pay and online hate and all this other stuff? It's to find people like us, to find some kind of community in the end, strangers connected through stories. It's for the fans, and I need every one I can get right now. So don't kill yourself! For serious. Don't leave me, Pilar. Don't leave me alone. *Don't be a shitty fan!*"

Tears were rolling down my face, and maybe a little bit of snot too. Pilar lowered the gun and shoved it into her waistband. She fished out a wadded Kleenex from her jeans pocket. We could hear shouts and heavy footsteps. Spinning police lights reflected off the sides of the storage units. Neither of us had noticed in the middle of our drama that Dirtbag had managed to struggle to his feet and limp away, but now we could hear the police yelling and chasing after him.

"Sorry," I said, wiping my eyes. "I've just had a really, really bad con."

"Really?" Pilar said. "This has been one of my better ones."

And then the cops burst in.

— — — —

Thwarted in their attempts to handcuff Pilar by her lack of a second hand, the officers cuffed her right wrist to my left one

and shoved us in the back of a squad car. They drove us to the
robin's-egg-blue police headquarters on Broadway and Fifteenth.
En route I learned that, with my usual luck, it turns out there's an
A1 24-hour U-Store on every corner; it's the Starbucks of storage
unit rentals. After Krystyna briefed them on my insane plan, the
cops went to intercept Dirtbag and me at the U-Store outside La
Jolla. By the time they realized their mistake, it would have been
too late were it not for Violent Violet's timely intervention.

Pilar and I got dumped in the corner of a cubicle bullpen
and sat there for a bladder-bustingly long time. We drifted in and
out of sleep, heads propped up against the wall and each other,
lulled by the soft sounds of trilling office phones, shuffling paper,
and buzzing fluorescent lights.

At one point we were joined by Krystyna, who looked like
she hadn't slept at all. She was carrying a clear plastic sleeve
holding some blank oversized pages marked in one corner with
the Atlas Comics single-A logo. They were yellowed from age
because they were a good two decades older than I was.

"They didn't take that from you as evidence?" I asked her
when she sat down next to us.

"Not yet."

"What is it?" Pilar yawned.

"It's what was in Danny Lieber's portfolio: Atlas paper from
the 1960s, taken from Ben K's apartment by Danny after the
Great One died. It's the only way Dirtbag's forgeries would pass
any kind of muster—they had to be drawn on paper that dated
from the period. Christine's whole scheme only worked because
Ben K was such a hoarder, he didn't even throw away his old art
boards." The Nothing that got transformed into Something—the

blank page, truly the most precious thing in all of art.

"I don't know who any of those people are," Pilar said.

"I'll tell you later."

I took out my sketchbook and with just the one free hand I was able to sketch out Violent Violet holding the pages while Krystyna watched.

"You still have that sketch you did of me?" Krystyna asked when I was done.

"Sure do."

"Maybe I'll take it now."

"Of course. Why now?"

She tugged long and hard on her e-cig. "Because now it means something."

- - - -

Near dawn a dazed-looking Dirtbag was rolled into the bullpen in a wheelchair, a hospital gown draped over his pants. Once he saw us he couldn't quite look at me. For the first time since entering the police station I saw Sam and Twitch emerge from an office, conferring with each other.

Then out of that same office I was surprised to see Brendan McCool. My eyes met his and our mutually dark gazes held each other for a full second.

McCool's look seemed to say, *You had your chance.*

I checked his look and raised him with one of my own that said:

I'd still rather be me than you.

Krystyna seemed to understand what was going on and reached over and took my hand and squeezed it. I was so grateful I wanted

to hug her right then and there, but that would've meant conceding the staring contest, and I was feeling stubbornly righteous.

McCool broke the stare, drawing up the full boulder of his bulk so his nose could be turned down on me from the loftiest possible height. He walked over to a gray door marked INTERVIEW ONE and waved at the uniform holding the wheelchair to roll Dirtbag inside. The Atlas Entertainment man shot me one final contemptuous look before closing the door behind them.

It didn't take much imagination to figure out the pitch that McCool was making to Dirtbag: Our understanding is that the Widow Kurtz had two surrogate sons. One has already rejected us, perhaps you're the more pliant prodigal. Tell Becca to play ball, finish what her husband started, finalize the settlement, accept our offer, and then we can help you out with your current legal troubles. Atlas is but a humble publisher of quaint funnybooks for impressionable youngsters, so it would be a bit difficult to make a murder two charge go away, but every defense team needs an alternative theory of the crime.

Like, gee, I don't know, what about the guy the police were looking at in the first place, the one who killed the man who slept with his wife and then killed his wife?

All I'm saying is, Randall—can I call you Randall instead of Dirtbag?—don't be so quick to decide who is Cain and who is Abel in this particular scenario.

I looked down at the sketchbook in my hands. I had already roughed out a five-issue arc for a new *Gut Check* series, a sequel of sorts that picked up the adventures of our hero many years later. He's been wandering the Earth like a masterless ronin, donning a mask in Guadalajara to take on an army of Chupacabra *luchadores* and battling bears in illegal SAMBO matches in the windswept Siberian taiga. But now, at last, he's been called back to help the love of his life, heel-turned-face-turned-heel-again Violent Violet, the one-armed Northern Irish GLOW whose abandonment was the cause of Gut's ringside diaspora. I already had the set pieces glowing in my head, they were all there in front of me, demanding to be brought to life. My fingers practically tingled without a pencil, stumps pining for phantom limbs. I wanted to start on this story immediately if not sooner because creating it would be the only way I could read it myself.

This is what I missed, I realized. I missed it more than a roof over my head that wasn't attached to a hotel, staying in the same city for more than a long weekend, a local bar, and even, God help me, a marriage:

The desire to create.

That is what the Terrys and the McCools and sadly the Dirt-bags and maybe even the Sebastian Mods of the world would never understand, forever lost in a fog of their own neediness and psychic wounds.

This was it. The work. It was all that ever mattered. Only the doing. It was magic. The Something that came out of Nothing.

More important than any fan's praise or glowing review or fat paycheck, it is in the *act* of creating that we transcend ourselves.

It was only in the drawing, I finally realized, that I was truly Home.

Krystyna cleared her throat and I became aware of something blocking my light. I looked up and saw Sam and Twitch standing over me, mildly annoyed, as if they had been waiting there for a while.

Twitch reached down and unlocked the handcuff linking Pilar and me.

"We're ready for Ms. Hernandez," Sam said.

"We'd like a statement from you too," Twitch said to me, "but we're going to ask you to give it to one of our colleagues, Lieutenant Yoo."

I nodded and stood. I looked back at Krystyna.

"Will you be here when I get out?"

She thought about it, then nodded.

"Good," I said.

"Let's go," Twitch said, and put his hand on my elbow, threatening to become a grasp.

Sam and Twitch led me past the first featureless interview room where, through the little window, I could see McCool using his hands animatedly to explain something to an entranced Dirtbag.

They put Pilar in the second interview room and closed the door, then brought me to your office, Lieutenant Yoo, and left me here.

"What's that?" you asked when I set the sketchbook on your desk.

"It's my Book of Special Thoughts," I said.

Then you said:

"So, tell me when you first heard about the murder."

"Which one?" I asked.

"Uh . . . " You looked down at your notes. "Start with the first death, then."

And so I said:

I heard about the first death from the girl who picked me up at the airport. She said her name was Violet and she was my biggest fan.

ACKNOWLEDGMENTS

I've met my best friends and some of the best people in the world in the comic book industry. I very much appreciate all my colleagues who talked to me about this novel in various stages of its development, especially Reilly Brown, Nate Cosby, Katie Cook, Alex Cox, Howard Chaykin, Danny Fingeroth, Kyle Higgins and Mike McKone. And most of all, I'd like to thank Tom Fowler for his friendship, advice, and wonderful illustrations.

Many thanks to my agent Jason Yarn, as well as Jason Rekulak and the whole team at Quirk Books for their invaluable support.

And infinite gratitude to my wife Crystal Skillman, and my family and friends, without whose love nothing would be possible.